A NE

MW00529027

A Nest of Nightmares

Lisa Tuttle

With a new introduction by
WILL ERRICKSON

VALANCOURT BOOKS

Dedication: For Megan

A Nest of Nightmares by Lisa Tuttle
Originally published by Sphere in 1986

Published by Valancourt Books, Richmond, Virginia
http://www.valancourtbooks.com

ISBN 978-1-948405-67-6 (*paperback*)
Also available as an electronic book.

Cover text design by M. S. Corley
Set in Dante MT

INTRODUCTION

The horror fiction genre that we readers hold so dear to our dark hearts did not spring forth from the ether fully formed. Its genesis was as an outgrowth of its literary predecessors, an embryonic gestation that slithered about beneath labels like science fiction, fantasy, gothic, suspense, thriller, mystery. Not even the authors themselves were privy to what lay beneath the works they were producing: 'I didn't think my stories were "horror stories" even when they were obviously not "science fiction",' Lisa Tuttle remarks about her earliest writing. 'Pre-Tolkienesque fantasy boom, pre-Stephen King and mass market horror fiction, science fiction kind of encompassed everything that was not the here-and-now or mundane or realist mainstream fiction.' A lifelong reader of supernatural tales, by the time Tuttle was twelve years old she had devoured her father's collection of Poe, Bierce, Saki, and 'anything with the words "ghost" or "supernatural" in the title.' This is the fertile earth from which horror writers are born and bred, and one can see its fruit in the stories collected here in *A Nest of Nightmares*, Tuttle's 1986 book that has, until now, been unavailable to most readers.

While in the very early Nineties I read some of Tuttle's output in various horror anthologies, it wasn't till reading Stephen Jones and Kim Newman's essential *Horror: 100 Best Books* in 1994 that I became aware of *A Nest of Nightmares*, and soon after learned that it had never been published in the United States. I had virtually no way of obtaining the book, and I didn't for nearly twenty years. When I did find it in a used bookstore in New Jersey, I devoured it at once, and was immensely pleased that each story slaked my horror fiction cravings. Her stories could be mean but not cruel, random but not meaningless, violent but not cheaply so. And the deliciously creepy birds on the cover – what an eye-catcher! (Artist Nick Bantock went on to create the bestselling *Griffin and Sabine Saga*.)

Tuttle began having her stories published in the very early 1970s, at the beginning of the *Paperbacks from Hell* era. Published in science fiction and fantasy magazines, it is obvious they had more in common with what would become the horror genre in a few short years. While she may not have thought she was writing horror, early tales like 'Dollburger' and 'A Stranger in the House' foreshadow the understated, realistic work that would come to be known as horror as the 1970s ended. Tuttle states that 'although I accepted it, I was not enamoured of the term "horror" for the genre' – a common enough objection by many a genre writer! 'My preference was for ambiguity,' she continues, 'and when dealing with "impossible" or supernatural elements I always felt that the further you pressed it, the more likely it was to start seeming ridiculous, and stop being genuinely disturbing or scary.'

Fortunately for us, Tuttle made sure she did not press too far with her scenarios, and virtually all of the stories end on a note of chilling realization that horror lurks beneath the domestic façade.

Born in Houston, Texas, in 1952, Tuttle moved to London in 1981. Her writing continued, including works with future *Game of Thrones* author George R. R. Martin, with whom she'd collaborated on a science fiction novel. At the very dawn of the 1980s she appeared in Kirby McCauley's earth-shaking tome *Dark Forces*, which showcased an all-star dream team of horrific talents of past and future: Robert Bloch, Ray Bradbury, Karl Edward Wagner, T.E.D. Klein, Dennis Etchison, Robert Aickman, and the King himself (the only other woman on the roster was the doyenne of literary mainstream fiction, the eternally prolific Joyce Carol Oates, whose own taste for and appreciation of horror has only grown). Tuttle's first novel, *Familiar Spirit*, was published by Berkley Books in 1983, a supernatural work about a demonic possession that slotted easily into the new paperback horror boom.

In late 1984, an editor from Sphere Books named Nann Du Sautoy approached Tuttle about putting together a collection of her short stories. Du Sautoy, horror fans should note, is credited with discovering Clive Barker, whose *Books of Blood* Sphere had published earlier that same year. The era-defining success of Barker's six-volume collection was unprecedented. Suddenly one-author short story collections, the bane of fiscally responsible publishers everywhere, were hot stuff, and Du Sautoy offered Tuttle an opportunity to pick her best stories for publication; thus was *A Nest of Nightmares* born. Although not a barn-burning success like *Books of Blood* – most likely, Tuttle supposes, the reason it was never published in America – it did have several European printings and was almost part of the fabled Dell Abyss horror line.

While she considers herself a Second Wave feminist, Tuttle did not write female-centered fiction as a reaction to the male-dominated horror genre ('Fiction is not and never has been about propaganda,' she states). In the late '80s she was infuriated by a high-profile horror anthology which contained only stories by men; in a genre pioneered by women, how could that be possible? She then edited her own title featuring solely women writers, *Skin of the Soul*, published by The Women's Press in 1990 and by Pocket Books at Halloween 1991 with a decidedly unsettling cat-woman gracing the cover. No surprise, then, that virtually all the stories in *A Nest of Nightmares* feature women as protagonists.

An astute chronicler of the female psyche, Tuttle peoples her stories with the lonely, the lost, the heartbroken; even those who are in relationships seem to have some chasm beneath and between. These are real women, scarred by the past and uncertain of the future, who bear the emotional burdens of domesticity. One may be reminded of Ramsey Campbell's unfulfilled protagonists going about their dreary Liverpudlian lives in damp, gloomy apartments; or of those wanderers and dreamers who populated Clive Barker's first fictions, when characters find meaning in their sudden doom or the appearance of the monstrous other (not for nothing then did George R.R. Martin team up Tuttle, Barker, and Campbell for the excellent third entry in the *Night Visions* anthology series). Tuttle is a master of the formula horror story, but not in a way that makes her work obvious, creaky, or clichéd; the recognizable scenarios – a traveling couple, a harried single mother, a woman's workaday drudge, a niece visiting her ailing aunt, two sisters buying and restoring a house – perfectly conceal a darkness our author sets about revealing.

One of the criticisms leveled against the horror genre is that it is too often a fantasy land of adolescent male aggression, obsessed as it is with the extremities of life and limb, madness and fear, sex and death, of killers and outcasts, monstrous egos and unstoppable rage. Horror becomes an endurance test, a game of one-upmanship: how far can the writer go, how much can the reader take? None of this for Tuttle. Here horror tiptoes, glides, smothers, appears in tiny details, climbing in at the corner of the page, lying in wait till the final sentences, then springing forth fully formed yet all too recognizable. Tension and suspense are present, but not unbearable; Tuttle's work is appealing, not off-putting.

A ghostly premonition of grief haunts 'Treading the

Maze,' in which a husband and wife witness a seemingly harmless pagan ritual, and the wife will come to realize it wasn't so harmless. In 'Horse Lord,' 'The Memory of Wood,' and 'The Other Mother,' children are a woman's undoing (ancient myths and possessed equines also appear). Can one be a mother and a full individual person at the same time? *'I don't know if I can manage it, not even with all the good examples of other women, or all the babysitters in the world,'* says a woman in the latter story. These are words mothers must not say aloud, for once spoken those forces will manifest themselves in otherworldly ways. Tuttle unleashes them, those inchoate fears at the bottom of women's minds, and lets them do their worst. These feelings are not fit for idle chat over coffee. The grotesque, flayed horrors of 'Sun City' appear in daylight, terrifying a woman already exhausted by her all-night employment. 'Sailing to Byzantium' is surely one of the most distressing portraits of the writing life, a nightmare of humiliation, indignity, and vulnerability: as mother always said, *'Don't think you're different, don't think you're special.'* The final tale, 'The Nest,' is a wise and heartbreaking account of loss about two sisters who are fixing up their new home. The haunting imagery – of a rubbish-strewn attic, of something black and unrecognizable flapping in a tree – perfectly encapsulates this collection's title.

Often the horror is all too recognizable: sadness, alienation, a not-belongingness, modern anxieties and disappointments that grow too large. Lisa Tuttle's characters suffer not just these pains but also the ineffable and unpredictable slings and arrows of the supernatural, the unexplainable, the uncanny. The sometimes predictable nature of some of the stories to me works not against them but in their favor: no matter how cozy we are in our rooms and our homes we are still most naked and vulnerable, and we cannot hide from the waiting world;

no matter how well we tend our nests for ourselves and our offspring, certain doom awaits within and without. All that is uncertain is when.

Will Errickson
October 2019

Will Errickson is a lifelong horror enthusiast. Born in southern New Jersey, he first encountered the paperback horrors of Lovecraft and Stephen King in the early 1980s. After high school he worked in a used bookstore during the horror boom of the '80s and early '90s, which deepened his appreciation for horror fiction. Many years later, in 2010, he revisited that era when he began his blog *Too Much Horror Fiction*, rereading old favorites, rediscovering forgotten titles and writers, and celebrating the genre's resplendent cover art. With Grady Hendrix in 2017, he co-wrote the Bram Stoker Award-winning *Paperbacks from Hell*, which featured many books from his personal collection. Today Will resides in Portland, Oregon, with his wife Ashley and his ever-growing library of vintage horror paperbacks.

CONTENTS

ACKNOWLEDGMENTS

'Bug House', 'Dollburger', 'Treading the Maze', 'The Memory of Wood', 'The Other Mother', 'The Horse Lord', and 'The Nest' were first published in *The Magazine of Fantasy and Science Fiction*. 'Flying to Byzantium' and 'A Friend in Need' were first published in *The Twilight Zone Magazine*. 'Community Property' first appeared in *Shayol*. 'Need' was first published by Doubleday in *Shadows 4* (1981). 'Sun City' was first published by Pan Books in *New Terrors* (1980). 'Stranger in the House' was first published by New American Library in *Clarion II* (1972).

BUG HOUSE

The house was a wreck, resting like some storm-shattered ship on a weedy headland overlooking the ocean. Ellen felt her heart sink at the sight of it.

'This it?' asked the taxi driver dubiously, squinting through his windshield and slowing the car.

'It must be,' Ellen said without conviction. She couldn't believe her aunt – or anyone else – lived in this house.

The house had been built, after the local custom, out of wood, and then set upon cement blocks that raised it three or four feet off the ground. But floods seemed far less dangerous to the house now than the winds, or simply time. The house was crumbling on its blocks. The boards were weather-beaten and scabbed with flecks of ancient grey paint. Uncurtained windows glared blankly, and one shutter hung at a crazy angle. Between the boards of the sagging, second-story balcony, Ellen could see daylight.

'I'll wait for you,' the driver said, pulling up at the end of an overgrown driveway. 'In case there's nobody here.'

'Thanks,' Ellen said, getting out of the back seat and tugging her suitcase after her. She counted the fare out into his hand and glanced up at the house. No sign of life. Her shoulders slumped. 'Just wait to be sure someone answers the door,' she told the driver.

Trudging up the broken cement path to the front door, Ellen was startled by a glimpse of something moving beneath the house. She stopped short and peered ahead at the dark space. Had it been a dog? A child playing? Something large and dark, moving quickly – but it was gone now or in hiding. Behind her, Ellen could hear the taxi idling. For a brief moment she considered going back. Back to Danny. Back to all their problems. Back to his lies and promises.

She walked forward again, and when she reached the porch she set her knuckles against the warped, grey door and rapped sharply, twice.

An old, old woman, stick-thin and obviously ailing, opened the door. Ellen and the woman gazed at each other in silence.

'Aunt May?'

The old woman's eyes cleared with recognition, and she nodded slightly. 'Ellen, of course!'

But when had her aunt grown so old?

'Come in, dear.' The old woman stretched out a parchment claw. At her back, Ellen felt the wind. The house creaked, and for a moment Ellen thought she felt the porch floor give beneath her feet. She stumbled forward, into the house. The old woman – her aunt, she reminded herself – closed the door behind her.

'Surely you don't live here all alone,' Ellen began. 'If I'd known – if Dad had known – we would have . . .'

'If I'd needed help I would've asked for it,' Aunt May said with a sharpness that reminded Ellen of her father.

'But this house,' Ellen said. 'It's too much for one person. It looks like it might fall down at any minute, and if something should happen to you here, all alone . . .'

The old woman laughed, a dry, papery rustle. 'Nonsense. This house will outlast me. And appearances can be deceiving. Look around you – I'm quite cozy here.'

Ellen saw the hall for the first time. A wide, high-ceilinged room with a brass chandelier and a rich oriental carpet. The walls were painted cream, and the grand staircase looked in no danger of collapse.

'It does look a lot better inside,' Ellen said. 'It looked

deserted from the road. The taxi driver couldn't believe anyone lived here.'

'The inside is all that matters to me,' said the old woman. 'I have let it all go rather badly. The house is honeycombed with dry rot and eaten by insects, but even so it's in nowhere near as bad shape as I am. It will still be standing when I'm underground, and that's enough for me.'

'But, Aunt May . . .' Ellen took hold of her aunt's bony shoulders. 'Don't talk like that. You're not dying.'

That laugh again. 'My dear, look at me. I am. I'm long past saving. I'm all eaten up inside. There's barely enough of me left to welcome you here.'

Ellen looked into her aunt's eyes, and what she saw there made her vision blur with tears. 'But doctors . . .'

'Doctors don't know everything. There comes a time, my dear, for everyone. A time to leave this life for another one. Let's go in and sit down. Would you like some lunch? You must be hungry after that long trip.'

Feeling dazed, Ellen followed her aunt into the kitchen, a narrow room decorated in greens and gold. She sat at the table and stared at the wallpaper, a pattern of fish and frying pans.

Her aunt was dying. It was totally unexpected. Her father's older sister – but only eight years older, Ellen remembered. And her father was a vigorously healthy man, a man still in the prime of life. She looked at her aunt, saw her moving painfully slowly from cupboard to counter to shelf, preparing a lunch.

Ellen rose. 'Let me do it, Aunt May.'

'No, no, dear. I know where everything is, you see. You don't. I can still get around all right.'

'Does Dad know about you? When was the last time you saw him?'

'Oh, dear me, I didn't want to burden him with my

problems. We haven't been close for years, you know. I suppose I last saw him – why, it was at your wedding, dear.'

Ellen remembered. That had been the last time she had seen Aunt May. She could hardly believe that woman and the one speaking to her now were the same. What had happened to age her so in only three years?

May set a plate on the table before Ellen. A pile of tuna and mayonnaise was surrounded by sesame crackers.

'I don't keep much fresh food on hand,' she said. 'Mostly canned goods. I find it difficult to get out shopping much anymore, but then I haven't much appetite lately, either. So it doesn't much matter what I eat. Would you like some coffee? Or tea?'

'Tea, please. Aunt May, shouldn't you be in a hospital? Where someone would care for you?'

'I can care for myself right here.'

'I'm sure Dad and Mom would love to have you visit . . .'

May shook her head firmly.

'In a hospital they might be able to find a cure.'

'There's no cure for dying except death, Ellen.'

The kettle began to whistle, and May poured boiling water over a teabag in a cup.

Ellen leaned back in her chair, resting the right side of her head against the wall. She could hear a tiny, persistent, crunching sound from within the wall – termites?

'Sugar in your tea?'

'Please,' Ellen responded automatically. She had not touched her food, and felt no desire for anything to eat or drink.

'Oh, dear,' sighed Aunt May. 'I'm afraid you'll just have to drink it plain. It must have been a very long time since I used this – there are more ants here than sugar grains.'

Ellen watched her aunt drop the whole canister into the garbage can.

'Aunt May, is money a problem? I mean, if you're staying here because you can't afford – '

'Bless you, no.' May sat down at the table beside her niece. 'I have some investments and enough money in the bank for my own needs. And this house is my own, too. I bought it when Victor retired, but he didn't stay long enough to help me enjoy it.'

In a sudden rush of sympathy, Ellen leaned over and would have taken her frail aunt in her arms, but May fluttered her hand in a go-away motion, and Ellen drew back.

'With Victor dead, some of the joy went out of fixing it up. Which is why it still looks much the same old wreck it was when I bought it. This property was a real steal because nobody wanted the house. Nobody but me and Victor.' May cocked her head suddenly and smiled. 'And maybe you? What would you say if I left this house to you when I die?'

'Aunt May, please don't – '

'Nonsense. Who better? Unless you can't stand the sight of it, but I'm telling you the property is worth something, at least. If the house is too far gone with bugs and rot you can pull it down and put up something you and Danny like better.'

'It's very generous of you, Aunt May. I just don't like to hear you talk about dying.'

'No? It doesn't bother me. But if it disturbs you, then we'll say no more about it. Shall I show you your room?'

Leading the way slowly up the stairs, leaning heavily on the banister and pausing often in her climb, May explained, 'I don't go upstairs anymore. I moved my bedroom downstairs because the climb was too much trouble.'

The second floor smelled strongly of sea-damp and mold.

'This room has a nice view of the sea,' May said. 'I thought you might like it.' She paused in the doorway, gesturing to Ellen to follow. 'There are clean linens in the hall closet.'

Ellen looked into the room. It was sparely furnished with bed, dressing table, and straight-backed chair. The walls were an institutional green and without decoration. The mattress was bare, and there were no curtains at the French doors.

'Don't go out on the balcony – I'm afraid parts of it have quite rotted away,' May cautioned.

'I noticed,' Ellen said.

'Well, some parts go first, you know. I'll leave you alone now, dear. I'm feeling a bit tired myself. Why don't we both just nap until dinner time?'

Ellen looked at her aunt and felt her heart twist with sorrow at the weariness on that pale, wrinkled face. The small exertion of climbing upstairs had told on her. Her arms trembled slightly, and she looked grey with weariness.

Ellen hugged her. 'Oh, Aunt May,' she said softly. 'I'm going to be a help to you, I promise. You just take it easy. I'll look after you.'

May pulled away from her niece's arms, nodding. 'Yes, dear, it's very nice to have you here. We welcome you.' She turned and walked away down the hall.

Alone, Ellen suddenly realised her own exhaustion. She sank down on the bare mattress and surveyed her bleak little room, her mind a jumble of problems old and new.

She had never known her Aunt May well enough to become close to her – this sudden visit was a move born of desperation. Wanting to get away from her husband for a while, wanting to punish him for a recently discovered infidelity, she had cast about for a place she could escape to – a place she could afford, and a place where Danny would not be able to find her. Aunt May's lonely house on the coast had seemed the best possibility for a week's hiding.

18

She had expected peace, boredom, regret – but she had never expected to find a dying woman. It was a whole new problem that almost cast her problems with Danny into insignificance.

Suddenly she felt very lonely. She wished Danny were with her, to comfort her. She wished she had not sworn to herself not to call him for at least a week.

But she would call her father, she decided. Should she warn him against telling Danny? She wasn't sure – she hated letting her parents know her marriage was in trouble. Still, if Danny tried to find her by calling them, they would know something was wrong.

She'd call her father tonight. Definitely. He'd come out here to see his sister – he'd take charge, get her to a hospital, find a doctor with a miracle cure. She was certain of it.

But right now she was suddenly, paralyzingly tired. She stretched out on the bare mattress. She would get the sheets and make it up properly later, but right now she would just close her eyes, just close her eyes and rest for a moment . . .

It was dark when Ellen woke, and she was hungry.

She sat on the edge of the bed, feeling stiff and disoriented. The room was chilly and smelled of mildew. She wondered how long she had slept.

Nothing happened when she hit the light switch on the wall. So she groped her way out of the room and along the dark passage toward the dimly perceived stairs. The steps creaked loudly beneath her feet. She could see a light at the bottom of the stairs, from the kitchen.

'Aunt May?'

The kitchen was empty, the light a fluorescent tube above the stove. Ellen had the feeling that she was not alone. Someone was watching. Yet when she turned, there was nothing behind her but the undisturbed darkness of the hall.

She listened for a moment to the creakings and moanings of the old house, and to the muffled sounds of sea and wind from outside. No human sound in all of that, yet the feeling persisted that if she listened hard enough, she would catch a voice . . .

She could make out another dim light from the other end of the hall, behind the stairs, and she walked toward it. Her shoes clacked loudly on the bare wooden floor of the back hall.

It was a nightlight that had attracted her attention, and near it she saw that a door stood ajar. She reached out and pushed it farther open. She heard May's voice, and she stepped into the room.

'I can't feel my legs at all,' May said. 'No pain in them, no feeling at all. But they still work for me, somehow. I was afraid that once the feeling went they'd be useless to me. But it's not like that at all. But you knew that; you told me it would be like this.' She coughed, and there was the sound in the dark room of a bed creaking. 'Come here, there's room.'

'Aunt May?'

Silence – Ellen could not even hear her aunt breathing. Finally May said, 'Ellen? Is that you?'

'Yes, of course. Who did you think it was?'

'What? Oh, I expect I was dreaming.' The bed creaked again.

'What was that you were saying about your legs?'

More creaking sounds. 'Hmmm? What's that, dear?' The voice of a sleeper struggling to stay awake.

'Never mind,' Ellen said. 'I didn't realize you'd gone to bed. I'll talk to you in the morning. Good night.'

'Good night, dear.'

Ellen backed out of the dark, stifling bedroom, feeling confused.

Aunt May must have been talking in her sleep. Or perhaps, sick and confused, she was hallucinating. But it made no sense to think – as Ellen, despite herself, was thinking – that Aunt May had been awake and had mistaken Ellen for someone else, someone she expected a visit from, someone else in the house.

The sound of footsteps on the stairs, not far above her head, sent Ellen running forward. But the stairs were dark and empty, and straining her eyes toward the top, Ellen could see nothing. The sound must have been just another product of this dying house, she thought.

Frowning, unsatisfied with her own explanation, Ellen went back into the kitchen. She found the pantry well stocked with canned goods and made herself some soup. It was while she was eating it that she heard the footsteps again – this time seemingly from the room above her head.

Ellen stared up at the ceiling. If someone was really walking around up there, he was making no attempt to be cautious. But she couldn't believe that the sound was anything but footsteps: someone was upstairs.

Ellen set her spoon down, feeling cold. The weighty creaking continued.

Suddenly the sounds overhead stopped. The silence was unnerving, giving Ellen a vision of a man crouched down, his head pressed against the floor as he listened for some response from her.

Ellen stood up, rewarding her listener with the sound of a chair scraping across the floor. She went to the cabinet on the wall beside the telephone – and there, on a shelf with the phone book, Band-Aids, and light bulbs was a flashlight, just as in her father's house.

The flashlight worked, and the steady beam of light cheered her. Remembering the darkness of her room, Ellen also took a light bulb before closing the cabinet and starting upstairs.

Opening each door as she came to it, Ellen found a series of unfurnished rooms, bathrooms, and closets. She heard no more footsteps and found no sign of anyone or anything that could have made them. Gradually the tension drained out of her, and she returned to her own room after taking some sheets from the linen closet.

After installing the light bulb and finding that it worked, Ellen closed the door and turned to make up the bed. Something on the pillow drew her attention: examining it more closely, she saw that it seemed to be a small pile of sawdust. Looking up the wall, she saw that a strip of wooden molding was riddled with tiny holes, leaking the dust. She wrinkled her nose in distaste: termites. She shook the pillow vigorously and stuffed it into a case, resolving to call her father first thing in the morning. May could not go on living in a place like this.

Sun streaming through the uncurtained window woke her early. She drifted toward consciousness to the cries of seagulls and the all-pervasive smell of the sea.

She got up, shivering from the dampness which seemed to have crept into her bones, and dressed quickly. She found her aunt in the kitchen, sitting at the table sipping a cup of tea.

'There's hot water on the stove,' May said by way of greeting.

Ellen poured herself a cup of tea and joined her aunt at the table.

'I've ordered some groceries,' May said. 'They should be here soon, and we can have toast and eggs for breakfast.'

Ellen looked at her aunt and saw that a dying woman shared the room with her. In the face of that solemn, unarguable fact, she could think of nothing to say. So they sat in silence broken only by the sipping of tea, until the doorbell rang.

'Would you let him in dear?' May asked.

'Shall I pay him?'

'Oh, no, he doesn't ask for that. Just let him in.'

Wondering, Ellen opened the door on a strongly built young man holding a brown paper grocery bag in his arms. She put out her arms rather hesitantly to receive it, but he ignored her and walked into the house. He set the bag down in the kitchen and began to unload it. Ellen stood in the doorway watching, noticing that he knew where everything went.

He said nothing to May, who seemed scarcely aware of his presence, but when everything had been put away, he sat down at the table in Ellen's place. He tilted his head on one side and eyed her. 'You must be the niece,' he said.

Ellen said nothing. She didn't like the way he looked at her. His dark, nearly black eyes seemed to be without pupils – hard eyes, without depths. And he ran those eyes up and down her body, judging her. He smiled now at her silence and turned to May. 'A quiet one,' he said.

May stood up, holding her empty cup.

'Let me,' Ellen said quickly, stepping forward. May handed her the cup and sat down again, still without acknowledging the young man's presence. 'Would you like some breakfast?' Ellen asked.

May shook her head. 'You eat what you like, dear. I don't feel much like eating . . . there doesn't seem to be much point.'

'Oh, Aunt May, you really should have something.'

'A piece of toast, then.'

'I'd like some eggs,' said the stranger. He stretched lazily in his chair. 'I haven't had my breakfast yet.'

Ellen looked at May, wanting some clue. Was this presumptuous stranger her friend? A hired man? She didn't want to be rude to him if May didn't wish it. But May was looking into the middle distance, indifferent.

Ellen looked at the man. 'Are you waiting to be paid for the groceries?'

The stranger smiled, a hard smile that revealed a set of even teeth. 'I bring food to your aunt as a favour. So she won't have to go to the trouble of getting it for herself, in her condition.'

Ellen stared at him a moment longer, waiting in vain for a sign from her aunt, and then turned her back on them and went to the stove. She wondered why this man was helping her aunt – was she really not paying him? He didn't strike her as the sort for disinterested favours.

'Now that I'm here,' Ellen said, getting eggs and butter out of the refrigerator, 'you don't have to worry about my aunt. I can run errands for her.'

'I'll have two fried eggs,' he said. 'I like the yolks runny.'

Ellen glared at him, but realised he wasn't likely to leave just because she refused to cook his eggs – he'd probably cook them himself. And he *had* bought the food.

But – her small revenge – she overcooked the eggs and gave him the slightly scorched piece of toast.

When she sat down she looked at him challengingly. 'I'm Ellen Morrow,' she said.

He hesitated, then drawled, 'You can call me Peter.'

'Thanks a lot,' she said sarcastically. He smiled his unpleasant smile again, and Ellen felt him watching her eat. As soon as she could she excused herself, telling her aunt she was going to call her father.

That drew the first response of the morning from May. She put out a hand, drawing it back just shy of touching Ellen. 'Please don't. There's nothing he can do for me and I don't want him charging down here for no good reason.'

'But, Aunt May, you're his only sister – I have to tell him, and of course he'll want to do something for you.'

'The only thing he can do for me now is to leave me alone.'

Unhappily, Ellen thought that her aunt was right – still, her father must be told. In order to be able to speak freely, she left the kitchen and went back to her aunt's bedroom where she felt certain there would be an extension.

There was, and she dialled her parents' number. The ringing went on and on. She gave up, finally, and phoned her father's office. The secretary told her he'd gone fishing, and would be unreachable for at least two days. She promised to give him a message if he called, or when he returned.

So it had to wait. Ellen walked back towards the kitchen, her crêpe-soled shoes making almost no sound on the floor.

She heard her aunt's voice, 'You didn't come to me last night. I waited and waited. Why didn't you come?'

Ellen froze.

'You said you would stay with me,' May continued. Her voice had a whining note that made Ellen uncomfortable. 'You promised you would stay and look after me.'

'The girl was in the house,' Peter said. 'I didn't know if I should.'

'What does she matter? She doesn't matter. Not while I'm here, she doesn't. This is still my house and I ... I belong to you, don't I? Don't I, dearest?'

Then there was a silence. As quietly as she could, Ellen hurried away and left the house.

The sea air, damp and warm though it was, was a relief after the smoldering closeness of the house. But Ellen, taking in deep breaths, still felt sick.

They were lovers, her dying aunt and that awful young man.

That muscular, hard-eyed, insolent stranger was sleeping with her frail, elderly aunt. The idea shocked and revolted her, but she had no doubt of it – the brief conversation, her aunt's voice, could not have been more plain.

Ellen ran down the sandy, weedy incline toward the narrow beach, wanting to lose her knowledge. She didn't know how she could face her aunt now, how she could stay in a house where –

She heard Danny's voice, tired, contemptuous, yet still caring, 'You're so naïve about sex, Ellen. You think everything's black and white. You're such a child.'

Ellen started to cry, thinking of Danny, wishing she had not run away from him. What would he say to her about this? That her aunt had a right to pleasure, too, and age was just another prejudice.

But what about *him*? Ellen wondered. What about Peter – what did he get out of it? He was using her aunt in some way, she was certain of it. Perhaps he was stealing from her – she thought of all the empty rooms upstairs and wondered.

She found a piece of Kleenex in a pocket of her jeans and wiped away the tears. So much was explained by this, she thought. Now she knew why her aunt was so desperate not to leave this rotting hulk of a house, why she didn't want her brother to come.

'Hello, Ellen Morrow.'

She raised her head, startled, and found him standing directly in her path, smiling his hard smile. She briefly met, then glanced away from, his dark, ungiving eyes.

'You're not very friendly,' he said. 'You left us so quickly. I didn't get a chance to talk to you.'

She glared at him and tried to walk away, but he fell into step with her. 'You shouldn't be so unfriendly,' he said. 'You should try to get to know me.'

She stopped walking and faced him. 'Why? I don't know who you are or what you're doing in my aunt's house.'

'I think you have some idea. I look after your aunt. She was all alone out here before I came, with no family or friends. She was completely unprotected. *You* may find

26

it shocking, but she's grateful to me now. She wouldn't approve of you trying to send me away.'

'I'm here now,' Ellen said. 'I'm a part of her family. And her brother will come ... she won't be left alone, at the mercy of strangers.'

'But I'm not a stranger anymore. And she doesn't want me to leave.'

Ellen was silent for a moment. Then she said, 'She's a sick, lonely old woman – she needs someone. But what do you get out of it? Do you think she's going to leave you her money when she dies?'

He smiled contemptuously. 'Your aunt doesn't have any money. All she has is that wreck of a house – which she plans to leave to you. I give her what she needs, and she gives me what I need – which is something a lot more basic and important than money.'

Afraid she was blushing, Ellen turned and began striding across the sand, back toward the house. She could feel him keeping pace with her, but she did not acknowledge his presence.

Until he grabbed her arm – and she let out a gasp that embarrassed her as soon as she heard it. But Peter gave no sign that he had noticed. Having halted her, he directed her attention to something on the ground.

Feeling foolish but still a little frightened she let him draw her down to a crouching position. A battle had drawn his attention, a fight for survival in a small, sandy arena. A spider, pale as the sand, danced warily on pipe-cleaner legs. Circling it, chitinous body gleaming darkly in the sunlight, was a deadly black dart of a wasp.

There was something eerily fascinating in the way the tiny antagonists circled each other, feinting, freezing, drawing back, and darting forward. The spider on its delicate legs seemed nervous to Ellen, while the wasp was steady and single-minded. Although she liked neither

27

spiders nor wasps, Ellen hoped that the spider would win.

Suddenly the wasp shot forward; the spider rolled over, legs clenching and kicking like fingers from a fist, and the two seemed to wrestle for a moment.

'Ah, now she's got him,' murmured Ellen's companion. Ellen saw that his face was intent, and he was absorbed by the deadly battle.

Glancing down again, she saw that the spider was lying perfectly still, while the wasp circled it warily.

'He killed him,' Ellen said.

'Not he, she.' Peter corrected. 'And the spider isn't dead. Just paralyzed. The wasp is making sure that her sting has him completely under control before going on. She'll dig a hole and pull the spider into it, then lay her egg on his body. The spider won't be able to do a thing but lie in the home of his enemy and wait for the egg to hatch and start eating him.' He smiled his unpleasant smile.

Ellen stood up.

'Of course, he can't feel a thing,' Peter continued. 'He's alive, but only in the most superficial sense. That paralyzing poison the wasp filled him with has effectively deadened him. A more advanced creature might torment himself with fears about the future, the inevitability of his approaching death – but this is just a spider. And what does a spider know?'

Ellen walked away, saying nothing. She expected him to follow her, but when she looked back she saw that he was still on his hands and knees, watching the wasp at her deadly work.

Once inside the house, Ellen locked the front door behind her, then went around locking the other doors and checking the windows. Although she knew it was likely that her aunt had given Peter a key to the house, she didn't want to be surprised by him again. She was locking the side door, close by her aunt's room, when the feeble voice called, 'Is that you, dear?'

'It's me, Aunt May,' Ellen said, wondering who that 'dear' was meant for. Pity warred briefly with disgust, and then she entered the bedroom.

From the bed, her aunt gave a weak smile. 'I tire so easily now,' she said. 'I think I may just spend the rest of the day in bed. What else is there for me to do, except wait?'

'Aunt May, I could rent a car and take you to a doctor – or maybe we could find a doctor willing to come out here.'

May turned her grey head back and forth on the pillow. 'No. No. There's nothing a doctor can do, no medicine in the world that can help me now.'

'Something to make you feel better . . .'

'My dear, I feel very little. No pain at all. Don't worry about me. Please.'

She looked so exhausted, Ellen thought. Almost all used up. And looking down at the small figure surrounded by bedclothes, Ellen felt her eyes fill with tears. Suddenly, she flung herself down beside the bed. 'Aunt May, I don't *want* you to die!'

'Now, now,' the old woman said softly, making no other movement. 'Now, don't you fret. I felt the same way myself, once, but I've got over that. I've accepted what has happened, and so must you. So must you.'

'No,' Ellen whispered, her face pressed against the bed. She wanted to hold her aunt, but she didn't dare – the old woman's stillness seemed to forbid it. Ellen wished her aunt would put out her hand or turn her face to be kissed: she could not make the first move herself.

At last Ellen stopped crying and raised her head. She saw that her aunt had closed her eyes and was breathing slowly and peacefully, obviously asleep. Ellen stood up and backed out of the room. She longed for her father, for someone to share this sorrow with her.

She spent the rest of the day reading and wandering aimlessly through the house, thinking now of Danny and then of her aunt and the unpleasant stranger called Peter, feeling frustrated because she could do nothing. The wind began to blow again, and the old house creaked, setting her nerves on edge. Feeling trapped in the moldering carcass of the house, Ellen walked out onto the front porch. There she leaned against the railing and stared out at the grey and white ocean. Out here she enjoyed the bite of the wind, and the creaking of the balcony above her head did not bother her.

Idly, her attention turned to the wooden railing beneath her hands, and she picked at a projecting splinter with one of her fingernails. To her surprise, more than just a splinter came away beneath her fingers: some square inches of the badly painted wood fell away, revealing an interior as soft and full of holes as a sponge. The wood seemed to be trembling, and after a moment of blankness, Ellen suddenly realised that the wood was infested with termites. With a small cry of disgust, Ellen backed away, staring at the interior world she had uncovered. Then she went back into the house, locking the door behind her.

It grew dark, and Ellen began to think longingly of food and companionship. She realised she had heard nothing from her aunt's room since she had left her sleeping there that morning. After checking the kitchen to see what sort of dinner could be made, Ellen went to wake her aunt.

The room was dark and much too quiet. An apprehension stopped Ellen in the doorway where, listening, straining her ears for some sound, she suddenly realised the meaning of the silence: May was not breathing.

Ellen turned on the light and hurried to the bed. 'Aunt May, Aunt May,' she said, already hopeless. She grabbed hold of one cool hand, hoping for a pulse, and laid her

30

head against her aunt's chest, holding her own breath to listen for the heart.

There was nothing. May was dead. Ellen drew back, crouching on her knees beside the bed, her aunt's hand still held within her own. She stared at the empty face – the eyes were closed, but the mouth hung slightly open – and felt the sorrow building slowly inside her.

At first she took it for a drop of blood. Dark and shining, it appeared on May's lower lip and slipped slowly out of the corner of her mouth. Ellen stared, stupefied, as the droplet detached itself from May's lip and moved, without leaving a trace behind, down her chin.

Then Ellen saw what it was.

It was a small, shiny black bug, no larger than the nail on her little finger. And, as Ellen watched, a second tiny insect crawled slowly out onto the shelf of May's dead lip.

Ellen scrambled away from the bed, backward, on her hands and knees. Her skin was crawling, her stomach churning, and there seemed to be a horrible smell in her nostrils. Somehow, she managed to get to her feet and out of the room without either vomiting or fainting.

In the hallway she leaned against the wall and tried to gather her thoughts.

May was dead.

Into her mind came the vision of a stream of black insects bubbling out of the dead woman's mouth.

Ellen moaned and clamped her teeth together, and tried to think of something else. *It hadn't happened.* She wouldn't think about it.

But May was dead, and that had to be dealt with. Ellen's eyes filled with tears – then, suddenly impatient, she blinked them away. No time for that. Tears wouldn't do any good. She had to think. Should she call a funeral home? No, a doctor first, surely, even if she was truly past

31

saving. A doctor would tell her what had to be done, who had to be notified.

She went into the kitchen and turned on the light, noticing as she did so how the darkness outside seemed to drop like a curtain against the window. In the cabinet near the phone she found the thin local phone book and looked up the listing for physicians. There were only a few of them. Ellen chose the first number and – hoping that a town this size had an answering service for its doctors – lifted the receiver.

There was no dialling tone. Puzzled, she pressed the button and released it. Still nothing. Yet she didn't think the line was dead, because it wasn't completely silent. She could hear what might have been a gentle breathing on the other end of the line, as if someone somewhere else in the house had picked up the phone and was listening to her.

Jarred by the thought, Ellen slammed the receiver back into the cradle. There could be no one else in the house. But one of the other phones might be off the hook. She tried to remember if there was another phone upstairs, because she shrank at the thought of returning to her aunt's room without a doctor, someone in authority, to go with her.

But even if there were another phone upstairs, Ellen realised, she had not seen it or used it, and it was not likely to be causing the trouble. But the phone in her aunt's room could have been left off the hook by either her aunt or herself. She would have to go and check.

He was waiting for her in the hall.

The breath backed up in her throat to choke her, and she couldn't make a sound. She stepped back.

He stepped forward, closing the space between them.

Ellen managed to find her voice and, conquering for the moment her nearly instinctive fear of this man, said, 'Peter, you must go get a doctor for my aunt.'

32

'Your aunt has said she doesn't want a doctor,' he said. His voice came almost as a relief after the ominous silence.

'It's not a matter of what my aunt wants anymore,' Ellen said. 'She's dead.'

The silence buzzed around them. In the darkness of the hall Ellen could not be sure, but she thought that he smiled.

'Will you go and get a doctor?'

'No,' he said.

Ellen backed away, and again he followed her.

'Go and see her for yourself,' Ellen said.

'If she's dead,' he said, 'she doesn't need a doctor. And the morning will be soon enough to have her body disposed of.'

Ellen kept backing away, afraid to turn her back on him. Once in the kitchen, she could try the phone again.

But he didn't let her. Before she could reach for the receiver, his hand shot out, and he wrenched the cord out of the wall. He had a peculiar smile on his face. Then he lifted the telephone, long cord dangling, into the air above his head, and as Ellen pulled nervously away, he threw the whole thing, with great force, at the floor. It crashed jarringly against the linoleum, inches from Ellen's feet.

Ellen stared at him in horror, unable to move or speak, trying frantically to think how to escape him. She thought of the darkness outside, and of the long, unpaved road with no one near, and the deserted beach. Then she thought of her aunt's room, which had a heavy wooden door and a telephone which might still work.

He watched her all this time, making no move. Ellen had the odd idea that he was trying to hypnotize her, to keep her from running, or perhaps he was simply waiting for her to make the first move, watching for the tell-tale tension in her muscles that would signal her intentions.

Finally, Ellen knew she had to do something – she could

33

not keep waiting for him to act forever. Because he was so close to her, she didn't dare to try to run past him. Instead, she feinted to the left, as if she would run around him and toward the front door, but instead she ran to the right.

He caught her in his powerful arms before she had taken three steps. She screamed, and his mouth came down on hers, swallowing the scream.

The feel of his mouth on hers terrified her more than anything else. Somehow, she had not thought of that – for all her fear of him, it had not occurred to her until now that he meant to rape her.

She struggled frantically, feeling his arms crush her more tightly, pinning her arms to her sides and pressing the breath out of her. She tried to kick him or to bring a knee up into his crotch, but she could not raise her leg far enough, and her kicks were feeble little blows against his legs.

He pulled his mouth away from hers and dragged her back into the darkness of the hall and pressed her to the floor, immobilizing her with the weight of his body. Ellen was grateful for her jeans, which were tight fitting. To get them off – but she wouldn't let him take them off. As soon as he released her, even for a moment, she would go for his eyes, she decided.

This thought was firmly in her mind as he rose off her, but he held her wrists in a crushing grip. She began to kick as soon as her legs were free of his weight, but her legs thrashed about his legs, her kicks doing no harm.

Abruptly, he dropped her hands. She had scarcely become aware of it and hadn't had time to do more than think of going for his eyes, when he, in one smooth, decaptively casual motion, punched her hard in the stomach.

She couldn't breathe. Quite involuntarily, she half doubled over, knowing nothing but the agonizing pain. He, meanwhile, skinned her jeans and underpants down

34

to her knees, flipped her unresisting body over as if it were some piece of furniture, and set her down on her knees.

While she trembled, dry-retched, and tried to draw a full breath of air, she was aware of his fumbling at her genitals as scarcely more than a minor distraction. Shortly thereafter she felt a new pain, dry and tearing, as he penetrated her.

It was the last thing she felt. One moment of pain and helplessness, and then the numbness began. She felt – or rather, she ceased to feel – a numbing tide, like intense cold, flowing from her groin into her stomach and hips and down into her legs. Her ribs were numbed, and the blow he had given her no longer pained her. There was nothing – no pain, no messages of any kind from her abused body. She could still feel her lips, and she could open and close her eyes, but from below the chin she might as well have been dead.

And besides the loss of feeling, there was loss of control. All at once she fell like a rag doll to the floor, cracking her chin painfully.

She suspected she was still being raped, but she could not even raise her head and turn to see.

Above her own laboured breathing, Ellen became aware of another sound, a low, buzzing hum. From time to time her body rocked and flopped gently, presumably in response to whatever he was still doing to it.

Ellen closed her eyes and prayed to wake. Behind her shut lids, vivid images appeared. Again she saw the insect on her aunt's dead lip, a bug as black, hard, and shiny as Peter's eyes. The wasp in the sand dune, circling the paralyzed spider. Aunt May's corpse covered with a glistening tide of insects, crawling over her, feasting on her.

And when they had finished with her aunt, would they come and find her here on the floor, paralyzed and ready for them?

She cried out at the thought and her eyes flew open. She saw Peter's feet in front of her. So he had finished. She began to cry.

'Don't leave me like this,' she mumbled, her mind still swarming with fears.

She heard his dry chuckle. 'Leave? But this is my home.'

And then she understood. Of course he would not leave. He would stay here with her as he had stayed with her aunt, looking after her as she grew weaker, until finally she died and spilled out the living cargo he had planted in her.

'You won't feel a thing,' he said.

Why did he show her the wasp and spider? Wanted her understanding which was more than the spider had after the attack

36

DOLLBURGER

When she listened hard, Karen thought she could hear the men downstairs searching for dolls. Although she didn't know what they looked like, she thought of them as hairy troll-like men with the large square teeth of horses. She glanced at the attic door. All her dolls were safe in there. Surely the men would never come upstairs into her room?

The thought made her clutch the blankets to her chin, her body rigid with the effort of not breathing. The bed was safe, it had always been a sanctuary, but she didn't know the powers or limits of these doll thieves and could only guess at protection. She'd learned about them just that morning, from her father.

'Daddy, have you seen Kristina?'

'Let daddy read his paper, sweetie – he doesn't know which doll Kristina is,' her mother said, flipping pancakes.

Daddy dipped a piece of toast in his coffee and looked at it thoughtfully before biting. He replied with his mouth full.

'Did you leave her downstairs?'

'Yeah – I think.'

Daddy shook his head. 'Shouldn't have done that. Dangerous. Don't you know what happens to dolls that get left downstairs all night?'

Karen glanced quickly at her mother. Catching the half smile on her mother's face, Karen raised her eyebrows sceptically.

'No,' she said, in a tone that dared him.

Daddy shook his head again and consumed the last of the piece of toast.

'Well, if you leave your doll downstairs, you can just expect that when those men come looking –'

'What men?'

He looked surprised that she should need to ask. 'Why the men who eat dollburgers, of course!'

'Dollburgers?'

'Just like hamburgers. Only, of course, made out of dolls.'

'No.'

'No?'

'People don't eat dolls, and dollburgers are just tiny hamburgers, like what Mommy made on my last birthday, which you feed to dolls.'

'But dolls don't eat – people do.'

'You *pretend*,' Karen said, exasperated with him. He was shaking his head.

'I don't care what you call little hamburgers – but I happen to know about dollburgers. People eat them, and they're made out of dolls. There are people who just love them. Of course, they're illegal; so they have to sneak around, looking for houses where little girls have forgotten to put their dolls safely away. When they find abandoned dolls, they pop them into a sack until they collect enough to grind up into dollburgers.'

'That's a story,' Karen said.

Her father shrugged. 'I'm just trying to warn you so when you lose a doll you'll know what's happened to it and maybe you'll be more careful in the future.'

Her mother came to the table. 'No dollburgers in *this* house. Pancakes though. Karen, get your plate if you want some.'

Karen suddenly remembered where she'd left Kristina. Of course – last night before she went to bed, she and Kristina had been lost in the wilderness and had crawled into a cave to rest for the night – Kristina must still be in the cave.

'In a minute,' she said, and went purposefully into the living room.

The bridge table was the cave, but there was no doll underneath. Karen dropped to her hands and knees. Kristina was gone. Something gleamed in the corner by a table leg, and she picked it up.

A blue eye gazed impassively up from her hand. There were some shards of pink plastic on the carpet. Kristina?

'Karen, do you want pancakes or don't you?'

'In a minute,' she called, and carefully picked up each tiny piece and put it in her pocket. She looked at the eye again. Kristina's eyes were blue. She put the eye in her pocket.

'Daddy,' she asked over pancakes, 'do the people – the people who eat dollburgers – do they ever just, you know, eat dolls? I mean, right where they find them?'

Her father considered. 'I suppose sometimes they get so hungry that they might just crunch up a doll right there, with their teeth,' he said. 'You never know what they'll do.'

'I'm sure Kristina is perfectly safe,' said her mother. 'I'll help you find her after I do the dishes.'

After breakfast Karen went up to her room and examined the eye and the pieces of pink plastic, the last remains of Kristina. What Daddy had said about the dollburger eaters was real, then, and not just a story like the grizzly bear in the cedar closet.

Karen had the attic room. Her closet was actually the attic itself – without wallpaper, beams bare overhead and decorated with bits of discarded furniture and boxes of old clothes. She kept her toys there, and it was home to all her dolls. She took Kristina's eye there, climbed onto a rickety chair, and put it in a secret place atop a ceiling beam. It would do better than a funeral, she thought, since there was so little of poor Kristina left.

The dolls watched her steadily from their places. Karen looked around at all of them from her position atop the chair, feeling queen of all she surveyed, giant queen-mother to all these plastic, rag, and rubber babies.

Hard-faced Barbie sat stonily beside doltish Ken in front of their dream house. Her clothes spilled out of the upstairs bedroom; two nude teenagers (Barbie's friends) sprawled in the kitchen.

The bride doll sat next to Princess Katherine where she'd sat for months undisturbed. There was dust in her hair, and the shoulders of her white gown looked grimy. Princess Katherine's crown was bent, her green dress stained, and her lower right leg secured to the upper leg with Band-Aids and masking tape.

Raggedy Ann, Raggedy Andy, Aunt Jemima, and Teddy-bear slouched together in the rocking chair. The talking dolls, Elizabeth, Jane, and Tina sat grimly silent. The babydolls had been tossed into one crib where they lay like lumps. Susan, bald and legless, had been wrapped tenderly and put in the blue plastic bassinet.

Karen looked at the top of the old dresser, where Kristina used to sit with Beverly. Now Beverly sat there alone. Karen felt tears in her eyes: Kristina had been her favourite. She suddenly felt uncomfortable standing above her dolls, felt that they were blaming her for Kristina's disappearance.

She felt guilt, a heaviness in her stomach, and thought she saw grim indictment on the still, staring faces.

'Poor Kristina,' she said. 'If only someone had warned me.' She stepped down from her perch, shaking her head sadly. 'If only daddy had told me before – then I could have protected her. When I think of all the times I've left some of you out – well, now that I know I'll be sure to take good care.'

She looked around at the dolls, who had not changed

40

expression, and suddenly the silence of the attic became oppressive.

Louisa, Karen's best friend, called that afternoon. 'Would you and Kristina care to join me and Isabella in having a tea party?' she asked in her best society-lady voice.

Karen assumed a similar voice to reply. 'Oh, my deah, I would love to, but Kristina has been kidnapped.'

'Oh, how dreadful, my deah.'

'Yes, it is, my deah, but I think I shall bring my other child, Elizabeth.'

'Very good. I shall see you in a few minutes. Ta-ta.'

'Ta-ta, my deah.'

Elizabeth was one of the talking dolls, always her favourite until golden-haired Kristina had come as a birthday gift.

Louisa's little sister Anne and her ragdoll Sallylou were the other guests at the tea party, treated with faint disdain by Louisa and Karen for their lack of society manners.

'Why don't you let Elizabeth eat her own cookie?' Anne demanded as Karen took a dainty bite. Elizabeth had politely refused the treat.

'Be quiet, silly,' Louisa said, forgetting her role. 'Dolls don't eat cookies.'

'Yes, they do.'

'No, they don't.'

'Uh-huh.'

'They do not.'

'Well, if they don't, then what *do* they eat?'

'Nothing.'

'Pretend food,' Karen amended. 'They have to eat pretend food because they only have pretend teeth and pretend stomachs.'

Anne shook her head. 'Sallylou has *real* teeth, and so she has to eat real food.'

'Oh, she does not,' Louisa said. 'All you do is mash

41

cookies in her face so she gets crumbs all over her. Show me her teeth if she has them.'

'I can't, 'cause her mouth is closed,' Anne said smugly.

'You're just stupid.'

Later, when they were alone, Karen told Louisa what had happened to Kristina and watched her friend's eyes grow wider. This was no story; it was real and immediate, and the proof was the blue eye now lying on a bed of dust and staring unceasingly at the attic roof.

Karen's ears ached from trying to hear movement downstairs. She always lay awake at the top of the house, feeling silence and sleep wrap the house from the bottom up until it finally reached her and she slept. But now every distant creak of board, every burp of pipe, made her tense and listen harder. She'd left no dolls downstairs, of course, but what if those men should not be deterred by stairs but were lured on by the scent of dolls up in the attic?

She thought of Louisa across the street and wondered if she too lay awake listening. Louisa, she knew, had put all her dolls under the bed, the safest place she could think of.

Karen suddenly thought of her own dolls, more frightened than she, sitting terrified in the dark attic, listening to the sounds as she did and wondering if the next creaking board would bring a dark sack over their heads, labelling them dollburger meat. It was her duty to protect them.

She went on bare feet to the attic door, the full moon through her window giving her light enough to find her way. She opened the attic door and thought as she did so that she heard a movement inside, as if perhaps a doll had been knocked over.

She had to go inside the attic several feet to reach the light cord. Her bare foot nudged something as she did, and when the light came on, she looked down to see what it was.

Poor, bald, legless Susan lay naked on the floor, and Karen noticed at once that Susan now was not only legless, but armless as well. When she picked her up, small shards of pink plastic fell from the arm sockets.

Karen felt an almost paralysing fear. They were up here, somehow in the attic without having come past her bed, and already they'd begun on her most helpless doll. Holding Susan to her, she began to gather all the other dolls into her arms. She lifted the skirt of her nightgown to make a bag and tumbled the dolls in there. They were scattered around as if they'd been thrown, none in their right places. Barbie on the floor, Ken in the rocking chair with Raggedy Andy and the bride.

Every time she bent to pick up another doll, she was sure she could hear the muffled breathing of the hungry dollburger eaters and feel the pressure of their eyes against her back.

She began to pray, whispering and thinking, 'Oh, please, please, please, oh, please.'

Finally she had all the dolls together, and she stumbled to the door and closed it, leaving the light still burning in the attic. For safety she pushed her chair in front of the door.

Then she went to bed, arranging all the dolls around her, lying down, falling asleep sandwiched by their small hard bodies.

She may have dreamed, but she never woke as they began to move closer to her in the night, and she didn't see the crumbs of plastic that fell from Elizabeth's open, hungry mouth.

COMMUNITY PROPERTY

Ellis had to drive, which meant that Susie got to hold Gonzo on her lap. He hated her for that, among so many other reasons. He felt close to tears at the memory of Gonzo's plump, furry little body, the warmth of him, the sudden tension in his skinny legs when something outside the window caught his attention.

Ellis didn't want to lose his dog. Most of all, he didn't want to lose his dog to *her*.

The house, community property, would have to be sold. The car was his, and he would keep it along with his hunting rifles and stereo system. The dishes, records, and furniture had been, with the help of the lawyers, divided fairly, even if neither party was entirely satisfied. But how did you divide a dog? Unthinkable to sell him, as if Gonzo were no more than a piece of community property like a house or a television set. Equally unthinkable for either Ellis or Susie to give the dog up to the other. It was impossible, and humiliating, to imagine custody of the dog granted to one and only visitation rights to the other.

His lip rose in a sneer. Visitation rights, with Susie laying down the law to him about when and where? No thanks. Once the divorce was final, he intended never to see the bitch again.

'Don't hold him like that,' he said without looking at her. 'Let him put his head out the window.'

'And have him jump out after some other dog and get hit by a car? Christ, you'd love to hang *that* over me, wouldn't you?' Her voice was dry ice.

'He wouldn't jump out. He's a smart dog. You always underestimate his intelligence. He's wiggling like that because you're squeezing him.'

'Just watch the road, would you? And don't talk to me.'

The animal clinic came in view, and with the sight of it his heart seemed to freeze. His hands tightened on the steering wheel. He wanted to touch Gonzo, to roll him on the ground, to pull his ears, to scratch the white patch on his chest.

He thought of Gonzo as he had first seen him: a patch-work scrap small enough to fit in one cupped hand. There was a lump in his throat and the taste of salt in his mouth. He couldn't go through with it.

Susie let out an ugly snuffling whimper as he turned the car into the parking lot, and the lump in his throat dissolved. Listen to her – you'd almost think she was feeling something.

'We don't have to do this,' Ellis said, putting the car in park but leaving the engine running. 'Just say the word.'

'Say the word and let you take him, you mean.' Her voice was strangled with tears. 'Hell, no. If you're so big-hearted, *you* say the word and *I'll* keep him.'

'This was your idea in the first place,' Ellis said, and it had been. It was a horrible idea, too. But he could not bear the thought of seeing her win, of losing Gonzo to her. He could stand to lose, but not to see her win.

She said, speaking for them both, 'I'd sooner see him die than see you get him.'

'All right,' he said, and switched off the car.

Gonzo understood where he was now, and began to struggle in her arms.

'You'll drop him. Let me carry him inside,' Ellis said, reaching for the writhing dog. Susie clutched Gonzo more tightly and backed away. Driven by a feeling of unfairness – she'd got to hold the dog all the way here – he followed, but she fled to the doorstep. With bad grace, but not wanting the people waiting with their pets inside to see him struggling with his wife, Ellis opened the door and let her carry the dog in.

'We have an appointment,' Ellis said to the receptionist. 'And we don't have time to wait all day.'

'Um, what's the problem?' The receptionist was young and seemed intimidated by him.

'We'll tell that to the vet.'

Blushing, the girl went to find a vet.

Gonzo had stopped struggling, but he was trembling violently now, and the whites of his eyes showed. A temporary truce went into effect between husband and wife under the watching eyes of all the other pet-owners present, and they both stroked Gonzo, their hands occasionally colliding, and murmured words meant to soothe him.

'Dr Blake will see you,' the receptionist said when she returned. Ellis had never met Blake before – a young man, he was presumably new to the clinic.

'What seems to be the problem?' he asked, his manner a nice mixture of cheerfulness and sobriety.

Silence for a moment, neither husband nor wife wanting to be the one to say the words. Finally, setting his jaw and hating her for making him do it, Ellis said, 'We want you to put our dog to sleep.'

'Oh? Is he ill? Young dog, isn't it?' The vet reached out and Susie retreated, arms closing more tightly about the animal. Ellis hissed her name and she stopped and let the vet take the frightened dog from her arms. She was trembling almost as much as the animal.

'You know,' said the vet, looking at her kindly, 'many problems people think are serious often aren't, really. We can cure many diseases that . . .'

'He's not ill,' Susie said. 'We just want you to, please, put him to sleep.'

'Kill him? But why?'

'I really don't think that's any of your business,' Ellis said coldly. 'We'll pay whatever it costs, of course. It's not as if we're asking you to do something illegal.'

The vet stiffened, and Ellis knew he had used the wrong tone of voice. 'Not illegal, perhaps,' said the vet. 'But I find it immoral to kill a healthy young dog for no good reason.'

'But we have a good reason,' Susie protested. 'We don't want him to suffer. He wouldn't be happy without us – he'd suffer if we gave him away to strangers. But if you put him to sleep – it really would be just like putting him to sleep, wouldn't it? – he wouldn't feel any pain, he wouldn't know what happened.'

Ellis could see that had thawed the vet a bit. Susie's earnest, almost child-like manner coupled with her beauty would thaw any man – until he got to know her too well.

'If a dog *is* suffering, then frequently the best thing is to put it to sleep. But I'm talking about physical suffering – I doubt the anguish he'd suffer at being parted from you and your husband would be great enough to justify euthanasia. He wouldn't be in any physical pain, and he'd soon get used to a new home and have a long life ahead of him.'

'I think we know what's best for our dog,' Ellis said. 'If you're not willing to put him to sleep, I'm sure we can find someone who is.'

'I doubt that,' said Dr Blake. 'I doubt you'll find any reputable vet willing to kill a perfectly healthy dog.' He stroked Gonzo's trembling flank. 'Look, if you can't keep the dog, why not give him away? He seems like a nice, friendly little dog. Why don't you let me take him? I'll find him a good home.'

'No. Absolutely not. We don't want to give him away,' Ellis said. 'There's no point in wasting your time – there are plenty of other vets in town.'

'But if you can't find one who'll agree?'

Ellis shrugged angrily. 'That's ridiculous. They gas dozens of dogs down at the pound every day. It wouldn't be as quick and painless as you could do it here, but . . .'

'But at the pound there would be a chance of someone else finding him and giving him a good home.'

'That's out of the question. We don't want anyone else to have our dog.'

Dr Blake shrugged. 'I think you better get used to the idea. I think I can guarantee you won't find a vet in town to go along with you. You'll have to take your dog to the pound.'

Ellis stared at the vet. 'If you won't make it easy for me,' he said quietly, 'think of this: there's no law that says a man can't shoot his own dog.'

Susie whimpered. 'Oh, he would,' she said, gazing at the vet for help. 'He would shoot Gonzo. Please . . . I don't want Gonzo to suffer.'

'All right,' the vet said, his lips tight. 'I'll save your dog from that.' Grim-faced, he put the dog on a metal table and motioned to Ellis to hold the dog still.

'He won't feel any pain,' Ellis said, as the vet prepared the needle.

'It's better this way, for all of us,' Susie said almost prayerfully.

They were both stroking the dog, on either side of some invisible property line, when it died.

The woman burst into tears and snatched up the body, keening over it while Ellis pulled at her arms, trying to get the body for himself.

Disgusted, the vet called in his assistant and managed to get the dog's body away from the weeping pair. 'City health regulations,' he said, as the assistant carried it out to dispose of it.

Ellis looked at the vet through a glaze of pain and tears and suspected that he lied, but it didn't matter. There was no point in fighting over the body now. Gonzo was gone.

'Some people,' said the vet bitterly as they turned to leave, 'shouldn't be allowed to have pets.'

They sat in the car; Susie weeping inconsolably, Ellis too drained to start the car. His grief had dissolved the hatred he felt for his wife. He no longer blamed her, any more than he blamed himself. The dog's death now seemed some unavoidable, senseless tragedy, some act of God which had destroyed the life they had built together.

Susie was sobbing the dog's name like a prayer. After a moment he joined her, weeping without shame. He forgot where they were, he forgot how Gonzo's death had come about, he forgot how much he hated his wife, forgot everything except this immense, dreadful loss which united them. He put his arms around her and they rocked back and forth in their shared grief, their tears running together.

Later, in the house they no longer officially lived in, the house largely stripped of furniture and soon to go on the market, they shared a bottle of plum brandy that had been left behind, unwanted or unnoticed, in a cabinet.

All they could think of was Gonzo. The memory of the dog still made Susie break out in fresh tears from time to time, but Ellis was through with his crying. He thought about Gonzo deliberately, testing himself, probing at the sore memory as if it were a wound just starting to heal.

'I loved that dog more than anything,' he mused aloud. 'Much more than I care for most people. I'd have given up anything for that dog.'

'You!' She was shocked out of her tears. 'You think you were the only one? How about me? Don't you know how I loved him? He was just like a child to me – the child *you* didn't want.'

He remembered then just why they had taken Gonzo,

49

the dog that had become so much a part of their lives that it was hard to remember a time without him.

Ellis had been laid off, bringing in $68 a week in unemployment while he looked for another job. She was making $125 a week as a receptionist, and complaining bitterly about having to work. They were quarrelling a lot – not always about money – and the subject of divorce had come up more than once.

Then Susie had got pregnant. Worse – she wanted to quit her job and have the baby. It would make them a family. It would keep the marriage together. On $68 a week.

Ellis had, after more hair-raising scenes and threats than he cared to remember, finally convinced her to have an abortion.

Three days after the abortion, while she was still lying in bed weeping and using up her sick leave, Ellis had gone to the pound and picked out the cutest puppy he could find.

It had been intended as a gift to cheer his wife up. He hadn't expected how much he would come to love the flippantly named Gonzo, how important the dog would become to both of them.

'I should never have let you make me have that abortion,' Susie said. 'If I'd had a baby I'd still have it – and we might not even be getting divorced. Somebody else would have taken Gonzo from the pound and he'd still be al-l-l-l-live.' She burst into tears yet again.

He moved across the couch to comfort her. Just then, he would have done anything to get Gonzo back. But that was one thing he could not do. He felt very close to Susie, knowing that she was feeling the same sorrow and loss that he felt. Suddenly he wanted her, more than he had in a very long time.

He began unbuttoning her blouse, consoling her with

his flesh. She forgot her tears and began responding to his urgency.

Sprawled across the couch she suddenly whispered, 'I don't have anything – I stopped taking the pill when I moved out.'

'It doesn't matter,' he said recklessly, suddenly seeing the answer to their irreplaceable loss. 'I love you; I want to be with you. We were crazy to think about a divorce.'

'We'll start all over again,' she murmured happily.

'We'll have a baby,' he said. 'We'll have a baby as we should have before. We'll start it right now.'

One photograph angered him the most. It showed Susie with little Jessica on her lap, as smug as she could be about having the child all to herself. Doling out the minutes to him only when it pleased her, while she could be with Jessica whenever she wanted.

'Of course, if you think you've got a case,' his lawyer had said. 'But I'd better warn you – the court nearly always lets the child stay with the mother, unless we can provide some compelling reason why not.'

He would find a compelling reason. Ellis flipped through the photographs again. All harmless. The first detective hadn't been able to get anything on her. She was keeping clean – at least until the divorce was final. But that careful morality wouldn't last long – she'd soon be sleeping around. He would keep a detective on her – a really good one, this time – until he had the proof he needed to get his child away from her.

He stared at the photograph. He wouldn't let that bitch get the better of him.

The house, community property, would be sold. They each had a car and their personal belongings, and the rest of the property had been divided up after many arguments and consultations with both lawyers. Neither was entirely happy about the result, but it was fair, they agreed, a fair division of property.

But how could you divide a child? You couldn't. Somebody had her, and somebody didn't. Unless nobody had her.

He looked across the room at his gun rack and crumpled the photograph in his fist.

FLYING TO BYZANTIUM

successful Eastern Roman empire, withstood fall of western Rome

Byzantine: complex, murky

The steady noise and pressurized atmosphere inside the plane made everything seem slightly unreal. Was she really going back to Texas?

She thought of flat, coastal plains, mosquitoes whining in the humid night air, dirty white plumes of smoke rising from industrial stacks, her mother's house, and the dreary brightness of the Woolco, and a familiar misery possessed her.

No. Her hands clenched in her lap. She was going back to Texas, but not to the stagnant little town on the Gulf Coast where she had grown up; she was flying to Byzantium.

The name of the town made her smile: how the dreams of the pioneers became the lies of property developers! She didn't know Byzantium. She had never heard of it before the invitation to spend the weekend as a guest of honour at a science fiction convention held there. According to the map, Byzantium was more than five hundred miles west of the southeastern swamp where she had grown up. West Texas to her meant deserts and dust, cowboys and rattlesnakes, rugged mountains etched against postcard sunsets: it was the empty space between Houston and Los Angeles, traversed by air.

She lived in Hollywood now, and Texas was no longer home. She was Sheila Stoller, author of *Moonlight Under the Mountain*, and her fans were paying for the privilege of meeting her.

Sheila pulled her traveling case from beneath the seat and took out her notebook, thinking of Damon. He had been impressed by her invitation to Byzantium, more than she was herself. But then he was an actor. Public appearances were something he understood, a sign of success. It had never occurred to him that Sheila might not accept – perhaps that was why she had. Away from him, though, she felt her confidence flag. She knew nothing about science fiction. Wouldn't the others at the convention see her as a fraud? She had written a speech in her notebook, the story of how she had written *Moonlight Under the Mountain*, but the speech was a fraud, too, a carefully constructed fiction. She stared down at the page wondering if she would have the nerve to read it.

The notebook had been a gift from Damon. 'For your next novel,' he had said, giving it to her with his famous, flashing smile. And she had taken it, unable to tell him that there would not be a next novel.

Ordinary people had ordinary jobs in Hollywood, as they did everywhere else, as sales assistants, as waiters, as secretaries and caretakers, but in Hollywood the jobs were always temporary; the people in them were *really* actors, directors, dancers, singers, producers, writers waiting for the main chance. Damon had been an actor working as a waiter until his pilot took off: now he had a minor but regular role in a weekly comedy series. He was the wisecracking roommate's best friend. Viewing figures and audience response were both good, and he was on his way up.

He thought that Sheila was on her way up, too. It was true she made her living doing temporary secretarial work, but she'd had one novel published, and surely it was only a matter of time until she was well-paid and famous: all she had to do was to keep on writing.

But Sheila didn't write anymore. She no longer felt the need.

Writing, for Sheila, had always been a means of escape. It took her out of herself, away from loneliness, dull school

54

classes, and the tedium of working behind a counter at the local Woolco. When she was writing she could forget that she wasn't pretty, didn't have a boyfriend or an interesting job, had no talents and no future. She'd had no friends because she never tried to cultivate any. Girls her own age thought she was a weird, stuck-up bookworm – she thought they were boring, and didn't bother to hide her opinions. Her quirky intelligence made her reject most of the people and things around her, but did not make her special enough to be forgiven. Despite her reading, she was an indifferent student, lazy in the classroom and inept at sports. She tried to write for the school magazine and newspaper, but after several cool rejections she learned to keep her writing to herself.

She wrote another world into existence. It was a fairy-tale world full of monsters and treasures, simpler, starker, and more beautiful than the reality she felt suffocating her, and she escaped into it whenever she could. Her universe contained a vast and dangerous wasteland spotted with small, isolated villages. One of the settlements had a mountain rising from its centre, towering over everything, dominating the landscape and the lives of those who lived there. For beneath the mountain was a series of maze-like tunnels where dwelt the evil, powerful grenofen. They kept the townspeople in terror until a young girl, Kayli, won her way through a series of adventures, battles, and enchantments to triumph over the grenofen and steal their sacred treasure for herself.

Sheila shared her world with no one, and never thought of publication, except as a vague fantasy. It was her mother who brought it about, indirectly. Sheila knew she was a disappointment to her mother – she almost took pleasure in it. Something in her seemed to compel contradiction, and as long as her mother nagged her about her appearance Sheila would eat too much, forget to wash her hair, and dress in unattractive, poorly fitting clothes. Her mother thought scribbling in notebooks was a waste of time, and it was her disparaging comment on a 'writers' weekend' being held at a local college which made Sheila consider attending. And it was there that Sheila met the editor who ultimately published *Moonlight Under the Mountain*.

She didn't make a lot of money from the book – the reality wasn't like her fantasy – but it gave her enough to leave Texas, to fly to Los Angeles and buy a used car and find her own apartment before she had to look for work. On the West Coast, in the sunshine, far from her mother's nagging, Sheila blossomed. She took an interest in the way she looked, bought fashionable clothes, joined a health spa, had her hair permed, and exchanged her heavy, smudged glasses for a pair of tinted contact lenses.

Damon met her while she was temping in his agent's office. He admired her clear, emerald eyes, her smooth, tanned skin, and slim figure, but those things were the norm in California – it was her book which caught his attention. He admired writers, and liked the idea of dating one so much that Sheila didn't know how to tell him the truth. She had written a book, but that didn't make her a writer in the way that he was an actor. Writing was one of the things – like baby fat, acne, and bad manners – she had left behind her in Texas.

They were like ghosts of her past, standing there waiting for her in the Campbell County Airport. Sheila knew them at once, without any doubt, and knew she had been wrong to come.

'Sheila Stoller?'

They knew her, too, and that was another bad sign; like calling to like. She wished she could deny her name, but she nodded stiffly, walking toward them.

There were two of them: a fat one swathed in purple,

and a thin one in a lime-green polyester trouser suit and teased, bleached-blonde hair. She knew them – they were the unwanted. They were the sort of people she had been lumped in with at school, always the last to be chosen for teams or dances. Her mother had pushed them on her, inviting them to parties, but Sheila had preferred loneliness to their company. She always shunned them rather than admit that she was like them.

'How do you do,' said the thin one. 'I'm Victoria Walcek, and this is Grace Baxter.'

Victoria would be smart, Sheila knew. Too smart for her own good. A bookworm with a sharp tongue and too many opinions, no one would like her, but she would exert a special influence over one or two followers; dull, timid outcasts like her fat friend.

'Your plane was late,' said Victoria.

The tone was reproving and before she could catch herself Sheila said, 'I'm sorry.'

Victoria smiled. 'That's all right. We didn't mind waiting. Do you have much luggage coming?'

'Only this.' She indicated the small case.

Victoria gave a dainty shriek. 'That's all? How do you manage? I couldn't possibly . . . my hot-curlers and makeup would just about fill that little bag. I always need a big garment bag whenever I go anywhere. I suppose I worry too much about the way I look . . . I like to have everything just right. It's much more sensible to travel light and just not think about that.'

'Sheila looks very nice,' said Grace with so much emphasis that it sounded like a lie. Sheila tried not to mind, but she wished Grace hadn't felt obliged to defend her. She knew how she looked: more fashionable and far more comfortable in her pink and grey tracksuit than Victoria in her ugly green polyester and high-necked ruffled blouse.

'Of course she does,' said Victoria. 'I didn't mean to

imply otherwise! Only with that little bag . . . well, there can't be more than one change of clothes in there.'

'I'm only staying the weekend.'

'Oh,' said Grace, sounding surprised. 'We thought you'd want to stay . . . being from Texas, and all.'

'I only came for the convention. I can't afford – I need to get back.'

'To your writing?' asked Grace.

The lie came easily. 'Yes, I've started a new book.'

'Oh, please tell us about it!'

'Wait until we get to the car,' said Victoria – her sharpness might have been directed at either of them or both. 'We've still got a long way to go.' She turned with a twitch of her narrow shoulders which said she didn't care if she was followed or not, and Sheila felt trapped into hurrying after.

'How far are we from Byzantium?'

'Fifty miles,' said Grace, huffing and puffing beside her.

'Fifty! I had no idea – '

Victoria glanced over her shoulder. 'I thought you came from Texas?'

'Not this part.'

Victoria exhaled sharply. It sounded like disbelief, but Sheila couldn't imagine why.

Outside, the darkness and heat disoriented Sheila, who remembered the cool, blue Los Angeles evening she had so recently left. She knew nothing about this place, she thought as Victoria steered the big car away from the lights and out into the unrelieved blackness of the vast country night. There was nothing on which she could focus but the stars winking in the distance, or the bright, white line down the centre of the highway.

'Now tell us about your new book,' said Grace from behind her. 'Is it a sequel to *Moonlight Under the Mountain*? I loved that book so much!'

'No, how could it be? Kayli escapes at the end – she's found the secret of the grenofen and can travel. She's free at last. How could there be a sequel?'

'Well, she might have to go back. Maybe there could be a friend she wants to rescue. Or she could be kidnapped . . . most of the grenofen are still under the mountain.'

'It would just be boring to send her back,' said Sheila. 'The new book will be something completely different.'

'Grace writes too,' said Victoria. 'Maybe you would be kind enough, while you are visiting here, to read something of hers and critique it.'

Sheila stared into the blackness, wondering what sort of landscape the night concealed. Suddenly the headlights swept across a small herd of jackrabbits by the side of the road. One of them was sitting up on his haunches and gazing, with dazzled eyes, directly at her. A thrill of strangeness made her smile. Here was something to tell Damon!

'Of course I will, if Grace wants me to. How about you Victoria – do you write, too?'

'Oh, no. My talents lie in another direction,' said Victoria primly. 'In my own small way I am something of an artist. My interests are in painting, sketching, and in fashion and costume design. You'll see my latest efforts at the convention.'

'Wait'll you see!' cried Grace, bouncing hard on the back seat.

'Sit still!'

Grace subsided as if bludgeoned. Sheila felt sorry for her, and yet contemptuous, for she invited such treatment by allowing it. As mile after dark mile passed and Sheila felt civilization – even if only represented by the Campbell County airport – growing more distant, she realised that she was even more dependent upon Victoria's goodwill than Grace was. She could be trapped here in this strange desert, with no car, no money, no friends, no knowledge of

59

her surroundings if Victoria decided Sheila wasn't deserving of her attention. It was a crazy notion, sheer paranoia, and yet she knew nothing about these people. Why had they invited her? Why had she come?

Out of the darkness came the familiar, cheery glow of a Ramada Inn sign, and Sheila felt a rush of relief that made her smile. Whatever was out there in the darkness, whoever these two people were, she knew, now, where she was.

The clock above the registration desk showed nearly midnight, and Sheila yawned reflexively, reminding herself that it was an hour earlier in Los Angeles, and wondering what Damon was doing. Was he thinking of her?

Victoria's melodramatic shriek sliced into her thoughts.

'I did,' said Grace in a high, terrified voice. 'I did reserve a room, honestly I did!'

'Yes, I know,' said the desk clerk. 'And I'm really sorry. But we couldn't keep it for you. Our check-in time is seven P.M. It's the same all over the country. You can request us to hold the room for as many hours after that as you like, but unless the request is made, after seven P.M. we assume the registered guest is a no-show, and we give the room to someone else. And all our rooms are taken tonight.'

'But I didn't know,' Grace wailed. 'It's not my fault that I didn't know.'

'It is your fault,' said Victoria in arctic tones. 'I gave you the responsibility of reserving the room, and that includes finding out check-in times.'

Sheila had the feeling that they would go on arguing whose fault it was all night, and she would still be without a place to sleep. 'Isn't there some other hotel?' she asked.

'Are you kidding?' said Victoria.

'There's one over by Taylor,' said the desk clerk. 'It's a Holiday Inn, but I'd be happy to make a phone call to check if they've got a room for you.'

'No,' said Victoria sharply. 'Taylor's thirty miles from here. I'm not driving all that way there and back. You can stay with me tonight. Luckily, I have two beds in my room. I know it won't be as nice for you, and I'm sorry about this. I apologize for Grace's stupidity – shut up, Grace. You won't mind sharing a room with me, will you?'

'Well, I don't think I really have a choice, do I?' said Sheila. She knew she was being ungracious and forced herself to sound grateful. 'It's very nice of you to offer. Thank you.'

The town of Byzantium was four miles farther down the highway, and in the darkness Sheila received no clear impression of it. A yellow bug-light on the porch revealed Victoria's house as an ordinary, one-story, white-painted frame house of the sort she'd often seen elsewhere. There was nothing special or unusual about it.

But the moment she stepped inside she broke into a sweat of fear. It was only Victoria's physical presence at her back which kept her from bolting, and after another moment she realised that it was the smell of the house she had responded to so powerfully. It was the smell of her mother's house, as if she had fallen back in time. But there was nothing mysterious or even unlikely about it – just an unfortunate combination of a particular brand of furniture polish, air freshener, and a whiff of bacon grease.

'Keep quiet,' Victoria breathed at her ear. 'Just follow me. Mom's asleep.' Still shaken by the physical force of memory, Sheila obeyed. Victoria had told her in the car that she lived with her widowed mother.

'Welcome to my sanctum sanctorum,' said Victoria, and closed the bedroom door. Sheila was not usually bothered by claustrophobia, but as the door closed she felt her throat tighten and she began to have trouble breathing. The room was so crowded with books, furniture, and clutter that it felt more like a storage closet than a place to live. Sheila looked around, trying to relax by taking in details.

There was a fussy, pink and white dressing table with a lighted mirror; narrow twin beds separated by a chest of drawers; a slant-topped, professional drawing table and adjustable chair; and bookshelves covering two walls, overstuffed with books and seeming to strain at their moorings. Sheila looked at one of the beds and at the burdened shelves above it, and hoped that nothing would fall on her in the night. Where there was wall space not covered with books, paintings and photographs had been mounted. Sheila recognized various famous movie and television stars in customary poses, but the paintings were uninspired: landscapes in unlikely colours, and stiff, mannered depictions of dragons, unicorns, and strangely dressed people.

'Most of the art is mine,' said Victoria. 'But I won't bore you with my creations right now.' She giggled. 'Oh, it's so exciting, having a real, live author in my very own room!'

Sheila realised suddenly that the bossy Victoria wasn't as self-confident as she pretended – that she was actually shy – but the understanding didn't change her feelings. Of course, it wasn't Victoria's fault that this house reminded her of her own past, or that in Victoria's nagging and bossing of Grace Sheila heard her mother's disappointment: *Would it kill you to show a little interest? To be friendly?*

Yes, she thought now, it *would* have killed her. If she had made friends and found contentment in the life her mother wanted for her it would have killed her soul. She would never have written. She would have felt no need to escape.

She looked at Victoria's pinched, sourly hopeful face. Victoria was trapped, even if she didn't know it, but Sheila had escaped. She could afford to show a little kindness.

'It's a very nice room,' she said. 'You'll have to show me your designs in the morning . . . not right now because I'm too tired to appreciate anything but bed.'

'Oh, silly me! Of course you're tired – I forgot how late it is. It's just that I'm so excited.'

Sheila decided she liked Victoria even less when she was giggly and excited, but there was no escape from her now except into silence and herself: the same old thing.

'It's like being a kid again, having someone spend the night,' Victoria said in the darkness. 'Didn't you used to love going to slumber parties?' *what happened to Grace?*

Sheila had been to only one slumber party, attending under pressure from her mother. She did now what she had done then and pretended to sleep. But she lay awake for what seemed hours, listening to Victoria's adenoidal breathing and hearing, behind it, her mother's voice: *Think you're better than all the other girls? Too good to talk to them? You think you're different?*

She knew she was different. She knew she was better. The hard part was to hang on to that knowledge, and resist all those who tried to make her ordinary.

Sheila woke feeling as exhausted as if she had been struggling rather than sleeping all night, and when she saw herself in the bathroom mirror it was clear that she had lost the struggle.

There were days when she liked her face, but this was not one of them. Makeup didn't really help, and her hair was hopeless. Confronted with the change in atmosphere and the dry, gritty wind of West Texas, it seemed the permanent had given up, leaving her with a lank, lifeless, mousy brown mop.

Her clothes, which had looked so fresh and fashionable in California, now looked drab and badly cut. They were wrinkled from having been packed, and they no longer fitted: the fabric of the skirt stretched unattractively tight across stomach and hips, while the blouse simply hung on her. Sheila had the eerie feeling that she had changed *wouldn't change but in one day* shape overnight. She sucked in her stomach as hard as she could and turned away from the mirror, not ready to face Byzantium, but having no other choice.

Daylight revealed what had been hidden by the night: towering above ordinary frame houses and scrubby trees was a vast, looming presence, a rugged brown peak.

'What's that?'

Victoria smiled disbelievingly. 'What do you think? It's the mountain.'

She was finding it hard to breathe – probably the effect of holding in her stomach, but it felt as if she was afraid. Of the mountain? That was silly. 'I just didn't realize there would be a mountain here.'

'Oh, come on!'

'No, really. I thought this part of Texas was all flat.'

Another hard look from Victoria. 'But it's the most famous thing about Byzantium, our mountain.'

That made Sheila laugh, despite her unease. 'Look, no offense, but "famous" is not a word I'd use about Byzantium! I'd never even heard of your town until you wrote me.'

'Really? And you've never been here before?'

'Never.'

'Well. That is a surprise. I'd better show you why. We'll go up where you can see it all . . . why don't you close your eyes until I tell you to look? It'll be more impressive that way.'

Most of the drive was a gradual ascent – too gentle to be up the mountain, and it seemed to Sheila that the car was travelling away from the peak. It was not long before the car pulled to a stop and Victoria said, 'You can open your eyes now.'

They were outside of town, up on a ridge, in a roadside parking area created especially for the view: there were coin-operated telescopes there, and a map mounted behind plastic, with the state highway department seal on it. Sheila took in the view mechanically, eyes scanning the distance, the hazy blue sky and a line of faraway mountains, then, just below, on the flat valley floor, the town of Byzantium, buildings clustered around the single peak rising like some rough, hunched beast furred brown and green.

And then she saw what she was seeing. She knew this landscape – she had been here many times before. She had invented the town, the mountain, and the wasteland beyond. She had written it into existence.

'You see?' said Victoria. 'You had to come here.'

The Ramada Inn had what they called a conference centre, and it was there – a detached, windowless, concrete building on the other side of the swimming pool that the First Byzantium Science Fiction Convention was held.

When Sheila and Victoria arrived, they found Grace sitting behind a table near the door, with a cashbox and a list of names.

'We've had fifteen people so far,' she said, looking apprehensively up at Victoria. 'I think that's pretty good for the first hour.'

'How many are you expecting?' Sheila asked.

'A lot,' said Victoria. 'Science fiction is big business these days, and there's never been a convention in this part of the state. I'm sure it'll be a big success. Here, put this nametag on. I designed it especially, so people can pick you out as the Guest of Honour.'

'What am I supposed to do?'

'This evening you'll judge the costume contest. Until then, just enjoy yourself. Give the fans a chance to talk to you. Be friendly.'

Sheila felt tired and uncertain of herself. She wanted to retreat, having seldom felt less like talking to strangers.

But she had agreed to come and must make an effort. She moved away from the registration desk to begin her tour of the convention.

The conference centre consisted of the small reception area where Grace sat, three small seminar rooms, and one big hall. In one seminar room Sheila found four boys and two girls huddled in a circle with dice and notebooks, playing Dungeons and Dragons. They didn't even look up when she entered, too involved with their fantasy to notice her.

The next seminar room contained eight or ten dark shapes gazing at a large television screen upon which flickered an episode of *The Prisoner*.

The main hall had a podium and microphone set up at the far end, unused. At the near end several tables had been set up and people were selling used paperbacks, comics, posters, little clay and metal figurines, and other paraphernalia. Some artwork was displayed, and Sheila recognized the paintings as Victoria's work.

People of both sexes, most of them apparently in their teens or early twenties, milled around the room. Sheila noticed a very fat man in a kilt, with a plastic sword belted at his side, and a skinny young woman in a black knitted mini-dress, who might have been attractive beneath the layer of green paint she wore over all exposed flesh. But even the people not in costume – the boy reading a paperback novel on the floor, frowning in fierce concentration; the acned young man whose shirt-pocket bulged with different coloured pens; the girl talking into a tape-recorder – seemed to exist in some other, private universe, and even if she had found any of them the slightest bit attractive, Sheila could not have approached without feeling herself an intruder.

'Excuse me, are you Sheila Stoller?'

Sheila turned to see an ordinary-looking teenager, a

girl in blue jeans and a pink T-shirt, holding up a copy of *Moonlight Under the Mountain* in much the way that people in horror films presented crosses to vampires. She smiled with relief and pleasure. This was what she was here for, after all: to be the author.

'Yes, I am.'

'Oh!' The girl sounded surprised. 'I thought – I don't know – I thought you'd look more – like a writer.'

'How is that? With thick glasses and a typewriter tucked under my arm?'

'No, I thought you'd be more glamorous. Well, would you sign my book? Make it out to Lori.'

Sheila did as she was told. 'Did you like it?'

'Oh, I haven't read it yet. I bought it because somebody told me it was sort of like Anne McCaffrey. I love Anne McCaffrey. I've read everything she's ever written. I was hoping they could get her to come here, but ... Thanks for the autograph. It was nice meeting you.' She slouched away, leaving Sheila bemused. Was that it? Was that why she was here, to disappoint Anne McCaffrey fans and sign unread books?

She went back to the registration area to find Victoria and Grace, and was discouraged to find that even they were no longer interested in her. It was an effort to make them talk, and as she struggled she wondered why she was bothering.

'So ... Victoria, you're interested in art. Do you plan to study it professionally, go to art school, or ... were you an art major in college?'

Victoria looked at her coldly. 'I didn't *go* to college. As I told you last night. It wasn't possible. We couldn't afford it and mother couldn't really do without me. Mother has problems with her health. As I told you.'

Sheila felt herself getting hot. She didn't know how to apologize without making things worse. She should have been paying attention instead of daydreaming, as usual. 'I'm sorry . . . I was tired last night, and . . .'

'You were probably thinking of *me*,' Grace said. '*I* went to college.'

'And much good it did you,' said Victoria. 'You can't get a job with your history degree now, can you? I've got a job in cosmetics, at Eckard's Drugs. I get a discount on all my perfume and makeup. It's a good deal. And it's a pretty creative job, sometimes. It calls for someone like me with taste and a good eye for colour to tell the ladies what lipstick would suit them, and how to put on blusher to make the most of their own features. You should have seen the makeover I did for Grace! I don't know why she doesn't fix herself up like that all the time. It would only take a half hour in the morning, and it makes all the difference in the world.'

Grace was getting steadily redder, and glaring at her feet. Sheila tried to feel some sympathy for her, but was too repelled. Did she have to be so fat and her hair so greasy? Makeup would probably only aggravate her skin problems, but surely she could make *some* effort.

'It might even help you get a job,' Victoria went on. 'If you looked more . . .'

'Don't want a job,' Grace mumbled. She raised her head defiantly. 'I need time to write.' She looked at Sheila. 'Don't you? Don't you need time to write?'

Before Sheila could think of how to answer, Victoria spoke for her. 'But you also need to earn a living,' she said. 'You can't sponge off your parents forever. You're twenty-four.'

'So? They don't mind.'

'But for how long? And how long before you actually finish your novel? You're too comfortable; you think you've got all the time in the world. How many years have you been working on it? Three? Four?'

Sheila was beginning to feel Grace's discomfort as her own, as if Victoria's jabs had been aimed at her. This was a familiar, old quarrel, but it was nothing to do with her. She wouldn't even try to break it up. She only wanted to get away and leave them to it.

Looking at her watch, Sheila said, 'Maybe I should check into my room now. There doesn't seem to be too much going on, and I'd like a chance to put my things away and maybe have a shower.'

Victoria and Grace looked at each other in a way that made Sheila's heart sink.

'I'm not saying this is your fault,' said Victoria carefully. 'Don't get me wrong. But we haven't had as many people register for the convention as we had hoped for.'

'How could that be *my* fault?'

'Well, a big-name guest will draw more people ... but I'm not saying it is your fault, you understand. If people didn't come to see you, it's our fault for assuming that everybody would like *Moonlight Under the Mountain* as much as us ... but that's probably not the reason, anyway. Grace probably didn't coordinate the publicity and press releases well enough – never mind, Grace, I'm not blaming you.'

'I don't understand. If you don't think it's my fault, why are you telling me?'

'Well, of course it's not your fault! And no matter *how* much money we lose on this, Grace and I will feel that it was worth it to get you to come here. I knew when I wrote out the check for your airplane ticket that I probably wasn't going to get my money back, and that isn't important. The thing is, we just don't have that much money left over ... for non-essentials. And since I've got a spare bed anyway ...'

Sheila just stared at her, refusing to give in.

Victoria sighed. 'We just can't afford to pay for your

hotel room. I'm sorry about that. But you are more than welcome to go on sharing my room. Like last night. You didn't mind sharing, did you?'

She couldn't answer honestly; she was trapped. Sheila bowed her head, giving in. She was doing figures in her head, furiously, but she already knew she couldn't afford to rent her own hotel room. She thought, longingly, of Damon, wondering how he would handle the situation. But Damon would never be in such a situation, she felt certain. His agent would have arranged everything better than she had been able to do for herself.

'Excuse me for a few minutes,' she said. 'I have to make a phone call . . . I have to let my boyfriend know where I'll be.'

But Damon wasn't in. Of course, it was silly of her to have expected him to be sitting at home in the middle of the day, but that made no difference to her disappointment.

She hung around the lobby for another twenty minutes, unwilling to return to the convention, leaning against the wall by the telephone as if waiting for a call. She wondered if she was expecting too much of Damon. She thought of them as a couple – an awareness of him and what he would think informed all her actions – but to him, she thought reasonably, she was probably just another girlfriend. They had made no promises to each other. She knew it wasn't fair to blame him for anything – for this trip to Texas, for not being in when she needed him – that was like Victoria, always apportioning blame. But although she fought against it, that was the way she felt.

Wal her mother

'We'll take you out for a nice dinner,' Victoria said. 'Our treat.'

It wasn't Sheila's idea of a treat: a drive to Byzantium to feast, far inland, in a Long John Silver Seafood Shoppe. The fried fish and potatoes were almost tasteless, but

Sheila covered them with ketchup and ate her way steadily through the meal. It was a way of not thinking, of not caring that Victoria and Grace could chatter away about private concerns as if she were not there. She was still thinking, painfully, of Damon, and finally, when the food was gone and they lingered over large paper cups of iced tea, she couldn't keep it to herself any longer. She told them about Damon.

She didn't say a word about her doubts: she wanted to impress them. It was such a joy to speak of him possessively, casually, and to see the dim, faint envy on their faces. Any boyfriend at all was good, but Damon was a TV star. They knew how handsome he was, how desirable.

She was explaining how they had first met when Victoria interrupted. 'Come on, girls, we've got things to do. We've got to get back to the Ramada. We'll stop at the Dunkin' Donuts on the way for our dessert.'

Sheila was irritated at being cut off, but knowing Victoria's jealousy must be responsible made it easier to bear. She had proven just how different her life was from the lonely existence Victoria and Grace had to suffer, and Victoria couldn't like the reminder.

At the convention, Sheila was left alone with the box of donuts while Victoria and Grace went off to prepare for the costume contest. Sheila was the judge, but she didn't feel burdened: nothing was really at stake. The only prize was a scroll hand-decorated by Victoria.

There were only eight entries, and two of them were jokes more than costumes: an Invisible Man, and a Time Traveler in Authentic Costume of the 1980s. Sheila leaned on the podium in the darkened hall, unable to see the audience for the glare of the spotlights, and watched the contestants parade slowly past: a mangy Wookie, a scantily clad Amazon, a Vulcan couple who performed a pretend marriage ceremony, and the green-painted girl

71

she had noticed earlier, now wearing a diaphanous gown and huge, painted cardboard wings.

Victoria and Grace came last, and when they emerged from darkness into light Sheila did not recognize them. She saw, not strangers, but two characters she knew very well, her own creations come to life.

She saw Kayli, triumphant in red velvet, brandishing a gleaming sword, leading a hunch-backed, shaggy, conquered grenofen on a leash.

Her heart threatened to choke her, and she leaned forward, nearly dislodging the microphone, to peer against the dazzle of the spotlights, trying to see through the illusion.

Fake fur and a papier-mâché head could disguise Grace, but how on earth had the unattractive Victoria been transformed to Kayli, as noble, heroic, and beautiful as Sheila had always known her to be. Was it possible that Kayli was *real*? That she wasn't an invention, but a real person, a resident of Byzantium, and Victoria had found her? What magic was this?

But it was all illusion, even if she couldn't penetrate it. Of course Kayli and the grenofen were only Victoria and Grace, revealed when they came forward to accept their prize.

Later, sharing the few remaining donuts and listening to Grace's delight at having won, Sheila could hardly take her eyes from Victoria. The glamour of Kayli clung to her still, making her eyes shine and her cheeks glow, giving her plain, sharp features a beauty Sheila envied.

'Weren't the costumes just perfect?' Grace demanded again. 'Weren't they just exactly how you imagined they would look when you were writing the book, Sheila?'

Sick at heart, yet she could not deny it, Sheila pretended her mouth was too full to speak, and nodded. She knew her denial would have made no difference: Victoria had triumphed, and they both knew it.

Now Victoria smiled graciously. 'It's nice of you to say so, Sheila. Of course, this prize should be *yours* just as much as ours, because without you ... well, without you there wouldn't be a Kayli. You created her first, in your book. And then I was fortunate enough to be able to bring her to another kind of life.'

You stole her from me, Sheila wanted to say. *Kayli was mine, Kayli was me – you took her away and you had no right.* But although that was what she felt, Sheila knew well enough how it would sound. She could say nothing. Once *Moonlight Under the Mountain* had been published, anyone could know Kayli. There might even be someone, like Victoria, who had more claim on Kayli now than Sheila did. Sheila, after all, had scarcely thought of Kayli since she sent her in her book out into the world. She had not thought of her as a real person until she saw her in Victoria.

It wasn't until later, after they had dropped off Grace at her house and driven back to Victoria's, that Sheila realised she had been robbed of something more concrete than a fictional character.

'My suitcase!'

'What?'

'My overnight bag,' Sheila said, twisting feverishly around in the seat. 'Do you remember what I did with it? Did we put it in the trunk?' Even as she asked she could remember only too well how she had slung it into the back seat, and she could see that it was not there.

'You didn't say anything about it to me. Why on earth did you bring it? Why didn't you just leave it here at home?'

'Because I thought I would be staying in the hotel.'

'Oh, Sheila,' said Victoria in the weary tone she used so often with Grace. 'You don't mean to tell me you left it in my car all day – unlocked!'

'It's *your* car. I thought you'd lock it!'

'Don't shout at me. If you'd said anything, I would have

suggested we lock it in the trunk. I never imagined you'd leave something valuable in the car.'

'It wasn't valuable. It was just my clothes, my notebook –' the magnitude of her loss struck her and she stopped, struggling against tears. All lost. Everything she had owned in this desolate place.

'Now, don't cry,' said Victoria. 'That'll only make you feel worse. Things will look better in the morning. Let's go to bed.'

She let Victoria lead her to the house but balked at the bedroom door. 'I want to use the phone.'

'At this hour!'

'It's earlier in California. Please. I have to. It's important. The operator can bill me.'

'I do not think this is a good idea,' said Victoria in a tight, disapproving voice. 'But if you insist, the phone is in the kitchen. Try not to wake mother, please.'

Damon would be able to put everything into perspective. She knew that if she could only hear his voice things would be better. She would realize that she hadn't lost everything, only a few material possessions. She could buy herself new clothes, and Damon would give her another notebook. But she needed to hear him say so.

His service picked up the call. No, he wasn't in; no, he had left no message for her; no, she really couldn't say when he would be back. Sheila left her name with Victoria's phone number. 'Tell him to call me whatever time it is, morning or night. Tell him it's urgent.' She didn't care if the ringing of the phone woke the whole house. The most important thing was to make contact again with her life in California, to convince herself that it was real and this place the fantasy. The sound of Damon saying her name would wake her from this nightmare of loss and confusion.

She tried not to think of what would happen if Damon

didn't phone back. She told herself that she was over-tired and that things would look better in the morning, even if it was Victoria who had said so.

Things looked different in the morning, but not better.

It began when Sheila lost a contact lens down the drain. In three years she'd had no problems, but after one moment of sleepy carelessness in a strange bathroom she had no choice but to put on her old glasses. Then she saw herself – really saw herself – in the big bathroom mirror, and she wanted to scream in protest.

She was not, she refused to be, the person she saw in the mirror. That was the old Sheila blinking through thick, smudged lenses, the self she had outgrown, with lank, greasy hair, dandruff, and pimples. That Sheila was so fat she could scarcely fasten her skirt, despite the fact that it had fitted the day before.

Sheila reached out, and the creature in the mirror reached, too, until they were touching. They were the same. She didn't want to believe it, but she had no choice. She was trapped in that hateful body again, as if she had never been different.

Victoria's voice came through the door. 'Hurry up in there, we've got to get moving! Your guest-of-honour speech is scheduled for an hour from now!'

Her speech was inside the lost notebook. Sheila began to tremble. She had no idea what she had written, what the words said. She knew she couldn't give a speech without that text. She unlocked the door and told Victoria.

Victoria, dressed like a Victorian governess in a high-necked white blouse and a long grey skirt, her face made up like a doll's with smears of blue eye-shadow and rosy blusher, did not hesitate. 'You'll give the speech. I don't care what you say. But you will give the speech.'

'You can't make me.'

Victoria settled her glasses. She didn't look angry. There

75

was the hint of a smile about her mouth. 'We paid to bring you here, and people have paid to hear your speech. Those people aren't going to be let down. Somebody is going to give Sheila Stoller's speech, even if it has to be me.'

Sheila felt her mouth go dry.

'I can talk about your book as well as you can, probably better,' Victoria went on. 'I've read it four times; I *know* it. You saw how I was as Kayli. I could be the author of *Moonlight Under the Mountain* just as easily. I can tell them what they want to hear – better than you could.'

Sheila believed her. She shook her head.

'Oh, yes,' said Victoria. 'If you don't believe me –'

'I'll give the speech.'

Victoria's smile settled and hardened. 'I know you will.'

'I need to make a phone call,' Sheila said.

'Who?'

'My boyfriend.' She clung to that last, fragile hope. Even though he had not returned her call, he had to be in now – it was a Sunday morning – and as soon as he picked up the phone and heard who it was, his voice would go warm and teasing. Her fears would all vanish in the sunshine of his love. 'Damon,' she said, savoring his name. 'I told you about him yesterday –'

'Oh, come off it, Sheila! Nobody believes you. It's childish to pretend you know Damon Greene.'

'I'm not pretending!' She tried to laugh, but it sounded more like a sob.

'Oh, no? And did you have a nice little conversation with him last night?'

'I couldn't get through to him last night.'

'Well, I'm glad you're still in touch with reality to that extent.'

Sheila was shaking. She wished it was with anger, but it felt like fear. 'Look,' she said. 'I'm not lying to you, and I'm not crazy. I'm in love with Damon Greene, and –'

'Oh, yes, I'm not questioning *your* feelings. But that doesn't mean you can phone him up, or that you have any special privileges, you know.' Victoria's hands fastened claw-like on Sheila's shoulders and she steered her down the passage, into the bedroom. 'I'm going to show you something. Look there on the wall.'

She hadn't noticed it before – individual photographs tended to get lost among the many taped and tacked up around the room – but now she saw the picture which had appeared in *People Magazine*, the posed shot of Damon and three of his costars from the new series. Her heart beat faster at his familiar smile. 'Oh, yes, I know that picture –'

But already Victoria was turning her away from it, allowing her no comfort, turning her toward the frilly dressing table with its makeup mirror. 'Now look at that. Look at yourself. Do you expect me to believe that Damon Greene would even consider going out with something that looks like *that*?'

But that's not *me*, Sheila wanted to protest. That's not the Sheila Damon knows; that's not who I am in California, in my real life. It's this place which has changed me.

'What really disgusts me,' said Victoria, 'is the way you don't even make an effort. You could try to make something of yourself, the way I do. Learn to use makeup and how to do your hair, eat sensibly, and follow my advice on clothes. But, no, you'd rather stuff your face with food and sit around all day imagining that television stars are in love with you. You'll never change, and I don't know why I knock myself out trying to help you.'

Staring at the horror in the mirror, Sheila began to cry. The great, wrenching sobs reddened her face, making her even uglier, and she felt the button on her skirt pop, and cried even harder at the hopelessness of her life.

'Your own mother wouldn't know you,' said Victoria, satisfied, and Sheila gazed into the mirror thinking that she wouldn't have known herself, either. Victoria had made up her face, covering the spots and making her eyes look bigger; her hair was hidden beneath a brightly patterned scarf, and her body in a tent-like yellow dress borrowed from Grace. She felt uneasy with her new image, but at least it was an improvement on the old one.

When they reached the convention they found between twenty and thirty people gathered in the main hall, waiting for Sheila's speech – about half the number who had registered.

'Now, don't be afraid,' said Victoria. 'They're just ordinary people, like you. Say anything you want to them.'

'Anything,' said Sheila dazedly. 'What . . .'

'Tell them how you wrote your book.'

'I don't . . . I can't remember . . . what can I say?'

Victoria stared at her. 'Do you want me to give the speech?'

Sheila backed away, shaking her head. She couldn't remember why, but she knew she must do this herself. She must not give Victoria the chance to . . . what?

'What are you waiting for?' demanded Victoria. 'Go on, they're waiting.'

Sheila stumbled toward the podium. In the large room the sound of applause was feeble and sporadic. As it died away, she stared at them, her audience. Who were they? They all wore glasses; most of them looked adolescent. She was reminded, horribly, of the time her mother had pressured her into trying for the debating society, and how she had gone utterly blank in front of them all, without a word in her head. Just like now.

The silence stretched. The sound of her own breathing was horribly loud. Her hands clenched, and she realised she was holding something. When she looked down, her own name blazed up at her in yellow letters. It was her book, a copy of *Moonlight Under the Mountain*. With shaking fingers she opened it and began to read.

Gradually the familiar words, the well-known story, Kayli's presence, all soothed her, and she was dreaming aloud, the audience forgotten. At the end of a chapter she looked up, pausing because her throat was dry, and was startled by the burst of applause.

She thought it would be all right to leave then, but as she turned Victoria blocked her way. Her face was grim and Sheila backed away, feeling threatened.

'I'm sure we all enjoyed that very much,' said Victoria. 'And now, perhaps you'll say a few words about how you came to write what you've just read us?'

Sheila shook her head, incapable of speech.

But Victoria seemed to have expected that, and scarcely paused. 'Questions from the audience, then. Does anyone have a question they'd like to ask Sheila Stoller? No? Well, I'll start the old ball rolling, then. About the setting of your novel, Sheila . . . what made you choose Byzantium?'

'I didn't – I didn't choose it!'

'*It* chose you?' The audience laughed at Victoria's inflection and Sheila felt herself blushing. Victoria said kindly, 'I suppose it was a natural affinity. You felt a connection to this place and so you wrote about it. Writers do that all the time, turning their lives into fiction. And what about Kayli? What can you tell us about her? Is she based on someone real?'

It went on, with Victoria asking questions Sheila could not answer, and then answering them herself. Sheila no longer knew if she agreed or disagreed with the things Victoria was saying; she hardly knew what she was talking about, whose book or life they were discussing.

It ended, finally; not only the interrogation but the whole convention, and Sheila went with Victoria and Grace for lunch in the coffee shop. She was glad that they talked to each other and left her alone to eat, but when the meal was over she glanced at her watch and fidgeted, working up the courage to say, finally, 'Isn't it getting kind of late?'

'Late for what? Was there something on TV – you-know-who isn't on tonight, is he?'

Sheila felt herself blushing. She wasn't going to talk about Damon; she would pretend she hadn't heard. 'I just don't want to miss my plane,' she said.

Victoria stared in disbelief, and Sheila's certainty crumbled. 'It . . . is tonight, isn't it? Not tomorrow?' She couldn't spend another night with Victoria; another night and she might never get away, she thought.

'What are you babbling about, Sheila?' said Victoria, as wearily as if this was an old, old question.

Sheila dug in her bag for the ticket, praying that it had not been stolen, too. But there it was; she pulled it out, seeing the stiff blue folder enclosing the flimsy ticket, but when she looked at it more closely, she froze. It was a one-way ticket. There could be no mistake, yet she stared, willing herself to be wrong, reading it again and again. Had it changed in the same way and for the same occult reasons as she had herself? Why hadn't she noticed before? She was certain that she would not have left Los Angeles with only a one-way ticket in her hand – not a one-way ticket to Texas, and no money for her return.

'I can't stay here,' she said. 'I have to go back.'

'Where would you go back?'

'Home. Los Angeles.'

'That's not your home. What's in Los Angeles? Damon Greene? Your imaginary boyfriend? You really think he'll notice if you're in Los Angeles or in Texas?'

'But I live there – I have an apartment and a job –'

'You don't. You've been making things up again. People like you don't live in Hollywood. You wouldn't fit in.

80

You're much better off here, where you belong. You can stay in my room, and I might even be able to wangle you a job at Eckard's. It's not a bad place to work. You'll have time to write. You'll settle down.'

She wanted to argue, but everything she thought she knew had slipped away. What could she give as proof? Damon? The apartment? The series of temporary jobs in glamorous locations? All those things felt unreal now, as if she had only seen them on television. 'I won't stay here . . . you can't make me.'

'How ungrateful!' said Grace, and Sheila looked at her, really for the first time since she had met her. She was shocked by the envy and hatred she saw on the fat, white face.

'She doesn't mean to be rude,' said Victoria. 'She just doesn't understand.'

'Oh, yes I do,' said Sheila, although she didn't. 'I'm not stupid, I can see what you're doing to me. Changing me, confusing me, trapping me. All right, you've got me now, but not forever. Maybe I can't afford to leave now, with twenty dollars in my purse, but it won't take me long to get out of here. I'm not like you. I got away once before. It's not just dreaming. I had another life – the life I wanted. A life you'll never know. I wrote a book and had it published.'

'You think that makes you special?'

'I know it does. I'm different from you.'

Victoria adjusted her glasses, checked the top button on her blouse, and moistened her lips. 'You may be different,' she said in her thin, colourless voice, 'but you need us. Don't blame us for that. We didn't trick you into coming here; nobody forced you to use that ticket. You wanted to come back, so we helped you. Hollywood was no good for you. You couldn't measure up, and you couldn't write any-more. You wanted to escape but you didn't know where or how. So we helped you. You're safe here, and you can stay just as long as you like.' She looked down at her empty plate, wiped her mouth with a folded napkin, and said, 'I think we might as well go home now, don't you?'

Not my home, thought Sheila, but she followed them out to the car. During the dark, familiar drive back to Byzantium she was thinking furiously, planning her escape.

Money was the most important thing, so she would get a job, even if it meant working in a drugstore with Victoria. She didn't have to pay attention to her. And she would go on a diet and start exercising to lose this flab; get a facial scrub and do something about her hair, buy herself some more clothes, and when she was herself again she'd fly back to Los Angeles and take up her real life.

Sheila leaned back against the seat, feeling something inside her unknot. With all that out of the way, she could think about something more interesting. It was as easy as dreaming.

Kayli was under the mountain again, although Sheila wasn't sure exactly why. Kayli didn't know, either. Her mind was cloudy with drugs, and someone had tied her hands behind her and left her in this dark turning of one of the tunnels. She didn't know where she was or what she had to do, but she would triumph. Despite her confusion, despite the constraints, her will was unbroken. All through the night she planned her escape.

TREADING THE MAZE

We had seen the bed and breakfast sign from the road, and although it was still daylight and there was no hurry to settle, we had liked the look of the large, well-kept house amid the farmlands, and the name on the sign: The Old Vicarage.

Phil parked the Mini on the curving gravel drive. 'No need for you to get out,' he said. 'I'll just pop in and ask.'

I got out anyway, just to stretch my legs and feel the warmth of the late, slanting sun rays on my bare arms. It was a beautiful afternoon. There was a smell of manure on the air, but it wasn't unpleasant, mingling with the other country smells. I walked towards the hedge which divided the garden from the fields beyond. There was a low stone wall along the drive, and I climbed onto it to look over the hedge and into the field.

There was a man standing there, all alone in the middle of the field. He was too far away for me to make out his features, but something about the sight of that still figure gave me a chill. I was suddenly afraid he would turn his head and see me watching him, and I clambered down hastily.

'Amy?' Phil was striding towards me, his long face alight. 'It's a lovely room – come and see.'

The room was upstairs, with a huge soft bed, an immense wooden wardrobe, and a big, deep-set window which I cranked open. I stood looking out over the fields.

There was no sign of the man I had just seen, and I couldn't imagine where he had vanished to so quickly.

'Shall we plan to have dinner in Glastonbury?' Phil asked, combing his hair before the mirror inside the wardrobe door. 'There should still be enough of the day left to see the Abbey.'

I looked at the position of the sun in the sky. 'And we can climb the tor tomorrow.'

'*You* can climb the tor tomorrow morning. I've had about enough of all this climbing of ancient hills and monuments – Tintagel, St Michael's Mount, Cadbury Castle, Silbury Hill – '

'We didn't climb Silbury Hill. Silbury Hill had a fence around it.'

'And a good thing, too, or you'd have made me climb it.' He came up behind me and hugged me fiercely.

I relaxed against him, feeling as if my bones were melting. Keeping my voice brisk, mock-scolding, I said, 'I didn't complain about showing you all the wonders of America last year. So the least you can do now is return the favour with ancient wonders of Britain. I know you grew up with all this stuff, but I didn't. We don't have anything like Silbury Hill or Glastonbury Tor where I come from.'

'If you did, if there was a Glastonbury Tor in America, they'd have a lift up the side of it,' he said.

'Or at least a drive-through window.'

We both began laughing helplessly.

I think of us standing there in that room, by the open window, holding each other and laughing – I think of us standing there like that forever.

Dinner was a mixed grill in a Glastonbury café. Our stroll through the Abbey grounds took longer than we'd thought, and we were late, arriving at the café just as the proprietress was about to close up. Phil teased and charmed her into staying open and cooking for two last customers. Grey-haired, fat, and nearly toothless, she

84

lingered by our table throughout our meal to continue her flirtation with Phil. He obliged, grinning and joking and flattering, but every time her back was turned, he winked at me or grabbed my leg beneath the table, making coherent conversation impossible on my part.

When we got back to The Old Vicarage, we were roped into having tea with the couple who ran the place and the other guests. That late in the summer there were only two others, an elderly couple from Belgium.

The electric fire was on and the lounge was much too warm. The heat made it seem even smaller than it was. I drank my sweet milky tea, stroked the old white dog who lay near my feet, and gazed admiringly at Phil, who kept up one end of a conversation about the weather, the countryside, and World War II.

Finally the last of the tea was consumed, the biscuit tin had made the rounds three times, and we could escape to the cool, empty sanctuary of our room. There we stripped off our clothes, climbed into the big soft bed, talked quietly of private things, and made love.

I hadn't been asleep long before I came awake, aware that I was alone in the bed. We hadn't bothered to draw the curtains, and the moonlight was enough to show me Phil was sitting on the wide window ledge smoking a cigarette.

I sat up. 'Can't you sleep?'

'Just my filthy habit.' He waved the lit cigarette; I didn't see, but could imagine, the sheepish expression on his face. 'I didn't want to disturb you.'

He took one last, long drag and stubbed the cigarette out in an ashtray. He rose, and I saw that he was wearing his woollen pullover, which hung to his hips, just long enough for modesty, but leaving his long, skinny legs bare.

I giggled.

'What's that?'

'You without your trousers.'

'That's right, make fun. Do I laugh at you when you wear a dress?'

He turned away towards the window, leaning forward to open it a little more.

'It's a beautiful night ... Cor!' He straightened up in surprise.

'What?'

'Out there – people. I don't know what they're doing. They seem to be dancing, out in the field.'

Half-suspecting a joke, despite the apparently genuine note of surprise in his voice, I got up and joined him at the window, wrapping my arms around myself against the cold. Looking out where he was gazing, I saw them. They were indisputably human figures – five, or perhaps six or seven, of them, all moving about in a shifting spiral, like some sort of children's game or country dance.

And then I saw it. It was like suddenly comprehending an optical illusion. One moment, bewilderment; but, the next, the pattern was clear.

'It's a maze,' I said. 'Look at it, it's marked out in the grass.'

'A turf-maze,' Phil said, wondering.

Among the people walking that ancient, ritual path, one suddenly paused and looked up, seemingly directly at us. In the pale moonlight and at that distance I couldn't tell if it was a man or a woman. It was just a dark figure with a pale face turned up towards us.

I remembered then that I had seen someone standing in that very field, perhaps in that same spot, earlier in the day, and I shivered. Phil put his arm around me and drew me close.

'What are they doing?' I asked.

'There are remnants of traditions about dancing or running through mazes all over the country,' Phil said. 'Most of the old turf-mazes have vanished – people stopped keeping them up before this century. They're called troy-towns, or mizmazes . . . No one knows when or why they began, or if treading the maze was game or ritual, or what the purpose was.'

Another figure now paused beside the one who stood still, and laid hold of that one's arm, and seemed to say something. And then the two figures fell back into the slow circular dance.

'I'm cold,' I said. I was shivering uncontrollably, although it was not with any physical chill. I gave up the comfort of Phil's arm and ran for the bed.

'They might be witches,' Phil said. 'Hippies from Glastonbury, trying to revive an old custom. Glastonbury does attract some odd types.'

I had burrowed under the bedclothes, only the top part of my face left uncovered, and was waiting for my teeth to stop chattering and for the warmth to penetrate my muscles.

'I could go out and ask them who they are,' Phil said. His voice sounded odd. 'I'd like to know who they are. I feel as if I *should* know.'

I stared at his back, alarmed. 'Phil, you're not going out there!'

'Why not? This isn't New York City. I'd be perfectly safe.'

I sat up, letting the covers fall. 'Phil, don't.'

He turned away from the window to face me. 'What's the matter?'

I couldn't speak.

'Amy . . . you're not crying?' His voice was puzzled and gentle. He came to the bed and held me.

'Don't leave me,' I whispered against the rough weave of his sweater.

'' Course I won't,' he said, stroking my hair and kissing me. '' Course I won't.'

But of course he did, less than two months later, in a way neither of us could have guessed then. But even then, watching the dancers in the maze, even then he was dying.

In the morning, as we were settling our bill, Phil mentioned the people we had seen dancing in the field during the night. The landlord was flatly disbelieving.

'Sure you weren't dreaming?'

'Quite sure,' said Phil. 'I wondered if it was some local custom . . .'

He snorted. 'Some custom! Dancing around a field in the dead of night!'

'There's a turf-maze out there,' Phil began.

But the man was shaking his head. 'No, not in that field. Not a maze!'

Phil was patient. 'I don't mean one with hedges, like in Hampton Court. Just a turf-maze, a pattern made in the soil years ago. It's hardly noticeable now, although it can't have been too many years since it was allowed to grow back. I've seen them other places and read about them, and in the past there were local customs of running the maze, or dancing through it, or playing games. I thought some such custom might have been revived locally.'

The man shrugged. 'I wouldn't know about that,' he said. We had learned the night before that the man and his wife were 'foreigners', having only settled here, from the north of England, some twenty years before. Obviously, he wasn't going to be much help with information on local traditions.

After we had loaded our bags into the car, Phil hesitated, looking towards the hedge. 'I'd quite like to have a look at that maze close-to,' he said.

My heart sank, but I could think of no rational reason to stop him. Feebly I tried, 'We shouldn't trespass on somebody else's property . . .'

'Walking across a field isn't trespassing!' He began to

walk along the hedge, towards the road. Because I didn't want him to go alone, I hurried after. There was a gate a few yards along the road by which we entered the field. But once there, I wondered how we would find the maze. Without an overview such as our window had provided, the high grass looked all the same, and from this level, in ordinary daylight, slight alterations in ground level wouldn't be obvious to the eye.

Phil looked back at the house, getting in alignment with the window, then turned and looked across the field, his eyes narrowed as he tried to calculate distance. Then he began walking slowly, looking down often at the ground. I hung back, following him at a distance and not myself looking for the maze. I didn't want to find it. Although I couldn't have explained my reaction, the maze frightened me, and I wanted to be away, back on the road again, alone together in the little car, eating apples, gazing at the passing scenery, talking.

'Ah!'

I stopped still at Phil's triumphant cry and watched as he hopped from one foot to the other. One foot was clearly on higher ground. He began to walk in a curious, up-down fashion. 'I think this is it,' he called. 'I think I've found it. If the land continues to dip . . . yes, yes, this is it!' He stopped walking and looked back at me, beaming.

'Great,' I said.

'The grass has grown back where once it was kept cleared, but you can still feel the place where the swathe was cut,' he said, rocking back and forth to demonstrate the confines of the shallow ditch. 'Come and see.'

'I'll take your word for it,' I said.

He cocked his head. 'I thought you'd be interested. I thought something like this would be right up your alley. The funny folkways of the ancient Brits.'

I shrugged, unable to explain my unease.

'We've plenty of time, love,' he said. 'I promise we'll climb Glastonbury Tor before we push on. But we're here now, and I'd like to get the feel of this.' He stretched his hand towards me. 'Come tread the maze with me.'

It would have been so easy to take his hand and do just that. But overriding my desire to be with him, to take this as just another lark, was the fearful, wordless conviction that there was danger here. And if I refused to join him, perhaps he would give up the idea and come away with me. He might sulk in the car, but he would get over it, and at least we would be away.

'Let's go now,' I said, my arms stiff at my sides.

Displeasure clouded his face, and he turned away from me with a shrug. 'Give me just a minute, then,' he said. And as I watched, he began to tread the maze.

He didn't attempt that curious, skipping dance we had seen the others do the night before; he simply walked, and none too quickly, with a careful, measured step. He didn't look at me as he walked, although the pattern of the maze brought him circling around again and again to face in my direction – he kept his gaze on the ground. I felt, as I watched, that he was being drawn farther away from me with every step. I wrapped my arms around myself and told myself not to be a fool. I could feel the little hairs standing up all along my arms and back, and I had to fight the urge to break and run like hell. I felt, too, as if someone watched us, but when I looked around, the field was as empty as ever.

Phil had stopped, and I assumed he had reached the centre. He stood very still and gazed off into the distance, his profile towards me. I remembered the man I had seen standing in the field – perhaps in that very spot, the centre of the maze – when we had first arrived at The Old Vicarage.

Then, breaking the spell, Phil came bounding towards

me, cutting across the path of the maze, and caught me in a bear hug. 'Not mad?'

I relaxed a little. It was over, and all was well. I managed a small laugh. 'No, of course not.'

'Good. Let's go, then. Phil's had his little treat.'

We walked arm in arm back towards the road. We didn't mention it again.

In the months to come those golden days, the two weeks we had spent wandering around southwest England, often came to mind. Those thoughts were an antidote to more recent memories: to those last days in the hospital, with Phil in pain, and then Phil dead.

I moved back to the States – it was home, after all, where my family and most of my friends lived. I had lived in England for less than two years, and without Phil there was little reason to stay. I found an apartment in the neighbourhood where I had lived just after college, and got a job teaching, and, although painfully and rustily, began to go through the motions of making a new life for myself. I didn't stop missing Phil, and the pain grew no less with the passage of time, but I adjusted to it. I was coping.

In the spring of my second year alone I began to think of going back to England. In June I went for a vacation, planning to spend a week in London, a few days in Cambridge with Phil's sister, and a few days visiting friends in St Ives. When I left London in a rented car and headed for St Ives, I did not plan to retrace the well-remembered route of that last vacation, but that is what I found myself doing, with each town and village a bittersweet experience, recalling pleasant memories and prodding the deep sadness in me wider awake.

I lingered in Glastonbury, wandering the peaceful Abbey ruins and remembering Phil's funny, disrespectful remarks about the sacred throne and King Arthur's bones. I looked for, but could not find, the café where we'd had dinner, and settled for fish and chips. Driving out of Glastonbury with the sun setting, I came upon The Old Vicarage and pulled into that familiar drive. There were more cars there, and the house was almost full up this time. There was a room available, but not the one I had hoped for. Although a part of me, steeped in sadness, was beginning to regret this obsessional pilgrimage, another part of me longed for the same room, the same bed, the same view from the window, in order to conjure Phil's ghost. Instead, I was given a much smaller room on the other side of the house.

I retired early, skipping tea with the other guests, but sleep would not come. When I closed my eyes I could see Phil, sitting on the window ledge with a cigarette in one hand, narrowing his eyes to look at me through the smoke. But when I opened my eyes it was the wrong room, with a window too small to sit in, a room Phil had never seen. The narrowness of the bed made it impossible to imagine that he slept beside me still. I wished I had gone straight to St Ives instead of dawdling and stopping along the way – this was pure torture. I couldn't recapture the past – every moment that I spent here reminded me of how utterly Phil was gone.

Finally I got up and pulled on a sweater and a pair of jeans. The moon was full, lighting the night, but my watch had stopped and I had no idea what time it was. The big old house was silent. I left by the front door, hoping that no one would come along after me to relock the door. A walk in the fresh air might tire me enough to let me sleep, I thought.

I walked along the gravel drive, past all the parked cars, towards the road, and entered the next field by the same gate that Phil and I had used in daylight in another lifetime. I scarcely thought of where I was going, or why, as I made my way to the turf-maze which had fascinated Phil and frightened me. More than once I had regretted not taking Phil's hand and treading the maze with him when he had asked. Not that it would have made any difference in the long run, but all the less-than-perfect moments of our time together had returned to haunt me and given rise to regrets since Phil's death – all the opportunities missed, now gone forever; all the things I should have said or done, or done differently.

There was someone standing in the field. I stopped short, staring, my heart pounding. Someone standing there, where the centre of the maze must be. He was turned away, and I could not tell who he was, but something about the way he stood made me certain that I had seen him before, that I knew him.

I ran forward and – I must have blinked – suddenly the figure was gone again, if he had ever existed. The moonlight was deceptive, and the tall grass swaying in the wind, and the swiftly moving clouds overhead cast strange shadows.

'Come tread the maze with me.'

Had I heard those words, or merely remembered them?

I looked down at my feet and then around, confused. Was I standing in the maze already? I took a tentative step forward and back, and it did seem that I was standing in a shallow depression. The memory flooded back: Phil standing in the sunlit field, rocking back and forth and saying, 'I think this is it.' The open, intense look on his face.

'Phil,' I whispered, my eyes filling with tears.

Through the tears I saw some motion, but when I blinked them away, again there was nothing. I looked around the dark, empty field, and began to walk the path laid out long before. I did not walk as slowly as Phil had done, but more quickly, almost skipping, hitting the sides of the maze path with my feet to be certain of keeping to it, since I could not see it.

And as I walked, it seemed to me that I was not alone, that people were moving ahead of me, somehow just out of my sight (beyond another turn in the winding path I might catch them up), or behind. I could hear their footsteps. The thought that others were behind me, following me, unnerved me, and I stopped and turned around to look. I saw no one, but I was now facing in the direction of The Old Vicarage, and my gaze went on to the house. I could see the upper window, the very window where Phil and I had stood together looking out, the point from which we had seen the dancers in the maze.

The curtains were not drawn across that dark square of glass this night, either. And as I watched, a figure appeared at the window. A tall shape, a pale face looking out. And after a moment, as I still stared, confused, a second figure joined the first. Someone smaller – a woman. The man put his arm around her. I could see – perhaps I shouldn't have been able to see this at such a distance, with no light on in the room – but I could see that the man was wearing a sweater, and the woman was naked. And I could see the man's face. It was Phil. And the woman was me.

There we were. Still together, still safe from what time would bring. I could almost feel the chill that had shaken me then, and the comfort of Phil's protecting arm. And yet I was not there. Not now. Now I was out in the field, alone, a premonition to my earlier self.

I felt someone come up beside me. Something as thin and light and hard as a bird's claw took hold of my arm. Slowly I turned away from the window and turned to see who held me. A young man was standing beside me, smiling at me. I thought I recognised him.

'He's waiting for you at the centre,' he said. 'You mustn't stop now.'

Into my mind came a vivid picture of Phil in daylight, standing still in the centre of the maze, caught there by something, standing there forever. Time was not the same in the maze, and Phil could still be standing where he had once stood. I could be with him again, for a moment or forever.

I resumed the weaving, skipping steps of the dance with my new companion. I was eager now, impatient to reach the centre. Ahead of me I could see other figures, dim and shifting as the moonlight, winking in and out of view as they trod the maze on other nights, in other centuries.

The view from the corner of my eyes was more disturbing. I caught fleeting glimpses of my partner in this dance, and he did not look the same as when I had seen him face to face. He had looked so young, and yet that light, hard grasp on my arm did not seem that of a young man's hand.

A hand like a bird's claw . . .

My eyes glanced down my side to my arm. The hand lying lightly on my solid flesh was nothing but bones, the flesh all rotted and dropped away years before. Those peripheral, sideways glimpses I'd had of my dancing partner were the truth – sights of something long dead and yet still animate.

I stopped short and pulled my arm away from that horror. I closed my eyes, afraid to turn to face it. I heard the rustle and clatter of dry bones. I felt a cold wind against my face and smelled something rotten. A voice – it might have been Phil's – whispered my name in sorrow and fear.

What waited for me at the centre? And what would I become, and for how long would I be trapped in this monotonous dance if ever I reached the end?

I turned around blindly, seeking the way out. I opened my eyes and began to move, then checked myself – some strong, instinctual aversion kept me from cutting across the maze paths and leaping them as if they were only so many shallow, meaningless furrows. Instead, I turned around (I glimpsed pale figures watching me, flickering in my peripheral vision) and began to run back the way I had come, following the course of the maze backwards, away from the centre, back out into the world alone.

THE HORSE LORD

The double barn doors were secured by a length of stout, rust encrusted chain, fastened with an old padlock.

Marilyn hefted the lock with one hand and tugged at the chain, which did not give. She looked up at the splintering grey wood of the doors and wondered how the children had got in.

Dusting red powder from her hands, Marilyn strolled around the side of the old barn. Dead leaves and dying grasses crunched beneath her sneakered feet, and she hunched her shoulders against the chill in the wind.

'There's plenty of room for horses,' Kelly had said the night before at dinner. 'There's a perfect barn. You can't say it would be impractical to keep a horse here.' Kelly was Derek's daughter, eleven years old and mad about horses.

This barn had been used as a stable, Marilyn thought, and could be again. Why not get Kelly a horse? And why not one for herself as well? As a girl, Marilyn had ridden in Central Park. She stared down the length of the barn: for some reason, the door to each stall had been tightly boarded shut.

Marilyn realised she was shivering then, and she finished her circuit of the barn at a trot and jogged all the way back to the house.

The house was large and solid, built of grey stone a hundred and seventy years before. It seemed a mistake, a misplaced object in this cold, empty land. Who would choose to settle here. who would try to eke out a living from the ungiving, stony soil?

The old house and the eerily empty countryside formed a setting very much like one Marilyn, who wrote suspense novels, had once created for a story. She liked the reality much less than her heroine had liked the fiction.

The big kitchen was warm and felt comforting after the outside air. Marilyn leaned against the sink to catch her breath and let herself relax. But she felt tense. The house seemed unnaturally quiet with all the children away at school. Marilyn smiled wryly at herself. A week before, the children had been driving her crazy with their constant noise and demands, and now that they were safely away at school for nine hours every day she felt uncomfortable.

From one extreme to the other, thought Marilyn. The story of my life.

Only a year ago she and Derek, still newly married, were making comfortable plans to have a child – perhaps two – 'someday'.

Then Joan – Derek's ex-wife – had decided she'd had her fill of mothering, and almost before Marilyn had time to think about it, she'd found herself with a half-grown daughter.

And following quickly on that event – while Marilyn and Kelly were still wary of each other – Derek's widowed sister had died, leaving her four children in Derek's care.

Five children! Perhaps they wouldn't have seemed like such a herd if they had come in typical fashion, one at a time with a proper interval between.

It was the children, too, who had made living in New York City seem impossible. This house had been in Derek's family since it was built, but no one had lived in it for years. It had been used from time to time as a vacation home, but the land had nothing to recommend it to vacationers; no lakes or mountains, and the weather was usually unpleasant. It was inhospitable country, a neglected corner of New York state.

It should have been a perfect place for writing – their friends all said so. An old house, walls soaked in history, set in a brooding, rocky landscape, beneath an unlittered sky, far from the distractions and noise of the city. But Derek could write anywhere – he carried his own atmosphere with him, a part of his ingrained discipline – and Marilyn needed the bars, restaurants, museums, shops and libraries of a large city to fill in the hours when words could not be commanded.

The silence was suddenly too much to bear. Derek wasn't typing – he might be wanting conversation. Marilyn walked down the long dark hallway – thinking to herself that this house needed more light fixtures, as well as pictures on the walls and rugs on the cold wooden floors.

Derek was sitting behind the big parson's table that was his desk, cleaning one of his sixty-seven pipes. The worn but richly patterned rug on the floor, the glow of lamplight, and the books which lined the walls made this room, the library and Derek's office, seem warmer and more comfortable than the rest of the house.

'Talk?' said Marilyn, standing with her hand on the doorknob.

'Sure, come on in. I was just stuck on how to get the chief slave into bed with the mistress of the plantation without making her yet another clichéd nymphomaniac.'

'Have him comfort her in time of need,' Marilyn said. She closed the door on the dark hallway. 'He just happens to be on hand when she gets a letter informing her of her dear brother's death. In grief, and as an affirmation of life, she and the slave tumble into bed together.'

'Pretty good,' Derek said. 'You got a problem I can help you with?'

'Not a literary one,' she said, crossing the room to his side. Derek put an arm around her. 'I was just wondering if we couldn't get a horse for Kelly. I was out to look at the barn. It's all boarded and locked up, but I'm sure we could get in and fix it up. And I don't think it could cost that much to keep a horse or two.'

'Or two,' he echoed. He cocked his head and gave her a sly look. 'You sure you want to start using a barn with a rather grim history?'

'What do you mean?'

'Didn't I ever tell you the story of how my – hmmm – great-uncle, I guess he must have been – my great-uncle Martin, how he died?'

Marilyn shook her head, her expression suspicious.

'It's a pretty gruesome story.'

'Derek . . .'

'It's true, I promise you. Well . . . remember my first slave novel?'

'How could I forget? It paid for our honeymoon.'

'Remember the part where the evil boss-man who tortures his slaves and horses alike is finally killed by a crazed stallion?'

Marilyn grimaced. 'Yeah. A bit much, I thought. Horses aren't carnivorous.'

'I got the idea for that scene from my great-uncle Martin's death. His horses – and he kept a whole stable – went crazy, apparently. I don't know if they actually *ate* him, but he was pretty chewed up when someone found his body.' Derek shifted in his chair. 'Martin wasn't known to be a cruel man. He didn't abuse his horses; he loved them. He didn't love Indians, though, and the story was that the stables were built on ground sacred to the Indians, who put a curse on Martin or his horses in retaliation.'

Marilyn shook her head. 'Some story. When did all this happen?'

'Around 1880.'

'And the barn has been boarded up ever since?'

'I guess so. I remember the few times Anna and I came out here as kids we could never find a way to get inside. We made up stories about the ghosts of the mad horses still being inside the barn. But because they were ghosts they couldn't be held by normal walls, and roamed around at night. I can remember nights when we'd huddle together, certain we heard their ghostly neighing ...' His eyes looked faraway. Remembering how much he had loved his sister, Marilyn felt guilty about her reluctance to take in Anna's children. After all, they were all Derek had left of his sister.

'So this place *is* haunted,' she said. trying to joke. Her voice came out uneasy, however.

'Not the house,' said Derek quickly. 'Old Uncle Martin died in the barn.'

'What about your ancestors who lived here before that? Didn't the Indian curse touch them?'

'Well ...'

'Derek,' she said warningly.

'Okay. Straight dope. The first family, the first bunch of Hoskins who settled here were done in by Indians. The parents and the two bond-servants were slaughtered, and the children were stolen. The house was burned to the ground. That wasn't this house, obviously.'

'But it stands on the same ground.'

'Not exactly. That house stood on the other side of the barn – though I doubt the present barn stood then – Anna and I used to play around the foundations. I found a knife there once, and she found a little tin box which held ashes and a pewter ring.'

'But you never found any ghosts.'

Derek looked up at her. 'Do ghosts hang around once their house is burned?'

'Maybe.'

'No, we never did. Those Hoskins were too far back

in time to bother with, maybe. We never saw any Indian ghosts, either.'

'Did you ever see the ghost horses?'

'See them?' He looked thoughtful. 'I don't remember. We might have. Funny what you can forget about childhood. No matter how important it seems to you as a child . . .'

'We become different people when we grow up,' Marilyn said.

Derek gazed into space a moment, then roused himself to gesture at the wall of books behind him. 'If you're interested in the family history, that little set in dark green leather was written by one of my uncles and published by a vanity press. He traces the Hoskins back to Shakespeare's time, if I recall. The longest I ever spent out here until now was one rainy summer when I was about twelve . . . it seemed like forever . . . and I read most of the books in the house, including those.'

'I'd like to read them.'

'Go ahead.' He watched her cross the room and wheel the library ladder into position. 'Why, are you thinking of writing a novel about my family?'

'No. I'm just curious to discover what perversity made your ancestor decide to build a house *here*, of all god-forsaken places on the continent.'

Marilyn thought of Jane Eyre as she settled into the window seat, the heavy green curtains falling back into place to shield her from the room. She glanced out at the chilly grey land and picked up the first volume.

James Hoskins won a parcel of land in upstate New York in a card game. Marilyn imagined his disappointment when he set eyes on his prize, but he was a stubborn man and frequently unlucky at cards. This land might not be much, but it was his own. He brought his family and household goods to a roughly built wooden house. A more permanent house, larger and built of native rock, would be built in time.

But James Hoskins would never see it built. In a letter to relatives in Philadelphia, Hoskins related:

'The land I have won is of great value, at least to a poor, wandering remnant of Indians. Two braves came to the house yesterday, and my dear wife was nearly in tears at their tales of powerful magic and vengeful spirits inhabiting this land.

'Go, they said, for this is a great spirit, as old as the rocks, and your God cannot protect you. This land is not good for people of any race. A spirit (whose name may not be pronounced) set his mark upon this land when the earth was still new. This land is cursed – and more of the same, on and on until I lost patience with them and told them to be off before I made powerful magic with my old Betsy.

'Tho' my wife trembled, my little daughter proved fiercer than her Ma, swearing she would chop up that pagan spirit and have it for her supper – which made me roar with laughter and the Indians to shake their heads as they hurried away.'

Marilyn wondered what had happened to that fierce little girl. Had the Indians stolen her, admiring her spirit?

She read on about the deaths of the unbelieving Hoskins. Not only had the Indians set fire to the hasty wooden house; they had first butchered the inhabitants.

'They were disembowelled and torn apart, ripped by knives in the most hungry, savage, inhuman manner, and all for the sin of living on land sacred to a nameless spirit.'

Marilyn thought of the knife Derek had said he'd found as a child.

Something slapped the window. Marilyn's head jerked up, and she stared out the window. It had begun to rain, and a rising wind slung small fists of rain at the glass.

She stared out at the landscape, shrouded now by the

driving rain, and wondered why this desolate rocky land should be thought of as sacred. Her mind moved vaguely to thoughts of books on anthropology which might help, perhaps works on Indians of the region which might tell her more. The library in Janeville wouldn't have much – she had been there, and it wasn't much more than a small room full of historical novels and geology texts – but the librarian might be able to get books from other libraries around the state, perhaps one of the university libraries . . .

She glanced at her watch, realising that school had let out long before; the children might be waiting at the bus stop now, in this terrible weather. She pushed aside the heavy green curtains.

'Derek –'

But the room was empty. He had already gone for the children, she thought with relief. He certainly did better at this job of being a parent than she did.

Of course, Kelly was his child; he'd had years to adjust to fatherhood. She wondered if he would buy a horse for Kelly and hoped that he wouldn't.

Perhaps it was silly to be worried about ancient Indian curses and to fear that a long-ago event would be repeated, but Marilyn didn't want horses in a barn where horses had once gone mad. There were no Indians here now, and no horses. Perhaps they would be safe.

Marilyn glanced down at the books still piled beside her, thinking of looking up the section about the horses. But she recoiled uneasily from the thought. Derek had already told her the story; she could check the facts later, when she was not alone in the house.

She got up. She would go and busy herself in the kitchen, and have hot chocolate and cinnamon toast waiting for the children.

The scream still rang in her ears and vibrated through her

body. Marilyn lay still, breathing shallowly, and stared at the ceiling. What had she been dreaming?

It came again, muffled by distance, but as chilling as a blade of ice. It wasn't a dream; someone, not so very far away, was screaming.

Marilyn visualised the house on a map, trying to tell herself it had been nothing, the cry of some bird. No one could be out there, miles from everything, screaming; it didn't make sense. And Derek was still sleeping, undisturbed. She thought about waking him, then repressed the thought as unworthy and sat up. She'd better check on the children, just in case it was one of them crying out of a nightmare. She did not go to the window; there would be nothing to see, she told herself.

Marilyn found Kelly out of bed, her arms wrapped around herself as she stared out the window.

'What's the matter?'

Kelly didn't shift her gaze. 'I heard a horse,' she said softly. 'I heard it neighing. It woke me up.'

'A horse?'

'It must be wild. If I can catch it and tame it, can I keep it?' Now she looked around, her eyes bright in the moonlight.

'I don't think . . .'

'Please?'

'Kelly, you were probably just dreaming.'

'I heard it. It woke me up, I heard it again. I'm not imagining things,' she said tightly.

'Then it was probably a horse belonging to one of the farmers around here.'

'I don't think it belongs to anyone.'

Marilyn was suddenly aware of how tired she was. Her body ached. She didn't want to argue with Kelly. Perhaps there had been a horse – a neigh could sound like a scream, she thought.

'Go back to bed, Kelly. You have to go to school in the morning. You can't do anything about the horse now.'

'I'm going to look for it, though,' Kelly said, getting back into bed. 'I'm going to find it.'

'Later.'

As long as she was up, Marilyn thought as she stepped out into the hall, she should check on the other children, to be sure they were all sleeping.

To her surprise, they were all awake. They turned sleepy, bewildered eyes on her when she came in and murmured broken fragments of their dreams as she kissed them each in turn.

Derek woke as she climbed in beside him. 'Where were you?' he asked. He twitched. 'Christ, your feet are like ice!'

'Kelly was awake. She thought she heard a horse neighing.'

'I told you,' Derek said with sleepy smugness. 'That's our ghost horse, back again.'

The sky was heavy with the threat of snow; the day was cold and too still. Marilyn stood up from her typewriter in disgust and went downstairs The house was silent except for the distant chatter of Derek's typewriter.

'Where are the kids?' she asked from the doorway.

Derek gave her a distracted look, his hands still poised over the keys. 'I think they all went out to clean up the barn.'

'But the barn is closed – it's locked.'

'Mmmm.'

Marilyn sighed and left him. She felt weighted by the chores of supervision. If only the children could go to school every day, where they would be safe and out of her jurisdiction. She thought of how easily they could be hurt or die, their small bodies broken. So many dangers, she thought, getting her coral-coloured coat out of the front closet. How did people cope with the tremendous responsibility of other lives under their protection? It was an impossible task.

The children had mobilised into a small but diligent army, marching in and out of the barn with their arms full of hay, boards or tools. Marilyn looked for Kelly, who was standing just inside the big double doors and directing operations.

'The doors were chained shut,' she said, confused. 'How did you –'

'I cut it apart,' Kelly said. 'There was a hacksaw in the tool shed.' She gave Marilyn a sidelong glance. 'Daddy said we could take any tools from there that we needed.'

Marilyn looked at her with uneasy respect, then glanced away to where the other children were working grimly with hands and hammers at the boards nailed across all the stall doors. The darkness of the barn was relieved by a storm lantern hanging from a hook.

'Somebody really locked this place up good,' Kelly said. 'Do you know why?'

Marilyn hesitated, then decided. 'I suppose it was boarded up so tightly because of the way one of your early relatives died here.'

Kelly's face tensed with interest. 'Died? How? Was he murdered?'

'Not exactly. His horses killed him. They . . . turned on him one night, nobody ever knew why.'

Kelly's eyes were knowing. 'He must have been an awful man, then. Terribly cruel. Because horses will put up with almost anything. He must have done something so –'

'No. He wasn't supposed to have been a cruel man.'

'Maybe not to *people*.'

'Some people thought his death was due to an Indian

curse. The land here was supposed to be sacred; they thought this was the spirit's way of taking revenge.'

Kelly laughed. 'That's some excuse. Look, I got to get to work. Okay?'

Marilyn dreamed she went out one night to saddle a horse. The barn was filled with them, all her horses, her pride and delight. She reached up to bridle one, a sorrel gelding, and suddenly felt – with disbelief that staved off the pain – powerful teeth bite down on her arm. She heard the bone crunch, saw the flesh tear, and then the blood . . .

She looked up in horror, into eyes which were reddened and strange.

A sudden blow threw her forward and she landed face-down in dust and straw. She could not breathe. Another horse, her gentle black mare, had kicked her in the back. She felt a wrenching, tearing pain in her leg. When finally she could move she turned her head and saw the great yellow teeth, stained with her blood, of both her horses as they fed upon her. And the other horses, all around her, were kicking at their stalls. The wood splintered and gave, and they all came to join in the feast.

The children came clattering in at lunchtime, tracking snow and mud across the red-brick floor. It had been snowing since morning, but the children were oblivious to it. They did not, as Marilyn had expected, rush out shrieking to play in the snow, but went instead to the barn, as they did every weekend now. It was almost ready, they said.

Kelly slipped into her chair and powdered her soup with salt. 'Wait till you see what we found,' she said breathlessly.

'Animal, vegetable or mineral?' Derek asked.

'Animal AND mineral.'

'Where did you find it?' Marilyn asked.

The smallest child spilled soup in her lap and howled.

When Marilyn got back to the table, everyone was talking about the discovery in the barn: Derek curious, the children mysterious.

'But what is it?' Marilyn asked.

'It's better to see it. Come with us after we eat.'

The children had worked hard. The shrouded winter light spilled into the empty space of the barn through all the open half-doors of the stalls. The rotting straw and grain was all gone, and the dirt floor had been raked and swept clear of more than an inch of fine dust. The large design stood out clearly, white and clean against the hard earth.

It was not a horse. After examining it more closely, Marilyn wondered how she could have thought it was the depiction of a wild, rearing stallion. Horses have hooves, not three-pronged talons, and they don't have such a feline snake of a tail. The proportions of the body were wrong, too, once she looked more carefully. *the god of the curse*

Derek crouched and ran his fingers along the outline of the beast. It had been done in chalk, but it was much more than just a drawing. Lines must have been deeply scored in the earth, and the narrow trough then filled with some pounded white dust.

'Chalk, I think,' Derek said. 'I wonder how deep it goes?' He began scratching with a forefinger at the side of the thick white line.

Kelly bent and caught his arm. 'Don't ruin it.'

'I'm not, honey.' He looked up at Marilyn, who was still standing apart, staring at the drawing.

'It must be the Indian curse,' she said. She tried to smile, but she felt an unease which she knew could build into an open dread.

'Do you suppose this is what the spirit who haunts this land is supposed to look like?' Derek asked.

'What else?'

'Odd that it should be a horse, then, instead of some animal indigenous to the area. The legend must have arisen after the white man –'

'But it's not a horse,' Marilyn said. 'Look at it.'

'It's not a horse exactly, no,' he agreed, standing and dusting his hands. 'But it's more a horse than it is anything else.'

'It's so fierce,' Marilyn murmured. She looked away, into Kelly's eager face.

'Well, now that you've cleaned up the barn, what are you going to do?'

'Now we're going to catch the horse.'

'What horse?'

'The wild one, the one we hear at night.'

'Oh, that. Well, it must be miles away by now. Someone else must have caught it.'

Kelly shook her head. 'I heard it last night. It was practically outside my window, but when I looked it was gone. I could see its hoof-prints in the snow.'

'You're not going out again?'

The children turned blank eyes on her, ready to become hostile, or tearful, if she were going to be difficult.

'I mean,' Marilyn said apologetically, 'you've been out all morning, running around. And it's still snowing. Why don't you just let your food digest for a while – get out your colouring books, or a game or something, and play in here where it's warm.'

'We can't stop now,' Kelly said. 'We might catch the horse this afternoon.'

'And if you don't, do you intend to go out every day until you do?'

'Of course,' Kelly said. The other children nodded.

Marilyn's shoulders slumped as she gave in. 'Well, wrap up. And don't go *too* far from the house in case it starts snowing harder. And don't stay out too long, or you'll get frostbite.' The children were already moving away from her as she spoke. They live in another world, Marilyn thought, despairing.

She wondered how long this would go on. The barn project had held within it a definite end, but Marilyn could not believe the children would ever catch the horse they sought. She was not even certain there was a horse out in that snow to be caught, even though she had been awakened more than once by the shrill, distant screaming that might have been a horse neighing.

Marilyn went to Derek's office and climbed again into the hidden window seat. The heavy curtains muffled the steady beat of Derek's typewriter, and the falling snow muffled the country beyond the window. She picked up another of the small green volumes and began to read.

'Within a month of his arrival, Martin Hoskins was known in Janeville for two things. One: he intended to bring industry, wealth, and population to upstate New York, and to swell the tiny hamlet into a city. Second: a man without wife or children, Hoskins' pride, passion, and delight was in his six beautiful horses.

'Martin had heard the legend that his land was cursed, but, as he wrote to a young woman in New York City, "The Indians were driven out of these parts long ago, and their curses with them, I'll wager. For what is an Indian curse without an Indian knife or arrow to back it?"

'It was true that the great Indian tribes had been dispersed or destroyed, but a few Indians remained: tattered and homeless in the White Man's world. Martin Hoskins met one such young brave on the road to Janeville one morning.

' "I must warn you, sir," said the ragged but proud young savage. "The land upon which you dwell is inhabited by a powerful spirit."

' "I've heard that tale before," responded Hoskins, shortly but not unkindly. "And I don't believe in your heathen gods; I'm not afraid of 'em."

' "This spirit is no god of ours, either. But my people have known of it, and respected it, for as many years as we have lived on this land. Think of this spirit not as a god, but as a force . . . something powerful in nature which cannot be reasoned with or fought – something like a storm."

' "And what do you propose I do?" asked Hoskins.

' "Leave that place. Do not try to live there. The spirit cannot follow you if you leave, but it cannot be driven out, either. The spirit belongs to the land as much as the land belongs to it."

'Martin Hoskins laughed harshly. "You ask me to run from something I do not believe in! Well, I tell you this: I believe in storms, but I do not run from them. I'm strong; what can that spirit do to me?"

'The Indian shook his head sorrowfully. "I cannot say what it may do. I only know that you will offend it by dwelling where it dwells, and the more you offend it, the more certainly will it destroy you. Do not try to farm there, nor keep animals. That land knows only one master and will not take to another. There is only one law, and one master on that land. You must serve it, or leave."

' "I serve no master but myself – and my God," Martin said.'

Marilyn closed the book, not wanting to read of Martin's inevitable, and terrible, end. He kept animals, she thought idly. What if he had been a farmer? How would the spirit of the land have destroyed him then?

She looked out the window and saw with relief that the children were playing. They've finally given up their hunt, she thought, and wondered what they were playing now. Were they playing follow-the-leader? Dancing like Indians? Or horses, she thought, suddenly, watching their prancing feet and tossing heads. They were playing horses. *animals on the land*

Marilyn woke suddenly, listening. Her body strained forward, her heart pounding too loudly, her mouth dry. She heard it again: the wild, mad cry of a horse. She had heard it before in the night, but never so close, and never so human-sounding.

Marilyn got out of bed, shivering violently as her feet touched the cold, bare floor and the chilly air raised bumps on her naked arms. She went to the window, drew aside the curtains, and looked out.

The night was still and as clear as an engraving. The moon lacked only a sliver more for fullness and shone out of a cloudless, star-filled sky. A group of small figures danced upon the snowy ground, jerking and prancing and kicking up a spray of snow. Now and again one of them would let out a shrill cry: half a horse's neigh, half a human wail. Marilyn felt her hairs rise as she recognised the puppet-like dancers below: the children.

She was tempted to let the curtains fall back and return to bed – to say nothing, to do nothing, to act as if nothing unusual had happened. But these were *her* children now, and she wasn't allowed that sort of irresponsibility.

The window groaned as she forced it open, and at the faint sound the children stopped their dance. As one, they turned and looked up at Marilyn.

The breath stopped in her throat as she stared down at their upturned faces. Everything was very still, as if that moment had been frozen within a block of ice. Marilyn could not speak; she could not think of what to say.

She withdrew back into the room, letting the curtains fall back before the open window, and she ran to the bed.

'Derek,' she said, catching hold of him. 'Derek, wake up.' She could not stop her trembling.

His eyes moved behind their lids.

'Derek,' she said urgently.

Now they opened and, fogged with sleep, looked at her.

'What is it, love?' He must have seen the fear in her face, for he pushed himself up on his elbows. 'Did you have a bad dream?'

'Not a dream, no. Derek, your Uncle Martin – he could have lived here if he hadn't been a master himself. If he hadn't kept horses. The horses turned on him because they had found another master.'

'What are you talking about?'

'The spirit that lives in this land,' she said. She was not trembling, now. Perspiration beaded her forehead. 'It uses the . . . the servants, or whatever you want to call them . . . it can't abide anyone else ruling here. If we . . .'

'You've been dreaming, sweetheart.' He tried to pull her down beside him, but she shook him off. She could hear them on the stairs.

'Is our door locked?' she suddenly demanded.

'Yes, I think so.' Derek frowned. 'Did you hear something? I thought . . .'

'Children are a bit like animals, don't you think? At least, people treat them as if they were – adults, I mean. I suppose children must . . .'

'I *do* hear something. I'd better go –'

'Derek – No –'

The doorknob rattled and there was a great pounding at the door.

'Who is that?' Derek said loudly.

'The children,' Marilyn whispered.

The door splintered and gave way before Derek reached it, and the children burst through. There were so many of them, Marilyn thought, as she waited on the bed. And all she could seem to see was their strong, square teeth.

the spirit uses one subjugated against the subjugators

THE OTHER MOTHER

Across the lake, on the other shore, something moved: pale-white, glimmering. Tall as a person.

Sara looked up from her work, refocusing her eyes. She realised how dark it had become. It had been too dark, in the rapidly deepening twilight, to paint for the last half-hour, but she had been reluctant to admit it, give up, and go in.

There, again. A woman in a white gown? Gone again.

Sara frowned, vexed, and concentrated on the brushy land across the narrow expanse of dark water. She waited, listening to the crickets and frogs, and she stared so intently that the growing shadows merged, reforming in strange shapes. What had she really seen? Had that pale glimmer been a trick of the fading light? Why did she feel as if there was a stranger lurking on the other shore, a woman watching her who would let herself be seen only in glimpses?

Sara realised she was tired. She arched her back and exercised her aching arms. She still watched the other shore, but casually now, hoping to lure the stranger out by seeming inattentiveness.

But she saw nothing more and at last she shrugged and began to tighten lids on tubes of paint, putting her supplies away. She deliberately avoided looking at the painting she had been working on. Already she disliked it, and was annoyed with herself for failing again.

The house was stifling after the balmy evening air, and it reeked of the pizza she had given the children for dinner.

They had left chunks of it uneaten on the coffee table and were now sprawled on the floor in front of the television set, absorbed in a noisy situation comedy.

'Hello, sweethearts,' Sara said.

Michael gave a squirming shrug and twitched his mouth in what might have been a greeting; Melanie did not move. Her mouth hung open, and her eyes followed the tiny moving images intently.

Sara put her painting and supplies back in her bedroom and then began to clean up the leftover pizza and soft drinks, wanting to turn off the set and reclaim her children, but too aware of the tantrums that would ensue if she interrupted a program.

At the next commercial, to catch their attention, Sara said, 'I just saw a ghost across the lake.'

Michael sat up and turned to his mother, his expression intrigued but wary. 'Really?'

'Well, it looked like a ghost,' Sara said. 'You want to come with me and see if she's still there?'

'Not *she*, ghosts aren't girls,' Michael said. But he scrambled to his feet. Melanie was still watching the set: a domestic squabble over coffee.

'Why can't ghosts be girls?' Sara asked. 'Come on, Melanie. We're going outside to look for a ghost.'

'They just can't be,' Michael said. 'Come *on*.'

Sara took hold of Melanie's sticky little hand and led her outside after Michael. Outdoors, Michael suddenly halted and looked around. 'Did you *really* see a ghost?'

'I saw something,' Sara said. She felt relieved to be outside again, away from the stale, noisy house. 'I saw a pale white figure which glided past. When I looked more closely, it was gone. Vanished, just like that.'

'Sounds like a ghost,' said Michael. 'They float around, and they're all white, and they disappear. Did it make a noise?'

'Not that I noticed. What sort of noise does a ghost make?'

Michael began to produce a low moaning sound, gradually building in intensity and volume.

'Mommy, make him stop!' Melanie said suddenly.

'That's enough, Michael.'

They had reached the water's edge and they were quiet as they looked across the dark water. Almost nothing could be seen now of the opposite shore.

'Did you really see a ghost?' Michael asked, yet again. Sara felt his hand touching her blue-jeaned hip.

She put an arm around his shoulder and hugged him close. 'Maybe I imagined it. Maybe it was an animal of some kind. I just saw something from the corner of my eye, and I had the impression that it was, well, a woman in a long white gown, moving more quickly and quietly than any living person should. I felt she wasn't ready to let me really see her yet. So when I tried to find her, she had disappeared.'

Sara felt the hairs on the back of her neck prickle and was suddenly ashamed of herself. If she had made herself nervous, what must the children be feeling?

Melanie began to whimper for the light.

'She can't turn the light on here – we're outside, stupid,' Michael said. Sara suspected a quaver in his voice.

'Come on, kids. There's nothing out here. Let's go inside and I'll tell you a story before you go to bed.'

Michael broke into a run toward the safe harbour of the lighted house, and Melanie let go of her mother's hand to chase him.

Sara turned to follow her children but then paused, feeling that she was being watched. She turned and looked back across the lake. But even if someone were standing on the opposite shore, it was now much too dark to see.

After the children had bathed and were in their pajamas,

Sara told a story about a tricycle-riding bear, a character both the children loved, but which Michael was beginning to outgrow.

Melanie was good about going to bed, snuggling sleepily under the bedclothes and raising her round, sweet face for a good-night kiss.

'Now a butterfly kiss,' Melanie commanded, after exchanging several smacking kisses with her mother.

Sara, kneeling by the bed, bent her head and fluttered her eyelashes against her daughter's downy cheek. The sound of Melanie's sleepy giggle, her warmth, the good, clean smell of her inspired a rush of love, and Sara wanted to grab her daughter and hug her suffocatingly tight. But she only whispered, soft as a breath, 'I love you, sweetie,' before she drew away.

Michael was waiting for her in his room with a deck of cards. They played two games of Go Fish and one of Crazy Eights before his uncontrollable yawns gave him away. He agreed to go to bed, but insisted upon hearing a story first.

'A short one,' Sara said.

'A ghost story,' he responded, nodding impatiently.

'Oh, Michael,' Sara sighed, envisioning nightmares and demands for comfort later.

'Yes. A ghost story. About that ghost you saw across the lake today.'

Had she frightened him? Sara couldn't be sure. But this was her opportunity to make up for what she'd done, to remove the menace and the mystery of that unseen figure. She tucked him under the covers and settled herself at the end of his bed, and then, in a low voice, began to weave a comforting sort of ghost story.

The ghost was a sad but friendly figure, a mother eternally searching for her children. They had run off into the wilderness one day without telling her and had become lost, and she had been looking for them ever since. The story had the moral that children shouldn't disobey their mothers or run and hide without telling her where they were going.

Michael was still too young to protest against stories with morals; he accepted what he was told, smiling sleepily, and gave his mother a warm hug and kiss goodnight.

But if Sara had protected Michael against nightmares, she was unable to protect herself.

That night Sara dreamed of a woman in white, gliding along the lake shore, heading toward the house. She was not a ghost; neither was she human. Her eyes were large, round, and protruding, like huge, milk-white marbles. The skin of her face was greyish, her mouth narrow, her nose almost nonexistent. She wore a long, hooded, all-enveloping gown.

Sara saw then that Michael and Melanie were playing in the yard, unaware of the ghastly figure gliding steadily toward them.

Where is their mother? Sara wondered. *Where am* I? She could only watch helplessly, powerless to interfere, certain that she was about to see her children murdered before her eyes.

Dreaming, Sara sweated and twitched and finally cried out, waking herself.

She sat up in the dark, hot room, feeling her heart pounding. Only a dream. But she was still frightened. Somewhere in the darkness those dead white eyes might be staring at her.

Sara turned on the light, wishing for comfort. She wanted a lover, or even her ex-husband, some male figure whose solid, sleeping presence would comfort her.

What a baby I am, she thought, getting up and putting on her robe. *To be so frightened by a dream. To have to make the rounds of the house to be sure everything is normal.*

Michael was sleeping on his back, the covers kicked

away, breathing through his mouth. Sara found his snores endearing and paused to pull the sheet up to his waist.

As she reached the doorway to Melanie's room, something white flashed by the window. Sara stopped breathing, feeling cold to the bone. Then she saw the bird. It was just a white bird, resting on the window ledge. A second later it had flown away. Sara felt weak with relief and annoyed with herself for overreacting. Just a bird at the window, a white bird.

Melanie was sleeping soundly, curled into a ball, her fists beneath her chin. Sara stood beside the bed looking down at her for a long time. How infinitely precious she was.

The next morning the children were particularly obnoxious. They were up early, spilling milk and cereal on the floor, slapping each other, fighting over television programs, complaining of boredom and asking questions without pausing to hear the answers. Their high-pitched voices repeating childish demands affected Sara like a cloud of stinging insects. Her skin itched. She felt raw and old, almost worn out with the effort of keeping a lid on her anger.

Sara suggested new games and answered questions in a level voice. She cleaned up their messes and promised the children ice-cream cones at Baskin-Robbins if they were good and quiet in the car and in the grocery store. They were neither good nor quiet, but she bought them the ice cream anyway, to avert a worse outburst. She longed for Thursday, when a neighbor would take Michael into town for a birthday party, and looked toward Sunday – when the children's father would have them both all day – as to her hope of heaven.

After lunch Melanie blessedly fell asleep, and Michael occupied himself quietly with his plastic dinosaurs. Almost holding her breath for fear the spell of peace would be broken, Sara went to get her canvas.

But at the sight of it her tentatively building spirits plunged. The painting she had spent so much time on the previous day was dreadful, laboured, flat, and uninspired. She had done better in high school. There was nothing to be done about it, Sara decided. She had done too much to it already. She would wait for it to dry and paint over it with gesso. She felt despairing of all the time she had wasted – not only yesterday, but all the years before that in which she had not found time to paint. Perhaps it was too late now; perhaps she had lost whatever talent she once had.

But she would lose this afternoon, too, if she didn't snap out of it. Sara turned the canvas to the wall and looked around. Watercolours, perhaps. Something quick and simple, something to loosen her up. She had been too stiff, intimidated by the oils and canvas. She would have to work up to them.

'Can we go to a movie tonight?' Michael asked as she emerged from her room with the big, spiral-bound pad of heavy paper and her box of watercolours. He was marching a blue dinosaur across the kitchen table and through the fruit bowl.

'We'll see,' Sara said absently.

'What does that mean? Does that mean yes?'

'It means we'll see when the time comes.'

'What will we see? Will we see a movie?' He followed her outside.

'Michael, don't pester me.'

'What's *that*?'

There was a new tone to his voice. Sara turned to look. He was staring in the direction of the lake, astonished. 'Is that the ghost?'

Recalling her dream, Sara felt a chill. Shading her eyes against the sun, she peered across the lake. She saw a large white animal walking on the farther shore, too oddly shaped to be a dog, too small for a cow.

'It's a pig,' Sara said. She had never seen such a large, white pig before, and she wondered where it had come from. What was somebody's prize pig doing loose?

The pig had stopped its purposeful walk and turned toward the water to face them. Now it stood still and seemed to watch them. Sara took an involuntary step backward, her arm moving down and to the side as if to shield Michael.

'It sees us,' he said. Sara couldn't tell from his voice if he was frightened, pleased, or merely commenting.

'It can't get to us,' Sara said. 'There's all that water in between.' She spoke to comfort herself. She had never heard that pigs were dangerous, but it was a very large animal, and there was something uncanny about it, about the way it stood watching them.

Then, just as abruptly as it had come, the pig turned away from the water and began to trot away, following the shoreline until it was out of sight.

Sara was relieved to see it go.

That night, Sara painted. She got out her oils and a new canvas; she felt inspired. She was excited; she hadn't felt like this in years. The picture had come to her, a vision she felt bound to paint. She was in no mood for sketches or exercises, or 'loosening up' with watercolours. This was her real work, and she needed no more training.

The main figures in the painting would be a large white pig and a shrouded human figure. Sara hoped to express some of the terror she'd felt during her nightmare, and to recapture in the painting the unease she had felt upon seeing the pig on the shore in the midday sun. She planned to keep the robed figure's face hidden, fearful of painting something merely grotesque instead of terrifying.

She worked for hours, late into the night, until she realised that weariness was throwing off her sight and coordination. Then, pleased, exhausted, and looking forward to the next day's work, she went to bed.

The children let her sleep no later than they ever did in the morning, but Sara didn't mind. The hours spent painting seemed to have invigorated her, enabling her to thrive on less sleep.

When Mary Alice arrived to pick up Michael, she offered to take Melanie for the day, too, as company for her youngest. Sara gazed at her in mute gratitude, seeing her blonde, smiling friend as a beneficent goddess, the personification of good fortune. With both the children gone, she would be able to work.

'Oh! Mary Alice, that would be wonderful! Are you sure you don't mind having her along?'

'What's one more kid? Chrissie needs someone to play with. And besides,' she patted Sara's shoulder, 'it will give you some time to paint. Are you working on anything right now?'

It had been Mary Alice, with her ready sympathy and praise, who had encouraged Sara to take up painting again.

Sara smiled. 'I started something new last night. It's different. I'll show you what I've done when you get back.'

But despite her words and easy manner, Sara felt her stomach fluttering nervously when she went to bring out the uncompleted painting after the others had left. She was afraid of what she would find; afraid it would be clumsy or stiff or silly, and not at all what she remembered working on.

To her own surprise she was pleased by the sight of it. She felt a rising excitement and a deep satisfaction at the thought of having uninterrupted hours to work on it.

The pig and the shrouded woman stood on a misty shore. Nearby was a bush in which nested a large white bird.

Sara painted all day with an easy authority she had not known in years. She felt light and free and intensely alive. She didn't have to think about what she was doing; the work had its own existence.

'Unusual.'

Sara turned with a start to see Mary Alice. She felt as if she had been abruptly awakened. The children – her own, and Mary Alice's three – were roaring through the house like a hurricane. She looked back at the painting and saw that it was finished.

'Would you like some wine?' Sara asked.

'Please.' Mary Alice slumped into the old armchair and continued to study the canvas. 'I've never seen you do anything remotely like this. The White Goddess, right?'

In the kitchen, pouring wine, Sara frowned. 'What do you mean?' She brought two glasses into the family room.

'Well, it reminds me of Welsh mythology,' Mary Alice said, accepting her wine. 'Thanks. You know, the pig, the bird, the hawthorn bush. The hooded figure would be Cerridwen – white goddess of death and creation.'

Sara shivered and looked around. It was as if a door had been opened and shut quickly, letting in a chill wind.

'I don't know about any of that,' Sara said. 'I never heard of . . . what's-her-name. But I had a dream about this terrifying white figure, and then I saw this huge pig across the lake. I just . . . they fit together into a painting, some-how. The bird's just there to balance out the composition.'

'A dream,' said Mary Alice. She glanced at her watch and stood up. 'I suppose you don't have to know what a symbol means, to pick up on it.'

Sara also stood. 'Look, why don't you and the kids stay for dinner? It's just spaghetti, but there's lots of it.'

'Thanks, but Bill's expecting me back. He hates having to fend for himself.'

'Some other time, then,' Sara said, feeling oddly bereft.

She wanted adult conversation, adult companionship. It had been so long since she had eaten a leisurely meal with other adults.

Mary Alice touched Sara's arm and said, 'You'll have to come over for dinner some night soon – a late meal, after the kids have been put to bed. There's a friend of Bill's from the university that I've been wanting you to meet, and I could cook something really elaborate and make a party of it.'

'That sounds marvellous,' Sara said. She glanced at the painting again, then away, oddly disturbed. 'You know, I had no problems with this painting. I never had to stop and think, and I've never worked so fast and surely in my life. It was odd, coming right after so much discouragement. For months I haven't been able to finish anything I liked.'

'The muse takes her own time,' Mary Alice said. 'She's the White Goddess, too, you know – at least for poets.' She raised her voice to call her children.

Company gone, Michael and Melanie buzzed around Sara, tugging at her arms and reciting unintelligible stories about the adventures of the day. They were tired and hungry but keyed up to such a pitch by the events of the day that Sara knew she would have a hard time calming them. She put her completed but still wet painting back in her bedroom, out of reach of flailing arms and flying toys, and resigned herself to being a mother again.

On Sunday morning Sara rose even before the children. She felt as if she'd been in hibernation for the past forty-eight hours, dozing as she tended her children, cleaned the house, and ran errands, and only now was she awake again.

In a few hours the children's father would come for them and Sara would be free to paint and live her own life until Monday morning. She had found a few moments to sketch, and she was bursting with the urge to take up brush and paints and turn her grey preliminaries into colour.

Not even pausing for her usual cup of tea, Sara pulled on a bathing suit and rushed outside. The air was a blessing on her bare skin and smelled of honeysuckle. The grass was cool and slippery beneath her feet and there was a special taste in the air that exhilarated her. She began to run, her thoughts streaming out behind her until she knew nothing but sensation.

She plunged into the water as she had plunged into the morning and began swimming vigorously toward the other shore. She was panting so hard she felt dizzy when she arrived, but she grinned with delight.

'Come on out, oh Pig or Ghost or whatever you are!' she called as she walked ashore. 'I'm not afraid of you – show yourself!'

She began to shake herself like a dog, simply to feel the droplets of water flying off her. Then, somehow, she was dancing: a wild, primitive, arm-waving dance.

Finally, tired, she dropped to the rocky beach and rested. She gazed northward to where the narrow lake began to widen. Then she looked across the short stretch of water to her own house and to the others like it which dotted the shore. This early on a Sunday all was still and quiet.

Sara drank it all in: the sun, the clean, warm air with the scent of cedar in it, the songs of the birds, the solitude. Everything was as it should be.

She was cheerful when she returned, telling the kids funny stories and making blueberry-and-banana pancakes for breakfast. It was a special morning; even the children felt it.

'You're our good mommy, aren't you?' said Melanie, hugging Sara's bare legs.

'Of course I am, sweetie.' She put the butter and syrup on the table and dropped a kiss on her daughter's head.

Feeling the promise in the air, Michael said, 'Could we maybe rent a sailboat and go sailing today like you said maybe we could someday?'

'That will be up to your father,' Sara said blithely. 'Did you forget he's picking you up this morning? I'm going to stay home and paint.'

Michael's face was comical as he absorbed this: the conflict between the pleasure of going out with his father and disappointment that he couldn't make use of his mother's good mood was clearly written there. Sara laughed and hugged him.

After breakfast had been eaten and the dishes washed, Sara began to feel impatient. Where was Bruce? He always liked to get an early start, and the children were ready to go.

The telephone rang.

'Sara, I'm not going to be able to make it today. Something's come up.'

'What do you mean you're not going to be able to make it? Sunday's your day – you know that. We agreed.'

'Well, I can't make it today.' Already, annoyance had sharpened his tone.

Sara clenched one hand into a fist, wishing she had him in front of her. 'And why not? One day a week isn't so much. The kids have been counting on seeing you.'

'I haven't missed a week yet and you know it. Be reasonable, Sara. I just can't make it.'

'Why? Why can't you make it? What's so important on a Sunday? You've got a date? Fine, bring her along. I don't care. Just come and take the kids like you're supposed to.'

'Look, put the kids on and I'll explain it to them.'

'Explain it to *me*, damn it!'

A silence. Then he said, 'I'm in Dallas.'

Sara was too angry to speak.

'Tell the kids I'm sorry and I'll try to make it up to them next week.'

'Sorry! You *knew* – why'd you wait until now to call?'

'I don't have to explain myself to you. I'll be by to pick up the kids next Sunday, nine A.M.' He hung up.

Sara held on to the phone, still facing the wall. There were tears of frustration in her eyes, and her back and shoulders ached as if she'd been beaten. When she had regained some control she went to look for her children.

They were outside on the driveway, eager to catch the first glimpse of their father's car.

'Sweethearts,' Sara said. Her throat hurt. 'Your father just called. He's . . . he's not going to be able to come today after all.'

They stared at her. Melanie began to whine.

'Why?' Michael asked. 'Why?'

'He's in Dallas. He couldn't get back in time. He said you'd all do something extra-special next weekend to make up for missing this one.'

'Oh,' said Michael. He was silent for a moment, and Sara wondered if he would cry. But then the moment passed and he said, 'Can we go sailing, then?'

Sara sighed. 'Not today. But why don't you two put on your bathing suits and we'll go for a swim?'

To Sara's relief they accepted the change of plans without fuss. For the next hour Michael showed off his skills in the water while Sara gave Melanie another swimming lesson. Afterward, she got them started playing a board game and went off to her room to be by herself.

She felt exhausted, the euphoria of the early morning faded into the distant past. She sat on the bed and paged through her sketchbook, wondering why she had been so excited and just what she had intended to make of these rather mediocre sketches of a woman's face and details of tree branches. With a part of her mind she was still arguing with her ex-husband, this time scoring points with withering remarks which left him speechless.

Finally she stood up and took out her paints and the fresh canvas. As she set up the work in the bedroom, she could hear the children running in and out of the house, laughing, talking, and occasionally slamming the screen door. They seemed occupied and might not bother her until they grew hungry for lunch. After that, with luck, she might still have the afternoon to paint while Melanie napped and Michael played quietly by himself. She'd had such days before.

But it didn't matter: Sara didn't know what to paint. She was afraid to make a start, so sure was she that she would ruin another canvas. Her earlier certainty was gone. She stared at the blank white surface and tried without success to visualize something there.

Then, from the other room, Melanie screamed.

It wasn't a play scream, and it didn't end. Melanie was screaming in terror.

Sara went cold with dread and ran into the family room. She saw Melanie cowering against a wall while Michael shouted and leaped around. At first Sara could not make out what was happening. Then she heard the mad fluttering of wings and saw a pale blur in the air: a bird had somehow blundered inside and was now flying madly around the room.

Poor thing, thought Sara. *It can't find the way out again.*

Her relief that the crisis was nothing more dangerous than a confused bird turned her fear into irritation with the children. Why were they being so stupid, carrying on so and making matters worse?

'Calm down,' she shouted. 'Just shut up and keep out of the way. You're scaring it.'

She gave Michael a firm push and then opened the door, keeping it open by lodging the iron, dachshund-shaped foot-scraper against it.

'Melanie, be quiet! You're making things worse,' Sara said in a loud whisper.

Melanie's screams trailed away into noisy sobs. She was still cowering in a corner, head down and hands protecting it.

The bird flew three more times around the room, finally breaking out of that maddened, fluttering pattern to soar smoothly and surely out of the open door. Sara gazed after it, smiling. Then she turned to her children.

'Oh, Melanie, what is the matter? It was only a bird and it's gone now.' Annoyed but obligated, Sara crossed the room to crouch beside her younger child. 'Now, what's all this about?'

Gently she raised Melanie's face away from her hands and the tangle of her hair, and saw that she was covered with blood.

'My God! Oh, sweetheart.' Sara hurried the little girl down the passage to the bathroom. So much blood . . . was her eye hurt? She'd never forgive herself if . . .

A wet flannel, carefully used, revealed no great damage. There were two small cuts, one just above Melanie's left eye and the other on her left cheek. Melanie snuffled and breathed jerkily. She was obviously content to have her mother fuss over her.

Michael peeked around the doorframe as Sara was applying Band-Aids to Melanie's face. 'That bird tried to kill Melanie,' he said in a tone of gleeful horror. 'He tried to peck her eyes out!'

'Michael, *really*.' Sara sighed in exasperation. Melanie would be nervous enough about birds without his stories. 'It was an accident,' she said firmly. 'Birds aren't mean or dangerous – they don't try to hurt people. But that bird was frightened – it was in a strange place. Unfortunately, Melanie got in the way while it was trying to get out. If you'd both been more sensible, instead of jumping around like that –'

'It flew right at her,' Michael said. 'I saw it. It tried to get me next, but I wouldn't let it – I kept waving my hands around over my head so it couldn't get at my face like it wanted.' He sounded very self-important and pleased with himself, which annoyed Sara still more.

'It was an accident. The bird felt trapped and didn't know how to respond. It's not something you have to worry about because it's not likely ever to happen again. Now I don't want to hear any more about it.' She hugged Melanie and lifted her down from the sink ledge. 'Feel better?'

'Hungry,' said Melanie.

'Glad you mentioned it. Let's go and eat lunch.'

On Monday morning Sara took her children to play with Mary Alice's children. It was a beautiful day but already stiflingly hot. Sara felt lethargic and faintly sad. After Michael and Melanie had joined the other children in the safely fenced-in yard, she lingered to drink iced tea and talk with Mary Alice.

'I hope you got a lot of work done yesterday,' Mary Alice said, settling onto a brightly cushioned wicker couch.

Sara shook her head. 'Bruce copped out. He called at the last minute and said he couldn't come – he was in Dallas.'

Mary Alice's eyes went wide. 'That . . . creep,' she said at last.

Sara gave a short laugh. 'I've called him worse than that. But I should know by now that he's not to be counted on. The kids are starting to learn that about him, too. The worst thing about it is what I lost – or what I felt I lost. I woke up feeling great – I was ready to conquer the world, at least to paint it. I felt so *alive*. I felt – I don't know if I can explain how I felt. I think of it as my "creative" feeling, and I haven't had such a strong one since Michael was born – or

131

maybe even since I married Bruce. It's a mood in which everything has meaning, everything is alive, everything is possible.'

'There's a girl who sits for us sometimes,' Mary Alice said hesitantly. 'She's very young, but responsible, and she doesn't charge much. You could have her over some afternoons to take care of the kids while you . . .'

Sara shook her head, discarding the suggestion impatiently. 'They'd still be around. They'd still be – oh, calling to me, somehow. I don't know how to explain it. Sometimes I feel I'm just looking for excuses not to paint, but . . . there's just something about being both a mother *and* an artist. I don't know if I can manage it, not even with all the good examples of other women, or all the babysitters in the world.

'Art has never been a part-time thing for me. Art was all I cared about in school, and up until I met Bruce. Then the part of me that was an artist got submerged. For the past five years I've been a full-time mother. Now I'm trying to learn how to be a part-time artist and a part-time mother, and I don't think I can. I know that's very all-or-nothing of me, but it's how I feel.'

The two women sat quietly in the bright, sunlit room. The high-pitched voices of their children, playing outside, floated up to them.

'Maybe it's just too early,' Mary Alice ventured at last. 'In the fall, Michael will be in school. You could put Melanie in a nursery, at least during the mornings. Then you could count on having a certain amount of time to yourself every day.'

'Maybe,' Sara said. She did not sound hopeful. 'But even when the children aren't around, the pull is there. I think about them, worry about them, have to plan for them. And my art makes as many demands as a child – I can't divide myself between them. I don't think it can ever

132

be the same – I'll never have all my energy and thoughts and commitment to give to my art. There are always the children pulling at me.' She sighed and rubbed her face. 'Sometimes ... I wish I had it to do all over again. And I think that, much as I love them, I would never have chosen to have children. I would never have married.'

Silence fell again and Sara wondered if she had shocked Mary Alice. She was rousing herself to say something else about her love for her children, to find the words that would modify the wish she had just made, when the clamour of children filled the house, the sound of the kitchen door opening and slamming, the clatter of many feet on hardwood floors, and voices raised, calling.

Sara and Mary Alice both leaped to their feet as the children rushed in.

Melanie and Chrissie were crying; the boys were excited and talking all at once.

'It was the same bird!' Michael cried, tugging at Sara's arm as she knelt to comfort Melanie. 'It came and tried to kill us again – it tried to peck her eyes out, but we ran!'

Melanie seemed unhurt; gradually, bathed in her mother's attention, her sobs subsided.

The children all agreed with Michael's story: there had been a white bird which had suddenly swooped down on Melanie, pecking at her head.

'Why does that bird want to hurt us?' Michael asked.

'Oh, Michael, I don't think it does. Maybe you were near its nest; maybe it was attracted by Melanie's hair.' Helpless to explain and trying not to feel frightened herself, Sara hugged her daughter.

'Me go home,' Melanie muttered into Sara's blouse.

Sara looked up. 'Michael, do you want to go home now, or do you want to keep on playing here?'

'You kids can all go and play in Barry's room,' Mary Alice said.

The other children ran off. Sara stood up, still holding Melanie and staggering slightly under her weight. 'I'll take this one home,' she said. 'You can send Michael by himself when he's ready, unless ... unless he wants me to come and get him.'

Mary Alice nodded, her face concerned and puzzled. 'What's this about the bird?'

Sara didn't want to talk about it. As lightly as she could she said, 'Oh, a bird got trapped in the house yesterday and scared the kids. I don't know what happened outside just now, but naturally Michael and Melanie are a little spooked about birds.' She set Melanie down. 'Come on, sweetie, I'm not going to carry you all the way home.'

Keeping her head down as if she feared another attack, Melanie left the house with her mother and walked the half-mile home staying close by her side.

At home, Sara settled Melanie in her room with her dolls, and then, feeling depressed, went back to her own bedroom and stretched out on the bed. She closed her eyes and tried to comfort herself with thoughts of the children at school, a babysitter, a silent house, and time to work. It was wrong to blame the children, she thought. She could be painting now – it was her own fault if she didn't.

Thinking about what she would paint next, she visualized a pale, blonde woman. Her skin was unnaturally white, suggesting sickness or the pallor of death. Her lips were as red as blood, and her long hair was like silvery corn silk.

The White Goddess, thought Sara.

The woman drew a veil over her face. Then, slowly, began to draw it back. Sara felt a quickening of dread. Although she had just seen her face, she was afraid that another, different face would now be revealed. And then the veil was removed, and she saw the grey face with dead-white, staring eyes.

Sara woke with a start. She felt as if she had dozed off

for less than a minute, but she saw from the bedside clock that she had been asleep for nearly an hour. She sat on the edge of the bed and rubbed her eyes. Her mouth was dry. She heard voices, one of them Michael's, coming from outside.

She stood up and walked to the window and pulled back the heavy curtains, curious to see who Michael was talking to.

Michael was standing on the edge of the lawn near the driveway with a strange woman. Although there was something faintly familiar about her, Sara could not identify her as any of the neighbours. She was a brassy blonde, heavily made-up – even at this distance her lips seemed garishly red against an unnaturally pale face. Something about the way they stood together and spoke so intently made Sara want to intrude.

But by the time she got outside, Michael was alone.

'Hi,' he said, walking toward her.

'Where'd she go?' Sara asked, looking around.

'Who?'

'That woman you were just talking to – who was she?'

'Who?'

'You know who,' Sara began, then stopped abruptly, confused. She had just realised why the woman seemed familiar to her; she'd seen her first in a dream. Perhaps she had dreamed the whole incident?

She shook her head, bent to kiss Michael, and went with him into the house.

In the middle of the night Sara started up in bed, wide awake and frightened. The children? She couldn't pinpoint her anxiety, but her automatic reaction was to check on their safety. In the hall, on the way to their rooms, she heard the sound of a muffled giggle coming from the family room. There she saw Michael and Melanie standing before the window, curtains opened wide, gazing into the garden.

Sara walked slowly toward the window, vaguely dreading what she would see.

There was a white pig on the lawn, almost shining in the moonlight. It stood very still, looking up at them.

Sara put her hand on Melanie's shoulders and the little girl leaped away, letting out a small scream.

'Melanie!' Sara said sharply.

Both children stood still and quiet, looking at her. There was a wariness in their gaze that Sara did not like. They looked as if they were expecting punishment. What had they done? Sara wondered.

'Both of you, go to bed. You shouldn't be up and roaming around at this hour.'

'Look, she's dancing,' Michael said softly.

Sara turned and looked out of the window. The pig was romping on the lawn in what was surely an unnatural fashion, capering in circles that took it gradually away from the house and toward the lake. It wasn't trotting or running or walking – it was, as Michael had said, dancing.

On the shore of the lake it stopped. To Sara's eyes the figure of the pig seemed to become dim and blurred – she blinked, wondering if a cloud had passed across the moon. The whiteness that had been a pig now seemed to flow and swirl like a dense fog, finally settling in the shape of a tall, pale woman in a silver-white gown.

Sara shivered and rubbed her bare arms with her hands. She wanted to hide. She wanted to turn her gaze away but could not move.

It's not possible, she thought. *I'm dreaming.*

The harsh, unmistakable sound of the bolt being drawn on the door brought her out of her daze, and she turned in time to see Michael opening the door, Melanie close behind him.

'No!' She rushed to pull the children away and to push the door shut again. She snapped the bolt to and stood in front of the door, blocking it from the children. She was trembling.

The children began to weep. They stood with their arms half-outstretched as if begging for an embrace from someone just out of their reach.

Sara walked past her weeping children to the window and looked out. There was nothing unusual to be seen in the moonlit garden – no white pig or ghostly woman. Nothing that should not have been there amid the shadows. Across the lake she saw a sudden pale blur, as if a white bird had risen into the air. But that might have been moonlight on the leaves.

'Go back to bed,' Sara said wearily. 'She's gone – it's all over now.'

Watching them shuffle away, sniffing and rubbing their faces, Sara remembered the story she had told Michael on the first night she had caught a glimpse of the woman. It seemed bitterly ironic now, that story of a ghostly mother searching for her children.

'You can't have them,' Sara whispered to the empty night. 'I'll never let you hurt them.'

Sara woke in the morning feeling as if she had been painting all night: tired, yet satisfied and hopeful. The picture was there, just behind her eyes, and she could hardly wait to get started.

The children were quiet and sullen, not talking to her and with only enough energy to stare at the television set. Sara diagnosed it as lack of sleep and thought that it was just as well – she had no time for their questions or games today. She made them breakfast but let the dishes and other housework go and hurried to set up her canvas and paints outside in the clear morning sunlight.

begrudging
the children the loss of
her painting / purpose

Another cool night-time painting, all swirling grays, blue, and cold white. A metamorphosis: pale-coloured pig transforming into a pale-faced, blue-gowned woman who shifts into a bird, flying away.

The new creation absorbed her utterly and she worked all day, with only a brief pause when the children demanded lunch. At a little before six she decided to stop for the day. She was tired, pleased with herself, and utterly ravenous.

She found the children sitting before the television, and wondered if they had been there, just like that, all day. After putting her unfinished painting safely away and cleaning her brushes, she marched decisively to the television set and turned it off.

Michael and Melanie began a deprived wailing.

'Oh, come on!' Sara scoffed. 'All that fuss about the news? You've watched enough of that pap for one day. How would you like to go for a swim before dinner?'

Michael shrugged. Melanie hugged her knees and muttered, 'I want to watch.'

'If you want to swim, say so and I'll go out with you. If you don't, I'm going to start cooking.'

They didn't respond, so Sara shrugged and went into the kitchen. She was feeling too good to be annoyed by their moodiness.

The children didn't turn the television back on, and Sara heard no further sound from the family room until, the chicken cooking and a potato salad under construction, she heard the screen door open and close.

She smiled and, as she was going to check on the chicken, paused to look out of the window. What she saw froze her with terror.

The children were running toward the lake, silently, their bare arms and legs flashing in the twilight. Michael was in the lead because Melanie ran clumsily and sometimes fell.

138

Across the lake on the other shore stood the pale woman in white; on her shoulder, the white bird; and at her side, the pig. The woman raised her head slightly and looked past the children, directly at Sara. Her blood-red lips parted in a gleaming smile.

Sara cried out incoherently and ran for the door. Ahead of her she saw Michael leap into the lake with all his clothes on. She caught up with Melanie on the shore and grabbed her.

'Go back to the house,' she said, shaking the girl slightly for emphasis. 'Go on back and stay there. You are not to go into the water, understand?'

Then, kicking off her sandals, Sara dived in and swam after her son.

She had nearly reached him when she heard a splashing behind her, and her courage failed: Melanie. But she couldn't let herself be distracted by her worries about Melanie's abilities as a swimmer. She caught hold of her son in a lifesaver's neck-grip. He struggled grimly and silently against her, but he didn't have a chance. Sara knew she could get him across to the other shore if only she didn't have to try to save Melanie as well.

'Michael,' Sara gasped. 'Honey, listen to me. It's not safe. You must go back. Michael, please! This is very dangerous – she'll kill you. She's the one who sent the bird!'

Michael continued to thrash, kick, and choke. Sara wondered if he even heard her. She looked around and saw Melanie paddling slowly in their direction. And on the other shore the White Goddess stood, making no sound or motion.

'Michael, please,' Sara whispered close to his ear. 'Don't fight me. Relax, and we'll all be safe.' With great difficulty, Sara managed to pull him back toward the home shore.

Melanie swam with single-minded concentration and was within Sara's grasp before she could try to avoid her.

She thrashed about in Sara's armlock, but not as wild nor as strongly as her brother.

Sara had them both, now, but how was she to swim? She was treading water, just holding her own against the children's struggles and hoping they would soon tire when she felt a rush of air against her cheek, and Melanie shrieked.

It was the bird again. Sara caught sight of it just as it was diving for Michael's head. The sharp beak gashed his face below one eye. Michael screamed, and the bright blood streamed down his cheek.

Trying to help him, Sara relaxed her stranglehold. At once he swam away, kicking and plunging below the water.

'Michael, go back to the house – you'll be safe there!'

She swallowed a mouthful of lake water as she spoke, and choked on it. Letting go of Melanie, she managed to catch hold of Michael's flailing legs and pull him back close to her. Melanie, trying to avoid the bird which was still flapping around, screamed and cried, barely managing to keep herself afloat. Sara had no trouble catching her again.

Shouting at the bird, longing for a spare hand to strike at it, Sara pulled her children close to her, pressing their faces tightly against her breast. They struggled still to get away, but they were tiring and their struggles grew weaker. Sara knew she would win – she would save them from the bird and from the goddess; she would protect them with her own body.

Finally, the bird flew away. In the sudden calm, Sara realised that her children were much too quiet, much too still. She relaxed her tight hold, and their bodies slipped farther into the water.

She stared down at them, slow to understand. Their eyes were open, looking up through a film of water, but they did not see her. She looked up from their sweet, empty faces and across the silver water to where the white-faced figure still stood, her pale eyes staring out at death, her favourite offering.

Sara saw it all as a painting. The pale figure on the shore glowed against the deep blue twilight, and the water gave off its own shimmering light. The woman in the water, also dressed in white, was a terrible, pitiable figure with her two drowned children beside her, their hair floating out around their heads like fuzzy halos; an innocent murderess.

I was the one they were afraid of, thought Sara.

She threw back her head and howled her anguish to the empty world.

she doesn't
protect them
when it matters;
her unexpired times
are at odds with
when they need her,
they aren't part of
her "feeling alive"
times, so instead
they're dead-

NEED

After ballet, Corey liked to walk home through the cemetery. The grounds were large and well tended and offered the visitor a wealth of picturesque monuments and sentimental gravestone inscriptions, some of them dating back before the Civil War. There were columns, slabs, and spheres in abundance of the pinkish marble that was quarried locally, and among the mausoleums built to look like temples, chapels, and houses was one defiant pink pyramid.

The walk through the cemetery, like the ballet class that preceded it, was one of the few things Corey enjoyed, something she did because she wanted to and not because she was expected to or thought she should.

On this October afternoon, crunching through the dead leaves and breathing in the crisp, autumn-scented air, Corey felt pleasantly tired, and looked forward to reaching her apartment where she could have a cup of hot tea and some sandwiches before settling down to write her usual evening letter to her fiancé.

But although she looked forward to those simple things, there was also pleasure in being able to delay them. With no one waiting for her and no schedule to follow, there was no reason to hurry back. It was a beautiful day, and she knew she had at least an hour before it would begin to get dark. So she turned aside from the main path and wandered the sloping, uneven ground among stone angels and headstones until she came to her favourite spot, discovered on a previous walk.

This was a bench beneath a large old oak tree with a

view of a cluster of elaborately carved tombstones all commemorating various members of the Symonds family, and a statue of a gentle-faced young woman holding a baby, with a second child clutching at her stone draperies, half turned as if looking longingly at the graves.

'It's as if she were saying, "Why did you abandon me, and leave us here alone?"' said a voice behind her.

Corey jumped up and turned to see a young man in a bright blue windbreaker. He had a pleasant, rather weak-looking face, and seemed about her own age.

'I'm sorry,' he said. 'I didn't mean to scare you.'

'I thought I was alone. I didn't hear you walk up,' she said, and realised she had pressed one hand against her heart; she let it drop, feeling embarrassed.

'And in a cemetery ... I don't blame you for being frightened.'

'I'm not,' Corey said. 'I was just startled, that's all. I like cemeteries. I like this one, anyway. It's peaceful. I often walk here.'

'I know,' he said. 'I do, too. I spend a lot of time here. I've seen you, although I don't suppose you ever noticed me. I've seen you, always by yourself, and I suppose I got to thinking that I knew you. That's why I came up and spoke like I did. It was stupid of me, and rude – I'm sorry.'

'It's all right, really, I understand,' Corey said. 'You don't have to keep apologizing.' He gave off such an aura of unhappiness and unease that she felt obliged to try to lessen it.

'I can tell you like this spot,' he said. 'It's one of my favourites. I love to sit on the bench and look at that woman with her children. She's so beautiful and so sad, really a tragic subject. Her husband has left her – and it's the ultimate desertion. He hasn't gone to another lover, but to Death. So she knows she can never win him back. But she stares at his grave and dreams, and asks him why.'

143

You'd think that her beauty and her obvious need would make any man change his mind – but it's too late, of course, for both of them.'

Corey felt uneasy now, her pleasant mood shattered. She had no desire to be standing in a cemetery, talking to an odd boy who had watched her without her being aware. But force of habit kept her polite.

'I have to be getting back soon,' she said. 'I have things to do.'

'You're from the South, aren't you?'

'North Carolina.'

'My parents live in Florida, so that's supposed to be my home now. But actually, I was born here in town. My family goes way back. In fact, I'll be buried right here in this cemetery when I die. There's a family plot, with a space reserved for me. But you're a long way from home. What made you come here?'

'It's a good school,' she said, her voice resentful. 'My parents thought I should have the opportunity to go to a first-rate school and see another part of the country. But I'm only here for a year. In May I'm going home. I'm getting married.'

'You're engaged.'

'That's right.'

'He's not here?'

'He's home, in North Carolina.'

'Ah.' He nodded quickly. 'I thought you were . . . it's the lonely who seek out the cemeteries. We have that in common.'

She wanted nothing in common with him. She wanted to get away, to escape to the dull confines of her furnished apartment and reread Philip's old letters. Blandly cruel, she said, staring at the bright blue of his jacket, 'In common? You mean you're engaged to someone who isn't here, too?'

'Engaged? Oh no, I . . . I don't have anyone. I don't have anyone at all except my dead friends here.'

'I've got to go,' Corey said, glancing at a wrist on which there was no watch. Anything not to see the misery on his face. She walked away quickly, deliberately crunching through fallen leaves. If he spoke again, or called after her, she might not hear him above the noise she made.

When the letter came, it had been five days without a word. Corey was so excited that her hands shook, and she tore the envelope in getting it open.

It wasn't very long. Just one page written in Philip's precise hand. She read it through to his signature without understanding, and then read it again, her mouth going dry and her stomach beginning to hurt.

He was releasing her from their engagement, he said. Their parents were right – they were too young to make such a momentous decision. He did love her, but he felt they should both date other people and get to know their own minds better. He was sure she would agree with him, but they could talk this over at greater length when they saw each other at Thanksgiving.

Corey dropped the letter on the floor and walked across the small room to stare unseeing at the wall. Less than two months they had been apart. He hadn't been able to last even two months.

She clenched her fists and pressed them against the sides of her head. Her mouth open wide, she breathed in ragged, tearing gulps, feeling as if she were drowning. She wept.

It was beginning to get dark, and still Corey remained slumped on the couch where she had spent most of the day since reading Philip's letter. She had tried to call him, and had left a message with his roommate. She didn't

145

know what she would say if he returned her call, but she had to talk to someone, and she could think of no one else to call.

She had come to this distant, northern town, this first-rate university, under protest, in order to satisfy her parents. She saw her agreed-upon year here as a time of trial, something that must be undergone before she could be united with Philip, and so she had taken a certain grim pleasure in refusing to do anything that would make the time easier on herself. She hadn't joined any organisations or tried out for plays, as she would have back home, and she had not made any friends. What was the point? She would be gone at the end of the year. Why should she pretend that this lonely interval had anything to do with her real life?

She didn't need dates, she didn't need friends, so long as she had Philip, no matter how far away he was. That was what she had thought. And now that she longed for a friend, anyone with a sympathetic ear, she had nowhere to turn.

She thought of the people from her classes who had spoken to her, and how she had always turned aside whatever gestures they had made towards friendship. She thought of the boy in the cemetery. He was as alone as she was now. Remembering how she had deliberately cut him, she felt deeply ashamed.

Abruptly she stood up. She had to get out. She had done nothing but sit and brood and cry alone all day, until the walls and furniture were so saturated with her grief that she could scarcely bear to look at them any longer.

She decided to go to the cemetery. It was a good place for walking, for brooding, for being alone. It was nearly dark, but that didn't bother her. She suspected a cemetery would be safer after dark than the campus.

Corey's apartment was one of four in an old house on the west side of the university. As she crept cautiously down the dark, narrow stairs, she hoped she wouldn't encounter any of her neighbours. Although she had heard them coming and going, she had never actually met any of the other occupants of the house; she wasn't even certain how many of them there were. They were only heavy footsteps on the stairs to her, and voices muffled by walls.

She walked quickly through the empty evening streets. The air was grey-blue with dusk and very still; she felt as if she were walking along the bottom of a deep, quiet pond. When she reached the cemetery she made her way towards the familiar bench and statue.

'You came.'

He didn't startle her this time. It was as if she had known he would be there, sitting on the stone bench and waiting for her as the day faded.

He stood when she approached. 'I knew you would come,' he said quietly. 'I knew that if I waited long enough, and thought about you hard enough, that you would understand and come to me.'

'How could you know?' Her voice was gentle.

'Because I needed you. I've come here every day, and hoped to see you. Today – I didn't know how much longer I could go on. Today I concentrated on you. I thought about you. I really needed you . . . and so you came. If you hadn't, then I would have known that it was all over, that what I needed didn't matter. But you came.'

'I came,' she agreed. It was an odd conversation, but it seemed almost appropriate under the circumstances. What else did one say to a strange boy at twilight in a cemetery? 'But I didn't know you would be here,' she said. 'How could I? I'm not sure why I came here. I guess I needed you, too.'

She heard him suck in his breath.

Feeling very tired, she sat down on the bench. After a moment he joined her.

'I didn't go to class today,' he said. 'I was up all night, thinking, and then I came here. I spent all day here, hoping I would see you. When it started to get dark I almost gave up. I'm glad I didn't.'

'You don't even know me,' she said. She turned her head to look at him. In the darkness she couldn't even tell what colour his eyes were. 'You don't even know my name.'

'But that doesn't matter. What matters is the kinship between us. I felt it long before I spoke to you. You feel it too, don't you?'

'I don't know.' She clutched her shoulders, folding her arms across her chest. 'I just didn't want to be alone any more. I don't have any friends here, I don't know anyone I can talk to.'

'You can talk to me,' he said. 'If I could help you – you don't know how happy that would make me. I'd do anything, anything to help you. Anything you need from me.'

His tone was disconcertingly intense, and Corey felt briefly the oddness of the situation. But anything was better than being alone right now.

'I'd like to talk to you,' she said. 'I need to talk – if you'd be willing to listen. Maybe we could go somewhere and have dinner together. I haven't eaten anything all day.'

'I'd like that very much,' he said quietly.

They went to an Italian restaurant near campus, and there, over plates of spaghetti and glasses of wine, she began to talk. The flood of her pent-up emotion rushed out and flowed over the young man who sat across the table from her, gazing at her as if she were a miracle. But she was past minding his disconcerting gaze or his odd speeches. He existed for her only as someone who kept her from being alone, a listening presence who served her need to talk in the same way that a glass of water relieved her mouth of dryness.

After their meal he walked her home and, noticing

the darkness of the hall, suggested firmly that it would be better if he saw her safely to her own door. She felt a pang – it was the sort of thing Philip would do – but smiled and thanked him. The front door, she discovered, was unlocked – a good, hard push would serve to open it. This was a common occurrence. It was an old door, slightly warped, and needed to be firmly shut, and most of the people who hurried in and out of the house did not bother to pause to make certain the latch had caught. She was slightly nervous as they walked up the dark stairs together, but he did not try to touch her or kiss her, and said good night politely when she had unlocked her door and turned on a light.

she wanted him to

'We'll see each other again?' he asked in a low, hopeful voice.

'Yes, of course,' she said. Exhausted from pouring out her troubles to him, she felt eager to get away from him.

'In the cemetery – tomorrow afternoon?'

'I'm not sure. I . . .'

'Then the next day. Or Saturday? Saturday afternoon, for sure?'

She nodded. 'Saturday.'

'I'm not trying to push you, or chase you, you understand. But I want to help you. And I think we need each other. It *is* mutual.'

'Thank you for listening to me tonight,' she said. 'It really helped. I hope it wasn't too boring for you.' She was uncomfortable again, aware of him as an individual, as an odd stranger who was now knowledgeable about her problems.

'You don't have to thank me. I'll be here for you whenever you need me, I promise. All you have to do is ask me, and I'll come. But I'll see you Saturday, for sure, in the cemetery. Our place.'

She nodded uneasily. When he had gone, she locked the

door and went to the telephone. Philip might have been trying to reach her while she was out.

But nothing could be learned or settled or changed by telephone, Corey found. Words went humming off into space and lost all connection with reality, with truth. Philip's voice, detached from Philip, was distant and unfamiliar. Was that impatience in his voice, or regret? Pain or indifference? Corey didn't like the sound of her own voice, which echoed in her ears, obscuring what Philip said and what she wanted to say.

She had to see him face to face and learn if he still loved her.

The money in her bank account, the money she was expected to live on for the next month, would more than cover the cost of a round-trip ticket. She didn't think about what she would do when she returned – her parents would provide.

She left Thursday evening, on the first flight she could get. It involved a change in Philadelphia as well as one in Charlotte, but Philip had agreed to meet her post-midnight flight. Despite her nervousness, she felt a greedy exhilaration. No matter what happened, she would have this weekend with Philip.

It was wretched.

At the end of it, Corey felt as if she and Philip were complete strangers. She was eager to leave, even to go back to a place she despised.

She returned on Sunday night, thinking about the boy from the cemetery, and remembered her broken promise – she had not met him on Saturday, after all. But surely he would understand when she explained, she thought. He knew, as no one else in this town did, something of her feelings. She would have to go and look for him the next day. She realised that she didn't know his name or where, besides the cemetery, she might expect to find him.

On Monday, she found out.

She paused by the student union to pick up a newspaper on her way to class, and noticed that the lead story was about a student who had committed suicide. It was not the student's name, but her own address that leaped out at Corey as she scanned the article – 501 Comstock. That was the house she lived in, and it was where the student, Harold Walker, had been found early on Sunday morning, dead of self-inflicted wounds. Shocked, she glanced at the accompanying photograph and recognised Harold Walker as the boy from the cemetery.

He must have spent his last hours of life waiting for her in the cemetery. And then he had come looking for her, needing her. And this time he had needed her in vain. She hadn't been home. And so he had killed himself outside her door.

'Oh, God,' she said. Heavy with guilt, she sat down on the steps of the Union. He had needed her, and she had failed him – betrayed him – and now he was dead. She began to cry. Other students, passing by on the steps, looked at her and then looked away. No one stopped to talk to her; no one knew her.

During the next few days Corey thought a lot about Harold Walker as she walked dazedly through her life. She saw his body interred in the family plot he had told her about; saw, but did not approach, his quiet, bewildered-looking parents. After the funeral she went to the place where they had first met, and sat alone on the bench where they had once sat together.

What horrified her most of all was the realisation that she could never atone. She had never before seen anything in her life as irrevocable. But Harold Walker was dead, and if she had not failed him when he needed her, he might now be alive. Beside his death, the loss of Philip faded into triviality. She scarcely thought of Philip now; it was Harold she dreamed of, mourned, and longed to see again.

Because she could not spend all her time in the cemetery, Corey continued to wander through her daily routine, but her mind was elsewhere. Gradually she accustomed herself to the idea of Harold's death – perhaps he was better off, he had escaped the life that had made him so unhappy. She mourned for herself, now, for her own loneliness.

On the last night of October, sitting alone in her small apartment, a bowl of soup rapidly cooling in front of her, Corey felt her grief turning to anger. The resentment must have been smouldering beneath the sorrow all along.

How *could* he kill himself like that? With all his talk of need, he must have known how she needed him, and realised what he would be doing to her by killing himself. If she had betrayed him, his betrayal of her had been far greater, because it was forever. It could not be recalled or apologised for. He had taken himself out of life, and out of her life, for all time.

'What about *me*?' she said aloud. The tears rolled slowly down her face.

It was Halloween night. People were out having a good time with their friends, attending parties all over campus. And Corey sat alone, talking to a dead man.

'I needed you,' she said. 'Did you think about that? Couldn't you have waited a little longer? Or weren't my needs as important as yours? All right; I wasn't there for you on Saturday, but I would have come back. You should have known that. But you can't come back – no matter how much I need you, you'll never come to me again.'

She went to bed early because there was nothing else to do, but she lay awake a long time. And when she did finally fall asleep, it seemed only a few minutes before something woke her.

She lay in the dark and listened. She could hear some-one moving about downstairs, and thought now that the sound which had wakened her had been the slamming of the front door. Probably one of her neighbours coming home drunk from a party. Whoever it was was making a very noisy job of climbing the stairs; in addition to the slow, heavy footfalls, Corey could hear a soft, erratic thump-and-slide sound, as if the climber had to support himself against the wall as he climbed.

There was something oddly disturbing about the sound. She was wide awake now, and she lay stiffly waiting for the noisy intruder to reach his journey's end.

Silence – the top of the stairs reached at last. Then more dragging footsteps. Then a thumping at her door.

She sat up in bed, clutching the covers. The pounding continued.

'No!' she cried. Then, feeling nervous and embarrassed (it was probably only a drunk who had made a mistake), she got out of bed and walked through the dark into the living room and called, 'You've got the wrong apartment; you're across the hall. Try the other door!'

She waited for the sounds of departure, but when the pounding stopped there was nothing, and the silence ate at her nerves.

Then the pounding began again, still at her door. It was not forceful at all, but neither was it controlled enough to be called knocking. It was heavy but unfocused, a loose, meaty slapping against the wood.

She shuddered. Remembering the downstairs door, and how it was often left unlocked, she realised that anyone might have got in.

'Who is that?' Corey called.

The pounding stopped. Silence again. Corey stared at the door, wondering who waited on the other side. Sud-denly she had a vivid image of Harold Walker crouching

153

outside her door on the night he died. Had he pounded and begged to be let in, imagining her hiding inside?

The pounding began again, making her jump. She bit her lip and tried to keep from crying. It wouldn't do to lose control. It was probably just some old drunk, or some kid trying to frighten her. But now that she had thought of Harold, she couldn't seem to get the thought of him out of her mind. It was absurd and impossible, but it seemed to her that Harold was on the other side of the door, making that terrible slapping sound with his weak, dead hands.

'Go away,' she cried, her voice high and shrill with fear. 'Go away, or I'll call the police!'

Silence again. A waiting silence. Whoever was there did not leave.

Harold, she thought. *I'm sorry. I'm sorry I wasn't here when you came looking for me.* She walked closer to the door. Cautiously, trying not to make a sound, Corey leaned against it, pressing her ear to the wood. She heard nothing, not even breathing, from the other side.

But as soon as she stepped back, the pounding began again.

She stared at the door, remembering something Harold had said: 'All you have to do is ask me, and I'll come.'

'But you're dead,' she said. It was barely a whisper, but again it stopped the pounding, as if whoever was in the hall was eager to hear anything she had to say.

'Go away,' she said more loudly. 'Go away, do you hear me? Go back to where you came from! Do you hear me? I don't need you! Go away!'

There was no more pounding after that. There was no sound of any kind. Corey slumped to the floor, facing the door, no more able to walk away from it than she was to open it. She was shivering and felt slightly sick.

If it was Harold, she thought, someone would find the body out there, sooner or later. And if it wasn't, if it had been only her imagination, her need, someone would find her and let her know; someone would call or someone would come. Sooner or later.

And so she sat, all through the night, waiting and listening for the sounds of the dead.

her grief and guilt @ her own betrayal of Harold + her anger @ him manifesting – imaginary based on her thoughts + experiences w/ him

Won't take responsibility for her role or guilt or acknowledge the guilt that killed him and that leaves him outside
↳ Harold is also immature + doesn't take responsibility for how he makes her feel by expecting too much from their "sameness"

THE MEMORY OF WOOD

It was a beautiful chest. The hard, dark old wood gleamed in the sunlight, looking rich and exotic against the bright green grass.

Helen and Rob saw it at the same time and glanced at each other swiftly, smiling in shared delight. Helen shifted the baby in her arms, looked down to see that Julian had not strayed, and followed her husband. They made their way among the furniture, the bits and pieces of a life scattered on the big front lawn, towards the thing they had, in that instant, made up their minds to buy.

'It's lovely,' she said softly, watching her husband run his hand across the smooth grain of the lid.

'It'll cost,' he said. His voice was dreamy.

'But we need it. Don't we?'

'We could keep blankets in it,' he said. 'Let me see how it opens.' He crouched on the grass and she moved near, standing over him. The chest wasn't locked; the hinged lid came up smoothly and quietly under his hands.

Helen clutched the baby closer and drew back, nearly stumbling. Her stomach twisted. The stench was horrible: sweet and rotten, with something nasty underneath. She made a small, despairing sound.

Rob looked up at her, frowning. 'I thought I –'

'That smell.'

'Yes ...' He was still frowning, puzzled. 'I thought I caught a whiff of something horrible, but – ' He sniffed loudly, obviously, moving his head above the open chest. 'Nothing, now.'

'Are you sure?' Cautiously, she breathed through her

156

nose again, and smelled nothing unusual, but she hesitated to move closer, to lean into the chest as Rob was doing.

'I'm sure,' he said.

She looked down at the chest, her pleasure broken.

Rob lowered the lid gently and stood up. 'It could go in the living room, beneath the Clarke print. Next to the red chair.'

'People would use it as a table then, put drinks down on it and spoil the finish.'

He smiled at her. 'We could put out coasters when we serve drinks.'

'Take baby for a minute, would you?' She flexed her arms when the weight was gone, and bent over the chest, stroking it with her finger tips. The wood was as sleek and satin-smooth as she had imagined. 'Whose estate was this?' she asked. 'Somebody really took care of this chest. She must have rubbed it with oil and polished it every week to get the wood like this.'

'Some old woman who just died,' Rob said, glancing up at the elaborate gingerbread of the house. 'She was all alone, no family, no children. An old maid.'

Helen hesitated, wanting to turn her back and walk away. She told herself she was being silly. Her fingers found the edge of the lid and she lifted.

They both sniffed, and looked at each other. They smelled nothing but the sun, the grass, the faint scents of musty furnishings exposed to the open air, the perfumes of people drifting around them.

'Maybe,' said Rob.

'We didn't imagine it.'

'No, but maybe it wasn't the chest at all. It might have been a coincidence that we smelled it when I first lifted the lid. Maybe it was someone passing by –'

Helen giggled. 'Anyone who smells like *that* and is still walking around – !' She lowered the lid.

'It'll cost,' said Rob. 'But not like it would if we bought it from a dealer.'

Julian let out a crow of pleasure and began running away at top speed on his fat, stumpy legs. Helen looked around and saw that he had sighted a leashed poodle. She winced, seeing his inevitable tumble a split second before it happened, and started after him, to comfort him. But Julian took the fall with his usual uncomplaining good nature; it was baby Alice, safe in her father's arms, who began to scream as Rob bent down to examine the chest again.

They spent more than they could realistically afford, but less – they were certain – than the beautifully made chest was worth. They were well pleased with themselves as they drove home from the estate sale, the chest in the back seat with Julian.

None of their furniture had been bought new; all of it had come as hand-me-downs from family or had been bought at garage sales, auctions, flea markets, and junk shops. What had started as economic necessity had grown into a point of pride. No shoddy, mass-produced contemporary furniture for Helen and Rob. They favoured dark wood, intricately carved high-backed sofas and chairs with velvet cushions, glass-fronted bookcases, and ancient, hand-made wardrobes. The chest was simple, but old and beautiful. It would fit in with the rest of their furniture.

When they had put it in place that night, in the living room near the red-velvet chair and the ornately tasselled floor lamp, beneath the black-and-white lithograph of a man on a lonely road, Helen opened the lid. Her hand flew to her mouth and she gagged at the rich and rotten smell of something dead. With an effort, Helen held back the rush of sickness, but tears came to her eyes.

'Rob,' she called weakly.

He came at once with the beers he had fetched to toast their new treasure. 'Darling, what's wrong?'

'The smell,' she said hopelessly.

Rob went to the chest and leaned into it. Watching, Helen felt the sudden urge to pull him back to safety. He looked around, shrugging. 'Honestly, darling, I can't smell anything. Some old dust, maybe.'

She let herself breathe again. He was right; the smell was gone. But it must be lurking within the chest, every opening releasing it.

'It was the same horrible smell,' she said. 'The minute I opened the chest, there it was.'

He gazed into the chest thoughtfully; put in one hand to stroke the interior. 'I suppose it could be something . . . maybe some food that went bad, or maybe a rat got inside and died there long ago. Wood holds a smell for a long time.'

Helen nodded bleakly. The odour, brief though it had been, had disturbed her profoundly. 'I wish we hadn't bought it. I can't bear that smell. I don't want it in the house.'

Rob frowned and said, 'You wanted it as much as I did. We agreed on it.'

'I know. I fell in love with the way it looked. But I didn't know – honestly, Rob, I can't live with it!'

'Do you smell anything now?'

She shook her head. 'No, but I did when I first opened it. I know I did. And if that's going to happen every time I open it –'

'It won't. We'll fumigate it. We'll clean it out with disinfectant and then put some of those whaddayacallems inside. Sachets. Oranges stuffed with cloves. I used to make them for my aunts every Christmas, and they'd put them in the big trunk where they kept the quilts. It's a great smell, that orange and clove among the blankets.'

He looked at her earnestly, eyes compelling her agreement. Weakly, to avoid an argument, Helen nodded. But she didn't believe his prediction. That horrible smell was somehow trapped in the chest, and it would not go away. Wood had a memory for smell that soap, disinfectant, and perfume could not erase.

She thought of the chest of drawers that was now in the baby's room. She had inherited it in college, when her roommate left to get married. Helen never knew whether Jenny had spilled perfume in the bottom drawer or if the smell had simply lingered from the clothes she had kept there – in either case, although Helen had cleaned out the drawer with soap and water and lined it with fresh paper, whenever she pulled out that bottom drawer she was tempted to look around, thinking that Jenny had come into the room. The fragrance was transmitted from the drawer to whatever clothes she kept there, although it was faint and did not last long. But the scent never left the wood, although it had been nearly six years since the chest had been Jenny's.

Wood remembers, she thought, and as if he had read her mind, Rob said, 'Look, as long as any of the bad smell lingers, we don't have to use it to store anything. It's still a beautiful-looking chest, even if we don't use it. We don't have to keep opening the lid. But I'm sure it won't last. Tomorrow why don't you teach Julian how to make a pomander out of an orange and cloves?'

She smiled at him, relieved that they weren't going to argue after all. 'Julian will only stick the cloves up his nose,' she said. 'If he doesn't eat them first.' She closed the lid.

A baby's crying woke Helen in the night. This was not unusual. What was unusual was that she didn't think it was Alice crying, and the sound didn't come from the nursery. Some odd trick of acoustics, or perhaps her sleepy mind, made the sound seem to come from the direction of the living room.

Nevertheless, Helen got up, tied her dressing-gown around her, and went into the next room to check. She found Alice sleeping soundly. As she looked down at the sleeping baby, she heard the crying again, distant and muffled.

A feeling of dread pushed at her heart. Moving slowly, she followed the sound. It had died away again by the time she stood in the living room, but it seemed still to ring in the air. She turned on a lamp and looked around the room, her eyes and attention drawn by the chest. It was no longer beautiful, but dark and menacing. Hastily, Helen switched off the light. Darkness was better. She didn't want to see the chest and think about opening it. She waited, praying she would not hear the crying again, praying that it had not come from the chest.

She waited long minutes in the darkness and the silence, and then went back to bed. In the morning she decided it had been a dream.

Helen was ironing in the kitchen half-listening to the soap opera on the television set out of sight in the next room. The baby was in her mechanical swing, creaking back and forth beside her, and Julian was playing in the living room. Helen's mind was just registering the fact that her son was being too quiet when from the living room came a soft but definite thud, and Julian made the noise he made to signify disgust or displeasure. Alice's face puckered and she began to cry. Helen caught a whiff of something rotten.

'Julian,' she said sharply. She set down the iron and rushed into the living room, ignoring the baby's cries.

She found her son standing before the open chest, a look of intense interest on his face as he stared down into it. Apprehension twisted her stomach and she caught

Julian's arms and pulled him away from whatever it was that so fascinated him. He cried out his annoyance and hit her ineffectually, squirming to get free. Helen held him tightly and turned him away from the chest. Then, curious, about what in that empty wooden box could have caught his attention, she turned back for a look.

It wasn't empty. For just a moment she saw – or thought she saw – the chest stuffed with bundles of old, yellowed newspapers. But when she frowned and began to move closer, she saw that of course it was empty. There was nothing inside it. The chest was empty as it had been when they brought it home the day before.

Helen turned her attention to her wriggling son. 'Julian,' she said, trying to keep her voice calm but firm. 'That's a no-no. You must not open the chest. Understand me? The chest is not a toy. You are not to open it. You must not play with it. Understand?'

He scowled up at her, obviously disagreeing but finding his small vocabulary inadequate to tell her so. Alice, in the kitchen, was still crying. Helen sighed.

'Go on and play with your toys, Julian. *Not* the chest. I mean it.'

She let go of him and went to close the lid. For a moment she stared down into the chest, wondering about the newspapers. What had made her imagine the chest was filled with newspapers, something wrapped in newspaper and packed away in the chest? No answer occurred to her, so she closed the lid, then went to see about the baby.

Alice simply wanted to be held and, after a few minutes of attention, she had calmed down and was agreeable to being put back in her swing. Helen went back to the living room to check on Julian.

And found him, as she had more than half-expected, again standing before the open chest, clearly fascinated by whatever he imagined he saw inside.

'Julian.'

Obviously he did not hear the threat in her voice, for he looked up brightly, blue eyes shining and round face puckered with interest. 'Baby,' he said.

'Julian, what did I tell you about that chest?' She advanced upon him.

The bright interest went out of his face, and he looked stubborn. 'Me see,' he said firmly.

'It's not a toy, Julian. I told you before you are not to play with it. You must not open it. Don't open it again.' She shut the lid.

'Me see,' he said again, his chubby hands creeping for the edge of the lid.

'No.' Helen caught his hands and held them. 'No. Leave the chest alone, Julian. I mean it. You're going to be in big trouble if you do that again.' She looked into his stubborn face and knew he would go to the chest as soon as her back was turned. Threats did not work with him, so she would have to distract him.

'Well, big boy,' she said cheerfully, hoisting him up in her arms. 'Why don't you play with your old mommy for a while? You want to play with your choo-choos? You want to play choo-choo trains with Mommy?' She carried him away, bouncing him slightly in her arms and asking questions, taking him away from the sight of the wooden chest.

For the rest of the day she kept an eye on Julian, never giving him the chance to go back to the chest. But in the evening, sitting with her family watching television, she was struck by how often Julian turned his head to look at the chest. In particular, she was struck by the way he looked at the chest.

Later, when Julian had been put to bed, she tried to explain her unease to Rob. 'He'd get a look on his face, as if he'd heard something, and then he'd turn and look straight at the chest. As if the sound came from the chest. Except that there wasn't any sound. Why is he so fascinated by it? Why does he want to keep opening it?'

'Because you've made such a big deal out of it,' Rob said easily. 'He opened it once, out of natural curiosity, and you hit the ceiling. Naturally that made him curious. He can't figure out what is so special about it. He's a kid who doesn't like to be told no, especially without a reason.'

'If you could have seen him, Rob, staring into … He was seeing something, I'm sure of it. But there's nothing there.' She stopped short of telling him what she had briefly, oddly imagined: the old, crumpled newspapers which seemed to fill the chest.

'So? It's big and dark and empty. To a kid, it's interesting. Why are you so worried about it?'

She saw from his face that he expected some irrational response, that he was ready to make fun of 'women's intuition'. She said calmly, 'Rob, he could get hurt. If he decided to play inside it, he might shut himself in and suffocate.'

'Oh come on, Helen. You'd hear him and find him long before that could happen.'

'What if the lid slammed down? It's heavy enough to break his hand.'

'Yeah, yeah,' Rob said. 'But there are lots of other ways he could get hurt around the house – more likely ways. It's silly to worry –'

'It's not silly! I've caught him opening the chest twice, and he'll try again, I know it.'

'All right, all right.' He held up a placating hand. 'Don't get upset. Maybe we could put something on the chest that he'd have trouble getting off.'

Helen nodded grudgingly and the discussion was over, but she was far from satisfied. She wished they had never bought the thing.

Something was wrong. Helen swam up out of sleep, drawn by the sound of a baby crying.

Then she was wide awake, listening and remembering. This was no dream. A baby was crying, somewhere in the house. It was not Alice – to Helen's ears the cry sounded like that of a much younger infant, a newborn child. The muffled sound came, she thought, from the living room.

She looked resentfully at Rob. He could sleep through anything. There had been a time, just after Julian's birth, when Helen had seen Rob's regular, undisturbed slumber as a sign of hostility towards her and their child. Logically, she knew he did not will his sleeping patterns. And she was used to it, now.

Gradually the crying was fading, and Helen thought she might be able to go to sleep after all. Then she heard the soft, unmistakable patter of Julian's feet in the hall, going towards the living room, and she sat up in bed. Had Julian heard the crying, too?

Heart thumping unpleasantly, Helen got up and went to check.

Julian was standing in the dark living room, a few feet from the chest. He turned and looked at his mother when she came into the room. He pointed to the chest. 'Baby,' he said.

Helen felt the hairs on the back of her neck prickle. 'No,' she said. 'No baby. Come back to bed, Julian. You must have been dreaming.'

He shook his head emphatically and walked closer to the chest. 'Baby,' he said firmly.

'No,' she said sharply, seeing Julian's hands straying to the lid. 'What did I tell you about that? Let Mommy open it.'

So now she had to. It was foolish to be afraid of opening the chest, Helen thought. She had opened it before and she knew there was nothing in it. She turned on the lamp, and

165

Julian flinched and squinted and put his hands to his eyes at the sudden flash of soft yellow light.

Helen raised the lid. She saw shadows, the faded yellow and black of old newspapers. Something deep inside that paper nest stirred faintly, and the packing rustled and settled around it.

The chest was empty. Helen stared into it, not trusting her eyes. Dark and deep and empty. She put her hand in and felt the smooth wood of the walls. Bile rose in her throat at the faint whiff of decay, but whether she had smelled it or only remembered smelling it, Helen could not have said.

Beside her Julian was silent, also staring into the chest.

'You see?' she said, making an effort. 'It's empty.'

Julian nodded and looked up at her gravely.

'There's nothing in the chest,' Helen said. 'It was only a dream. Now let's go back to bed.'

But it had been no dream, she thought, taking Julian's soft little hand in her own. They had both heard the baby cry.

The chest is haunted, Helen thought as she climbed back in bed beside her sleeping husband. There was a kind of relief in the thought: the problem had been identified. But her spirits sank again at the thought of trying to explain her certainty to Rob. He would be scornful of her silly fears; he would not understand. And yet she had to tell him, she had to make him believe her, because she would not go on living with that chest. There was something evil about it. The past, whatever its past had been, still lived on inside it, manifested in a baby's cry, a foul odour, and the teasing visual image of the chest packed with newspaper.

How to make Rob understand? She could already hear his objections, his refusal to sell the chest. It was a beautiful piece of furniture and they had paid a lot for it. Was she crazy?

Helen tossed and turned, wide awake, trying to find a way out. Perhaps she should say nothing to Rob and simply get rid of the chest while he was at work. Afterwards, she would face his anger as the lesser of two evils. At least then the chest would be gone. *casting their issues on the chest*

By morning, Helen had neither slept nor decided what to do. She watched Rob as he rose and moved around the room getting dressed.

'Do you believe things can be haunted?' she asked him.

He gave her a quizzical look. 'You mean like a house?'

'A house, a room, a piece of furniture.'

'I don't believe in ghosts.'

'All sorts of people have seen them, you know. At least, something they call ghosts. Don't you think that something, like a strong personality or a violent occurrence, could leave an impression, like a recording, on the place where it happened?'

He shrugged and sat down on the edge of the bed, buttoning his shirt. 'I heard some kind of theory about that. That ghosts are like photographs or movies or recordings that receptive people can tune in to.'

'Do you believe it?'

'I don't know. I've never seen one myself.'

'What if we lived in a haunted house. If we saw a ghost. Would you want to move?'

'Well, that depends on the ghost, and the house. How would this ghost make itself known?'

'It might cry and howl and wake us up at night.'

He laughed and patted her blanket-covered leg. 'Wake *you* up at night. I don't think it would bother me much.'

'It wouldn't bother you? To hear it crying all the time?' She was trembling and moved further beneath the covers, hoping he wouldn't notice.

Rob shrugged and stood up. 'I don't think I'd sell the

house on account of it. It doesn't sound like a problem the magnitude of our plumbing.'

'But what if it did something else? It might be dangerous,' Helen said. Rob was leaving the room, tired of the abstract discussion. Tears came to her eyes and she buried her face in the pillow. It was hopeless. He wouldn't understand. He wouldn't agree.

She dragged through the day after he had left, wanting a nap but not daring to leave Julian unattended. It seemed that every time her back was turned he escaped to the living room where she would find him raising the lid for another look inside, or pressing his ear against the chest, or simply standing before it, staring intently, as if it told him things no one else could comprehend. She could almost hear Rob scoffing at her for imagining things, but she knew Julian's interest in the chest was neither normal nor safe. She knew she had to get rid of the chest.

The baby was crying again. Helen's eyes came open on darkness. The muffled sound came from the living room, from within the wooden chest. She clenched her teeth together. It would pass. The sound would fade and die away. She wasn't going to get up this time and go to the living room and open the chest and assure herself it was still empty. She would wait it out. And tomorrow she would take the chest out and sell it to the first furniture-dealer she found, and worry about the lies or explanations for Rob later. She wondered if Julian was awake and listening, too. She could imagine him in the living room, crouching beside the dark bulk of the chest.

She shivered and moved closer to Rob's warmth. When would it stop crying? How long did she have to listen to it?

It occurred to her then that if Rob could hear it she would not be alone, and she would not be so afraid. And he might understand. Heartened, she sat up and began to shake her husband, calling his name. Waking him in the mornings on the rare occasions when he overslept was hard enough; waking him in the middle of the night was all but impossible.

'Rob! Wake up, wake up, wake up.' She tickled him and blew in his ear, but got in response only the sluggish motion as he moved away from her, still holding on to sleep.

'Rob, wake up. Wake up. This is important. Rob. Damn.'

Sighing noisily, Helen rose and went across the landing to the bathroom to fetch a wet towel. Drastic measures were called for. For a wonder, the crying had not died away. She hoped it would go on long enough for Rob to hear it. Returning from the bathroom, she glanced into Julian's room and saw his bed was empty. Well, she knew where he was. Right now the important thing was to wake Rob.

The wet towel did the trick. At last he was moving, fending her off, eyelids fluttering to reveal flashes of blue.

'Whatsamatta – whatsamatta – hey – Helen, what's wrong?'

She let out a sigh of relief as he sat bolt-upright in bed, indisputably awake. She clutched his arm. 'Hush. Listen. Tell me what you hear.'

He stared at her. 'What's wrong?'

'*Hush*, just listen,' she said. She could hear it still, but faintly – a distant, gasping cry that was fading.

Rob was silent for a moment frowning, then he shook his head. 'What did you hear?' he asked quietly. 'Someone at the door? Someone in the house?'

Helen shook her head, despairing. If he hadn't heard it, then he would not. The crying had faded altogether now; she could no longer hear it.

'A baby,' she said hopelessly. 'A baby crying.'

Rob swore and threw himself back on the bed. 'You

couldn't go and check on her yourself? You woke me for that?'

'Not Alice,' Helen said. 'It was another baby crying. I've heard it the past two nights. The sound doesn't come from Alice's room. It's in the living room. Inside the chest.'

Rob turned over, burying his face in the pillow, and did not answer. Helen had no heart to try to explain what she meant, to struggle with his anger and sleepy incomprehension. He had not heard and he would not understand. She lay back down, longing for the oblivion of sleep.

But she couldn't stop thinking of the chest. It was almost as if it was calling to her. She wanted to go to it and raise the heavy lid and look inside yet again, to assure herself that there was nothing there. But she knew there was nothing inside. How many times did she have to look before she believed?

There is no baby there, she told herself. No crying, no newspapers, nothing. I will stay here in my bed and go back to sleep.

Helen heard Julian's footsteps on the landing, going towards his room.

It's over, she told herself. Even Julian knows that. And this is the last night I will suffer this. In the morning the chest goes.

She did not sleep again. She lay in bed until it was light, and the thought of the chest was like a suffocating weight. When she heard Julian stirring in his room, she knew it was time to get up. While she was in the bathroom, she heard the front door open and slam and knew that Julian had run outside, as he often did, to bring the morning paper in for his parents.

In the kitchen she went through the motions of making a pot of coffee while her mind puzzled over the fact that she had not yet heard a sound from Alice, and the oddity that Julian had not rushed into the kitchen, eager to be praised for bringing her the paper. Moving slowly, wearily, Helen went back to check on her family.

Rob, she saw from the doorway, was still sacked out, the alarm buzzing steadily and to no effect directly into his ear. The interruption of his sleep during the night meant she would have another battle to wake him, and he would be grumpy all day.

And Alice –

– was not in her crib.

Helen stared down, disbelieving, at the bare sheet. Alice was much too small to have got out of bed on her own. 'Julian,' she called, rushing into the living room. 'Julian!'

He was sitting on the floor beside the open chest, the newspapers spread out around him. He was tearing the newspaper into strips and dropping them into the chest.

Already understanding, Helen stepped closer to the chest and looked down into it. It was no longer empty, but nearly half-filled with newspaper. The strips Julian had so industriously shredded lay like packing over and around the central bundle, something which had been wrapped in sheets of yesterday's paper. All the paper Julian had found in the house had not been enough to make the interior of the chest an exact replica of the image he had seen, but it was quite enough to do the same job the second time. Only there was no smell now. It was too soon for that.

As Helen reached down into the chest for the bundle, Julian let out a loud noise of displeasure and stood up. It wasn't supposed to be taken out; it was supposed to be hidden away in the chest forever. He tried, futilely, to get the bundle away from his mother.

She held it up out of reach. It was still warm. Her hands shaking, Helen began to unwind the many layers of newspaper that Julian had wrapped around her baby.

171

A FRIEND IN NEED

Photographs lie, like people, like memories. What would it prove if I found Jane's face and mine caught together in a picture snapped nearly twenty years ago? What does it mean that I can't find such a photograph?

I keep looking. My early life is so well documented by my father's industrious camera work that Jane's absence seems impossible. She was, after all, my best friend; and all my other friends – including one or two I can't, at this distance, identify – are there in black and white as they run, sit, stand, scowl, cry, laugh, grimace, and play around me. Page after page of birthday parties, dressing-up games, bicycle riding, ice-cream eating, of me and my friends Shelly, Mary, Betty, Carl, Julie, Howard, Bubba, and Pam. But not Jane, who is there in all my memories.

Was she ever really there? Did I imagine her into existence? That's what I thought for twelve years, but I don't believe that anymore.

I saw her in the Houston airport today and I recognised her, although not consciously. What I saw was a small woman of about my own age with dark, curly hair. Something about her drew my attention.

We were both waiting for a Braniff flight from New York, already five minutes late. A tired-looking man in uniform went behind the counter, made a throat-clearing noise into the microphone, and announced that the flight would be an hour late.

I swore and heard another voice beside me, like an echo. I turned my head and met her eyes. We laughed together.

'Are you meeting someone?' she asked.

'My mother.'

'What a coincidence,' she said flatly. 'We've both got mothers coming to visit.'

'No, actually my mother lives here. She went to New York on business. Your mother lives there?'

'LongIsland,' she said. It came out as one word; I recognised the New Yorker's pronunciation.

'That's where you're from?'

'Never west of the Hudson until two years ago.' Her sharp eyes caught my change of expression. 'You're surprised?'

'No.' I smiled and shrugged because the feeling of familiarity was becoming stronger. 'I thought I knew you, that's all. Like from a long time ago, grade school?'

'I'm Jane Renzo,' she said, thrusting out her hand. 'Graduate of Gertrude Folwell Elementary School and Elmont High, class of '73.'

Jane, Jane Renzo, I thought. Had I known someone by that name? There were distant resonances, but I could not catch them. 'Cecily Cloud,' I said, taking her hand.

'What a great name!'

Our hands unclasped and fell apart. She was grinning; there was a hint of a joke in her eyes, but also something serious.

'But it doesn't ring any bells?' I asked.

'Oh, it does, it definitely does. Sets the bells a-ringing. It's the name I always wanted. A name like a poem. I hated always being plain Jane.' She made a face.

'Better than Silly Cecily,' I said. 'The kids used to call me Silly until I got so used to it that it sounded like my real name. But I always hated it. I used to wish my parents had given me a strong, sensible name that couldn't be mispronounced or misspelled or made fun of – like Jane.'

Jane. Memory stirred, but it was like something deep in a forest. I couldn't get a clear sight of it.

'We all have our own miseries, I guess,' she said. She looked at her watch and then at me, a straightforward, friendly look. 'We've got time to kill before this flight gets here. You want to go and sit down somewhere and have some coffee?'

The rush of pleasure I felt at her suggestion was absurdly intense, inappropriate, as if she were a long-lost friend, returned to me when I had nearly given up hope of seeing her again. Trying to understand it, I said, 'Are you sure we haven't met before?'

She laughed – a sharp, defensive sound.

Hastily, afraid of losing our easy rapport, I said, 'It's only that I feel I know you. Or you remind me of someone. You never came to Houston when you were a kid?'

She shook her head.

'College?'

'Montclair State.' We had begun to walk together in search of a coffee shop, down the long, windowless, carpeted, white-lit corridor. It was like being inside a spaceship, I thought, or in an underground city of the distant, sterile future. We were in Houston, but we might as easily have been in New York, Los Angeles, or Atlanta for all the cues our surroundings gave us. It was a place set apart from the real world, untouched by time or season, unfettered by the laws of nature.

'It's like the future,' I said.

Jane looked at the curving walls and indirect lighting and gave me an appreciative smile. 'It is kind of *Star Trek*y,' she said.

We came to rest in a small, dim, overpriced restaurant which was almost empty, in contrast to the bar on one side and the fast-food cafeteria on the other. I saw by my watch that it was too late for lunch and too early for dinner. We ordered coffee, causing the middle-aged waitress to sigh heavily and stump away.

'Actually, I'd rather have a shot of Tullamore Dew,' said Jane. 'Or a large snifter of brandy.'

'Did you want –'

She shook her head. 'No, no. Better not. It's just that the thought of seeing my mother again has me wanting reinforcement. But I'd be less capable of dealing with her drunk than I am sober.'

I looked at her curiously because she had struck me from the first as a capable, almost fearless person. 'You don't get along with your mother?'

'Something like that. I moved out here to get away from her, and she still won't let me be. She calls me every night. Sometimes she cries. She won't believe that I'm grown up and that I have my own life to live, a life I've chosen. She's still waiting for me to give up this silliness and move back home. My sisters got away because they got married. But in her eyes I'm still a child.'

The waitress returned, setting our coffees down before us with unnecessary emphasis. I watched the dark brown liquid slide over the rim of my cup, to be caught in the shallow white bowl of the saucer.

'You're lucky if you and your mother can relate to each other as people,' Jane said.

I nodded, although I had never given the matter any thought; I'd simply taken it for granted. 'We have disagreements, but we're pretty polite about them,' I said.

This made Jane laugh. 'Polite,' she said. 'Oh, my.' She peeled the foil top off a plastic container of coffee whitener. 'You're so lucky ... to have had a happy childhood and a mother who knows how to let go.'

It seemed at first acceptable, the way she so calmly passed judgment on my life, as if she knew it; then, suddenly strange.

'I think I had a fairly normal childhood,' I said. 'Very ordinary. At least, it always seemed that way to me.' It had been suburban, middle-class, and sheltered. I saw my experiences reflected in the lives of my friends, and I found it hard to believe that Jane had come from a background terribly dissimilar. 'You were unhappy as a child?'

Jane hesitated, stirring her coffee from black to brown. Then she said, 'I don't remember.'

'What do you mean?'

'Just that. I don't remember my childhood. Most of it, anyway. It's as if I went to sleep when I was five and didn't wake up until I was twelve. The years in between are a blank.'

I stared at her, trying to understand. I couldn't believe it. I didn't doubt that I had forgotten much of my own childhood, but there remained a satisfyingly large jumble of memories that I could rummage around in when the need arose. Some of the things that had happened to me remained as vivid in my imagination as if they had just happened: the day I had broken my bride doll, a rabbit-shaped cake my mother had baked one Easter, the taste of water warm from the garden hose at the height of summer, the Christmas when I had been ill, games of hide-and-seek, classroom embarrassments . . . I had only to let down the barriers to be flooded by memories, most of them far more intense than the recollections of anything that had happened to me as an adult. To be without such memories was to be without a childhood, to lack a certain identity.

'I can remember a few things from when I was very young,' Jane said into my stunned silence. 'None of them pleasant. And my sisters have told me things . . . it's just as well I don't remember. The things I've forgotten can't hurt me.'

'But why? What happened to you? What was so terrible?'

'I'm sure other kids survived a lot worse. In fact, I know that for certain. There's no telling what will make one kid break and another survive, or what kind of defence mechanisms are needed. I work with emotionally disturbed children, and some of them have every right to be, given their backgrounds, while others come from loving families and just . . . crack over things that other kids take in their stride. All I can say about the things that happened to me – well, I had my way of dealing with them, whether it was a good way or not. Forgetting, blotting it out, was part of it.'

She sounded defensive and apologetic. I tried to look reassuring. 'You don't have to. If it makes you uncomfortable, don't talk about it.'

'No, that's it, I *do* want to talk about it. But I don't want to bore you. I don't want to burden you with my old stories.'

'I don't mind at all,' I said. 'I'm happy to listen, if it helps you to talk.'

'I think it might help. Well . . .' She cleared her throat and took a sip of coffee, looking at me self-consciously over the cup. 'One of my earliest memories is when I was about four. My mother was forty-nine and menopausal. She was crazy that year, more than usual. Any little thing could set her off, and when she got angry, she got violent. I can't remember what it was I did, but it was probably something as minor as interrupting her while she was thinking – I got swatted for that more than once. At any rate, she started screaming. We were in the kitchen. She grabbed the carving knife and came for me, yelling that she'd cut off my hands so I couldn't make any more trouble.'

'Jane!'

She shrugged, smiling wryly. 'I'm sure I remember the knife as bigger than it really was. And maybe she wouldn't have hurt me at all. But what did I know? I was a little kid. And when somebody comes at you with a knife, the

177

instinct is to get the hell away. She chased me all through the house. I finally hid in a cabinet and listened to her looking for me. One of my sisters got my father, and he managed to calm her down. But nobody knew where I was, and I was afraid to come out. I crouched there in the dark, beneath the bathroom sink, for hours, until I decided it was safe to come out. I hadn't heard her screaming for a long time, but I was afraid that she might be tricking me and that I'd open the door to find her on the other side, the knife in her hand and a horrible smile on her face.'

'Was she insane?' I asked quietly.

'No.' The denial came too quickly. Jane paused and shrugged. 'I don't know. Define the term. Generally, she could cope. Was she really over the edge, or just trying to scare me into being good? It's hard to decide even now. She was very unhappy at that time in her life, and she's always been a very self-dramatizing person. We all have our own ways of dealing with life. What's insane?'

'I don't know,' I said, although I thought I did. 'Was she violent toward you most of the time? Did you go in fear of your life?'

'Sometimes. It was hard to know where you stood with her. That's the worst thing for a kid. I couldn't count on her, I didn't know how to get the right responses. Sometimes she would be very loving, sometimes what I did would make her laugh. At other times the same thing would have her screaming at me. But more often she turned her anger against herself. She must have tried to kill herself – or at least she pretended to – half a dozen times. I remember her lying on the floor in the living room with an empty bottle of pills and a half-full bottle of vodka. She told us she was going to die, and she forbade us to call for help. We were supposed to sit there and watch her die, so that she could die looking at the faces she loved most. We didn't dare move. Finally she seemed to have passed out, and Sue, my oldest sister, tried to call Dad. But the second her hand touched the telephone, my mother sat up and started screaming at her for being a disobedient bastard.'

'Lord,' I said, when Jane paused to sip coffee. I tried to imagine it, but could not quite achieve the child's point of view. 'How did you survive?'

'Well, I blotted it out, mostly. I had my imaginary life.' She smiled.

'How do you mean?'

'When you were a kid, weren't there some things which seemed just as real to you as real life, although you knew they were different? The things you didn't tell grown-ups about, although they were every bit as real and important – if not more so – as life at school and at home?'

'You mean like pretend games?' I asked. 'I used to pretend – ' And suddenly I remembered. 'Of course! That's who you remind me of.' I laughed, feeling silly. 'Jane. I had an imaginary friend named Jane.'

Jane's smile was somewhat wistful. 'What was she like?'

'Oh, she was everything I wanted to be and wasn't. Practical and neat instead of dreamy and disorganized. Her hair was dark and curly instead of straight and mousy. She read a lot, like me, and knew all kinds of wonderful games. She had my favourite name, of course.' I shrugged and then laughed. 'She was like a real person. She didn't have any magical powers – except, of course, that she disappeared from time to time. She was actually rather like you, I guess. Isn't that funny, that my imaginary friend should remind me of you?'

Jane didn't look as if she found it particularly odd or amusing. She said, 'I had imaginary friends, too. Except, at the time, they weren't in the least imaginary to me. The life I made up for myself was more important to me than my real life. It was my escape. It was how I survived the childhood I don't remember – the things that *really* happened to me.' She paused to sip her coffee and then went on.

'I was six years old. I was wearing a brand-new brown velvet dress with a white lace collar. I'm not sure why, but I think I was going to a party later in the afternoon. I was feeling very special and happy, and I was sitting at the dining room table eating my lunch. My mother sat next to me and nagged me. She kept warning me to be careful. She kept telling me how expensive the dress was, and how difficult it would be to clean if I got it dirty. She told me not to be as clumsy as I usually was, and she warned me that I'd better not spill anything on myself. So of course, I did. I slopped a little bit of milk onto my dress. At that, she grabbed me and pulled me up out of my chair, screaming at me that I was messy, disobedient, and a complete disgrace. I didn't deserve to have nice clothes. I was an animal. I ate like a clumsy pig and I didn't deserve the nice meals she fixed for me. I should never have been born. Nobody could stand to be around me. I should be kept in a cage where I could spill my food all over me to my heart's content. Screaming all the way, she dragged me up to the attic and left me there to meditate on my sins.'

My stomach clenched with sympathy at Jane's level, matter-of-fact tone.

'But the odd thing,' Jane went on, 'the odd thing was that I *liked* the attic. I always had liked it. Being taken up there and left was no punishment at all. I was always begging to be allowed to play up there, but she would never let me. I could only go up there when my father went, to help him clean, or to get out the Christmas ornaments, or to store old clothes away. I suppose I liked the attic so much because it was outside her domain. She would send my father up for things instead of going herself. It was the only place in the house that didn't belong to her.

'And that was where she left me. Where I couldn't mess

up any of her things. I was left all alone up there under the roof. It was cold and quiet and filled with cardboard boxes. I was very far away from the rest of the house. I couldn't hear my family downstairs – for all I knew, they might have gone out, or just disappeared. And I knew my mother couldn't hear me or see me, either. I could do anything I wanted and not be punished for it. I could think or say whatever I liked. For the first time in my life, it seemed, I was completely free.

'So I pretended that my family didn't exist – or at least that I didn't belong to it. I made up a family I liked a lot better. My new mother was pretty and young and understanding. She never lost her temper and she never shouted at me. I could talk to her. My new father was younger, too, and spent more time at home with us. My real sisters were so much older than me that they sometimes seemed to live in another world, so my new sisters, in my made-up family, were closer to my age. I had a younger sister who would look up to me and ask me for advice, and I had a sister exactly at my age who would be my best friend. She was good at all the things I wasn't. And instead of being ugly, with kinky hair like mine, she was pretty with long, straight hair that she would let me braid and put up for her.' She stopped short, as if on the verge of saying something else. Instead, she sipped her coffee. I waited, not saying a word.

'I know I invented them,' she said. 'I know it was all a game. But still it seemed – it still seems – that I didn't make them up but found them somewhere, and found a way of reaching them in that faraway, warm place where they lived. I lived with them for a long time – nearly seven years. When I remember my childhood, it's the time I spent with my make-believe family that I remember. Those people.'

I wanted to ask her their names, but I said nothing,

almost afraid to interrupt her. Jane was looking at me, but I don't think she saw me.

'I sat all alone in that cold, dusty attic, and I could feel the house changing below me. I was in the attic of another house. I could hear the voices of my new family drifting up to me. I could imagine every room, how each one was furnished. When I had it all clear in my mind, I went downstairs to see for myself. It was the same size as my real house, but completely different. There was a small chord organ in the living room that my make-believe mother played in the evenings, all of us gathered around to sing old-fashioned songs. The family room had a cork floor with woven Indian rugs on it. There was a deer head over the television set; my make-believe father liked to hunt. The wallpaper in the kitchen was gold and brown, and the cookie jar was shaped like a rabbit dressed in overalls. There was a big oak tree in the back yard that was perfect for climbing, perfect for playing pretend games in. It could be a pirate ship, or – '

My skin was crawling. It was my house she was describing. My parents. My childhood. 'What about the front yard?' I asked.

'Another oak tree. We had lots of acorns in the fall. There was a magnolia tree on one side, and a big brick planter box built out of the front of the house. It was great to play in. I'm amazed those blue flowers managed to grow with us stomping on them all the time. Your mother – '

'It was you,' I said.

She shut up and looked down into her coffee.

'Why didn't you say?' I asked. 'Why this game? Why pretend you didn't know me? Did you think I'd forgotten? Jane?'

She gave me a wary look. 'Of course I thought you'd forgotten. I wasn't sure myself that any of it had happened. I never thought I'd see you again. I thought I'd made you up.'

'Made me up!' I laughed uneasily. 'Come on, Jane! What are you talking about? What's the point of this whole story?'

'It's not a story,' she said. Her voice was high and stubborn, like a child's. 'I knew you wouldn't believe it.'

'What is it you want me to believe? We were friends when we were children. We both remember that. But if you tell me that you grew up in New York, and I know that –'

'Why did you say you had an *imaginary* friend called Jane?'

'Because I thought – ' And I stopped and stared, feeling the little hairs prickling all over me as I remembered. 'Because you disappeared,' I said softly. 'Whenever you left to go home, you just vanished. I saw you come and go out of nowhere, and I knew that real people didn't do that.' I was afraid that I was sitting at a table with a ghost.

As if she read my thoughts, Jane reached across the table and gripped my hand. There was a sullen, challenging look on her face. Her hand was warm and firm and slightly damp. I remembered that, as a child, too, she had been solid and real. Once her firm grasp, just in time, had kept me from falling out of a tree. We had tickled each other and played tag and helped each other into dressing-up clothes. She had liked to braid my hair.

Jane took her hand away to look at her wristwatch. 'We'd better go,' she said.

I thought of the first time I had seen her, coming down the attic stairs. I was surprised to find a stranger in my house, but she had looked back at me, perfectly at ease, and asked me if I wanted to play. We were friends in that instant – although I couldn't remember, now, what we had said to each other or what we played. Only that first moment of surprise remains hard and clear and whole in my mind, like the last time I saw her disappear.

Usually when Jane left she simply walked away and I did not see where she went. She was different from my other friends in that I never walked her home and we never played at her house. I didn't even know where her house was; I knew only, from things she had said, that it was in a different neighbourhood.

But that last day, I remember, we had been playing Parcheesi on the floor of my bedroom. Jane said goodbye and walked out. A few seconds later I thought of something I had meant to ask or tell her, and I scrambled to my feet and went after her. She was just ahead of me in the hallway, and I saw her go into the living room. She was just ahead of me, in plain sight, in daylight – and then she wasn't. She was gone. I looked all through the living room, although I knew she hadn't hidden from me; there hadn't been time.

I couldn't believe what I had seen. Things like that didn't happen, except on *The Twilight Zone*. I was eleven-and-a-half years old, too old to have imaginary friends. I never saw Jane again.

Until today.

And now she was standing, preparing to leave me.

Hastily I stood up, pushing my chair away from the table. 'I don't get it,' I said. 'I don't understand what you're saying.'

She looked at me and shrugged. 'Why do you think I know? I thought I'd imagined you, and here you are. But I grew up in New York, you grew up in Texas. We *couldn't have* known each other as kids. But that's what we both remember.'

'And now what?'

She smiled at me ironically. 'And now the plane is coming in. Let's go.'

We walked together through the featureless corridors in silence. It felt right and familiar for me to be at her side, as if we'd never been apart, as if we'd walked together many times before.

'I wish she wasn't coming,' Jane said suddenly. 'I wish I could have told her no. I wish I didn't have to deal with her. Will I be running away from my mother all my life?'

I touched her arm. She was real. She was there. I felt very close to her, and yet I knew, sadly, that she must be lying to me, or crazy. One of us must be. I said, 'You'll be all right. You're strong. You're grown up now and you've got your own life. Just tell yourself that. Your mother's just another woman. She can't make you do anything you don't want to do.'

She looked at me. 'You always thought I was braver than I really was. It's funny, but your thinking that made me try to live up to it. In order to be as brave and strong as you thought I was, I did things that terrified me. Like the time I climbed from a tree up onto the roof of the house —'

'I was terrified!' I said. Her words brought it back vividly, those moments when, from my own precarious treetop perch, I had seen her thin, small figure drop to the dark shingles of the roof, the breath catching in my throat as if I were the one in danger.

'So was I,' she said. 'But it was worth it for the way you looked at me. I'd always been a quiet little coward, but to you I was wild and daring.'

Through the big window we saw a bright orange plane land and roll along the runway.

'Thank you,' said Jane. 'I needed a friend today.'

'Not just today,' I said. 'Now that we've found each other, we'll get together again, often.'

She smiled and looked away. I followed her gaze and saw the plane docking.

'That's ours,' I said, turning my head to look at her. She was gone.

I whirled away from the window, scanning the crowds for her dark hair, her white blouse, her particular way of moving. She was nowhere to be seen.

There hadn't been time. I had turned my head only for a moment. She had been right beside me; I could feel her presence. From one second to the next, she had simply vanished.

Feeling dizzy, I moved indecisively a few steps this way, a few steps that. There was no point in searching for her. I already knew I wouldn't find her. I wondered what airport she might be waiting in; I realised she had never said where she lived. Was she able to find me because our lives briefly intersected in the bland, anonymous limbo of an airport, or could she have come to me wherever I was, because of her need?

I am waiting, wondering if I will ever see her again. Jane is real; she exists; I know I didn't imagine her. But did she imagine me?

She didn't imagine Jane, Jane imagined her but Jane was the one who disappeared

*★ airport as liminal space, attic as liminal space
↳ Cecily is Jane's escape, one she creates to be away from her man and can only do so in/from places that can be painted/imagined how she wants*

STRANGER IN THE HOUSE

Sharon knew all the patterns of this neighbourhood. She was standing on the corner of Newcastle and Devon, near the house where she had once lived. She knew where she was, and what the women and children who would be home at this hour of a hot summer day would be doing, but she did not know why she was standing where she was. She felt dizzy and put a hand on top of her head, feeling the heat caught and reflected in her sleek dark hair, and wondered what were the realities of sunstroke.

She closed her eyes, trying to sort the confusion, but forcing memory made it more recalcitrant. She opened her eyes and again took in the familiarity of the neighbourhood she had lived in for the first twelve years of her life.

I must have blacked out for a minute, she thought. It was a temporary solution, not one she believed, but something to hold onto until she found the answer. It was not a serious problem, after all. She knew where she was.

She began to walk down Devon, towards the house she had once lived in. It seemed the logical place to go.

Bill drove with only one hand on the wheel. The other arm was draped across the back of the seat. 'You're the one who used to live here – so where do we go today?'

'I haven't been in Houston for years.' She shrugged. 'I don't know. What do you feel like doing?'

'It doesn't matter. What do you want to do?' When she didn't answer, or even look at him, his voice sharpened. 'Come on, there must be something here you want to see – or some place you want

to visit. You haven't been here for . . . how old were you when your old man left?'

She lit a cigarette. A mistake: he saw her hand tremble.

'Yeah, you told me once when you were drunk. The sad, sad story about your father skipping out. You don't remember telling me, huh? What are you always so –'

'Would you keep your eyes on the road?'

'Don't worry about it. I've been driving since I was twelve. I know – let's go see your old house. What do you think of that?'

She watched the buildings as they passed them, reading the signs, noticing a new shopping centre.

'Wouldn't you like to see your old home again? You can say hello to the rats and roaches – let 'em know you've come up in the world with one husband behind you already and working on –'

'Okay,' she said, to stop the growing bitterness of the argument.

'What?'

'I said yeah.'

The house had not changed. The oak and mimosa still stood in the front yard; the ivy and honeysuckle still battled for possession of the front flowerbed; the gutters were peeling yellow paint and the magnolia by the kitchen door was in bloom. In almost thirteen years the house and yard had managed to remain exactly as she remembered them. It didn't seem likely, but neither did the alternative: that her memory was faulty.

Sharon walked around to the side of the house where there were four windows. The first two were masked by curtains; the last two were the ones Sharon knew best, for they belonged to the room she had shared with her sister. She went to her old window and looked in.

Everything was so familiar, so right, that she did not at first feel surprise. Everything fit, everything was in its place: the scratched wooden play table in the centre of the

188

room; the two beds, one beneath each window; the sheets of Manila paper covered with crayoned designs and taped to the blue walls.

She was home again, and unsurprised, until she remembered that she was twenty-four years old and had not even seen this house for half that many years. Her mind must be playing tricks on her. She was seeing things and her mind was tricking her into thinking that she remembered those same things.

Déjà vu, she thought. *That's what it's called. It's normal, it's natural. I'm tired, the sun is hot, I've been smoking too much lately, and Bill...*

Bill. An image in her mind suddenly of a dark-haired, scowling man leaning against a bright-red Mustang. She knew then that she must have come here with Bill, to look at the old house. But where was Bill?

The answer came quickly: With the car. She set off down the street. He wouldn't have parked far away.

'*This seems like a pretty nice part of town. You never told me about your childhood.*'

She was still gazing out the window. So much had changed.

'*Talkative, aren't we?*'

She thought of the wine he had insisted upon with breakfast. She had said nothing then, and would say nothing now. She knew her silences infuriated him.

'*I guess your father had a good bit of money.*'

Those townhouses were new, and that office building.

'*You lived pretty well until the bastard skipped out.*'

She folded her arms, holding herself.

'*You can't blame me for guessing when you never tell me anything.*'

She turned the volume up on the tape-player: '*Home, where my thoughts are strayin'...*'

The car was not parked on the street. Other cars beamed reflected sun into her eyes, but there were no 1972 Mustangs. All the cars seemed to be at least ten years old. She went around the block, knowing that almost anything could have happened, for she could not remember the circumstances of their arrival.

A car drove past, an old green Ford that still looked shiny and new. She glanced at it, had a glimpse of a short-haired woman in sunglasses driving with two small girls bouncing in the back seat. The familiarity tugged at her mind.

The farther she walked without seeing either Bill or the car the lonelier she felt. It began to seem clear to her that they had quarrelled (their arguments had become too frequent lately), and she had demanded—— But, alone? Would he have left her alone?

Eventually she returned to the house on Devon. The green Ford was parked in the garage.

'Jesus Christ!' Bill pounded his horn; a woman glared. 'The worst drivers in the world, around here. The number of people in this city who are allowed to drive cars . . .'

'You ignored a yield sign,' she said. Not asking for an argument.

'The hell I did. If you're so good, Little Miss Silence, why don't you . . .'

'Just drive,' she said wearily.

'You're really suffering, aren't you? I mean, I really give you a pain. Well, listen, lady . . .'

When she saw the Ford in the garage she remembered being nine years old. The car had been new, then.

She heard the kitchen door open and slam, and two little girls came running from around the magnolia tree. She saw them mount bicycles in the garage and moments later they sailed past her as she stood, feet curling on the hot street. One girl was dark-haired and thin, pedalling fiercely. The other was a plump, blonde, happy-looking child.

Sharon knew the blonde child. It was her sister Ellen, fifteen years ago. But the skinny kid——

'That can't be me,' Sharon said aloud. Then she began to laugh.

'So which street is it?'
    'That one. No, you passed it now.'
    'Well, why didn't you tell me?'
    'You can circle the block.'
    'I know I can circle the block, goddammit; that's not what I'm talking about. I'm talking about you never telling me anything.'
    'You'll miss it again if you're not careful.'
    'Listen to me, you bitch,' he said, turning to glare at her.
    'Watch out . . . !'

When the two little girls came riding back, Sharon was resting beneath a tree in the yard next door. She stared at them, knowing where they had gone, who they had seen, and what games they had played. They pretended not to see her; either that, or they did not notice her. Sharon knew that, from shyness and parental warnings against strangers, they would feel themselves bound to ignore her. She watched the dark-haired child who pedalled with such single-minded intensity and felt no bond, no sympathy, no feeling of kinship. That little girl was not herself any more than she, Sharon, was again physically nine years old.

Not physically nine, no, but somehow she had come back to the happiest time of her life. She remembered the years between six and eleven as a sort of paradise where parents never quarrelled and little girls were never lonely or unhappy. She remembered fears, but they had been

191

fears banished by daylight or the presence of a comforting grown-up.

Sharon waited under the tree until the sun had almost set, shedding worries like used skin. Bill was gone, her former husband did not exist, and her father had never left. When she saw the two little girls, released from the dinner table, ride past her again, she stood up – wanting with a sudden intensity to be on her bicycle again – and walked to the house.

The sun was out of sight, but had not completely set. She stood before the front door, gazing at the dark varnished wood, and touched the doorknob. It was still slightly warm where the last rays of the sun had rested. She opened the door and stepped inside.

The foyer and living room were empty. She could hear sounds from the kitchen where her mother was washing dishes. She rejoiced in the smell of the house; partly her father's pipe from the den (she heard the crackle and rustle of newspaper), partly the lamb-chop-and-lima-bean smell left from dinner, partly indefinable but familiar.

Quick steps on the linoleum alerted her and she moved silently into her old hiding place: the space between the piano and the window. She felt awkward, too large for a space that had been fine when she was nine. As the room grew darker she made herself comfortable and hoped that a bit of protruding knee would not be noticed.

Time passed, and Sharon heard the two little girls come home laughing through the kitchen door. She tensed suddenly at the sound of a light footstep and then a sharp click. A light had been turned on. Sharon relaxed, knowing who it was. Sharon had always been frightened of the dark, and had liked, to the mystification of her mother, to have a light on in every room.

Sharon smiled slowly. The light wouldn't help. She knew that light often was dangerous, for in lighting up the

192

dark corners it forced the monsters to come out into the open. Nine-year-old Sharon still had a lot to learn.

Sharon stood up and stretched. From the den she could hear the television, and felt a sudden terrible loneliness that she could not run in and join her family. She could imagine her mother with Scott on her lap, her father with a detective magazine (through with his paper by now), and the two girls with red Popsicles, all watching television. They all belonged, and she was suddenly the outsider.

Sharon went into the hallway, and from there into her parents' bedroom. She felt no fear, although the room was dark. Happy in her freedom from fear, she moved farther into the room and walked around. She even stepped into the closet. As a child she had been afraid to enter the room when it was empty, and nothing could induce her to walk past the open closet door after dark. It had always seemed to her the most likely hiding place for whatever lunatic or burglar needed shelter. She had feared that someone would be lurking in the closet, waiting for her, ready to grab a little girl for some mysterious purposes. But Sharon was no longer afraid.

Scott's room was also dark. She walked past it and entered her bedroom. Both the ceiling light and the bed-side lamp were burning. She turned off the ceiling light at the door. Suddenly she was flooded with the desire to have everything again as it should be. The room was right, the setting was perfect. Only she herself was out of place, in a too-old body. Sharon longed to be able to go to the dresser (with the painted-daisy drawer knobs) and pull out her blue cotton nightgown. She would take off her clothes and pull the nightgown on over her head. Then she would turn down the covers on the bed, go get an apple (afterwards she would have to brush her teeth), and kiss everyone goodnight. And then . . .

Sharon remembered the ritual. Always afraid that

Something lurked under the bed – something with long arms and a penchant for grabbing small girls – she had devised a method of getting into bed safely. First, she would turn off the ceiling light. Then, beginning at the door, she would run towards the bed, leaping up and onto it from as far away as she could. That way her feet, her vulnerable legs, did not come too close to the edge of the bed, and nothing could grab them. Once in bed she would turn out the lamp and lie still, heart pounding, and wonder if perhaps tonight the thing under the bed would be able to come out and get her, sending long, bony arms up over the sides of the bed, creeping for her throat . . .

And then Sharon would dive under the covers, feeling that out of sight she was somehow safe. Ellen had never shared her fears, and Sharon had often envied her safety in ignorance.

But Sharon could not do that tonight. Now there was someone else to sleep in her bed, someone else who would be kissed goodnight and get to eat an apple. Her place was already filled. This was her home, the only place she wanted to be, and someone else had stolen her role.

Sharon felt dizzy. Her stomach growled. She had not eaten all day. And then she knew what she had to do.

She turned off the lamp and stood for a moment in darkness before rolling under the bed to wait. She did not mind waiting, and she was not afraid of the dark.

SUN CITY

It was 3.00 A.M., the dead, silent middle of the night. Except for the humming of the soft-drink machine in one corner, and the irregular, rumbling cough of the ice machine hidden in an alcove just beyond it, the lobby was quiet. There weren't likely to be any more check-ins until after dawn – all the weary cross-country drivers would be settled elsewhere by now, or grimly determined to push on without a rest.

Working the 11.00 p.m. to 7.00 a.m. shift was a dull, lonely job, but usually Nora Theale didn't mind it. She preferred working at night, and the solitude didn't bother her. But tonight, for the third night in a row, she was jumpy. It was an irrational nervousness, and it annoyed Nora that she couldn't pin it down. There was always the possibility of robbery, of course, but the Posada del Norte hadn't been hit in the year she had worked there, and Nora didn't think the motel made a very enticing target.

Seeking a cause for her unease, Nora often glanced around the empty lobby and through the glass doors at the parking lot and the highway beyond. She never saw anything out of place – except a shadow which might have been cast by someone moving swiftly through the bluish light of the parking lot. But it was gone in an instant, and she couldn't be sure she had seen it.

Nora picked up the evening paper and tried to concentrate. She read about plans to build a huge fence along the border, to keep illegal aliens out. It was an idea she liked – the constant flow back and forth between Mexico and the

United States was one of the things she hated most about El Paso – but she didn't imagine it would work. After a few more minutes of scanning state and national news, Nora tossed the paper into the garbage can. She didn't want to read about El Paso; El Paso bored and depressed and disturbed her. She couldn't wait to leave it.

Casting another uneasy glance around the unchanged lobby, Nora leaned over to the filing cabinet and pulled open the drawer where she kept her books. She picked out a mystery by Josephine Tey and settled down to it, determined to win over her nerves.

She read, undisturbed except for a few twinges of unease, until 6.00 a.m. when she had to let the man with the newspapers in and make the first wake-up call. The day clerk arrived a few minutes after seven, and that meant it was time for Nora to leave. She gathered her things together into a shoulder bag. She had a lot with her because she had spent the past two days in one of the motel's free rooms rather than go home. But the rooms were all booked up for that night, so she had to clear out. Since her husband had moved out, Nora hadn't felt like spending much time in the apartment that was now hers alone. She meant to move, but since she didn't want to stay in El Paso, it seemed more sensible simply to let the lease run out rather than go to the expense and trouble of finding another temporary home. She meant to leave El Paso just as soon as she got a little money together and decided on a place to go.

She didn't like the apartment, but it was large and cheap. Larry had chosen it because it was close to his office, and he liked to ride his bicycle to work. It wasn't anywhere near the motel where Nora worked, but Nora didn't care. She had her car.

She parked it now in the space behind the small, one-storey apartment complex. It was a hideous place;

Nora winced every time she came home to it. It was made of an ugly pink fake adobe, and had a red-tiled roof. There were some diseased-looking cactuses planted along the concrete walkway, but no grass or trees: water was scarce.

The stench of something long dead and richly rotting struck Nora as she opened the door of her apartment. She stepped back immediately, gagging. Her heart raced; she felt, oddly, afraid. But she recovered in a moment – it was just a smell, after all, and in her apartment. She had to do something about it. Breathing through her mouth, she stepped forward again.

The kitchen was clean, the garbage pail empty, and the refrigerator nearly bare. She found nothing there, or in the bedroom or bathroom, that seemed to be the cause of the odour. In the bedroom, she cautiously breathed in through her nose to test the air. It was clean. She walked slowly back to the living room, but there was nothing there, either. The whiff of foulness had gone as if it had never been.

Nora shrugged, and locked the door. It might have been something outside. If she smelled it again, she'd talk to the landlord about it.

There was nothing in the kitchen she could bear the thought of eating, so, after she had showered and changed, Nora walked down to the Seven-Eleven, three blocks away, and bought a few essentials: milk, eggs, bread, Dr Pepper, and a package of sugared doughnuts.

The sun was already blazing and the dry wind abraded her skin. It would be another hot, dry, windy day – a day like every other day in El Paso. Nora was glad she slept through most of them. She thought about North Carolina, where she had gone to college, reflecting wistfully that up there the leaves would be starting to turn now. As she walked back to her apartment with the bag of groceries in her arms, Nora thought about moving east to North Carolina.

The telephone was ringing as Nora walked in.

'I've been trying to get in touch with you for the past three days!'

It was her husband, Larry.

'I've been out a lot.' She began to peel the cellophane wrapping off the doughnuts.

'Do tell. Look, Nora, I've got some papers for you to sign.'

'Aw, and I thought maybe you'd called to say "Happy anniversary".'

He was silent. One side of Nora's mouth twitched upwards: she'd scored.

Then he sighed. 'What do you want, Nora? Am I supposed to think that today means something to you? That you still care? That you want me back?'

'God forbid.'

'Then cut the crap, all right? So we didn't make it to our wedding anniversary – all right, so *legally* we're still married – but what's the big deal?'

'I was joking, Larry. You never could recognise a joke.'

'I didn't call to fight with you, Nora. Or to joke. I'd just like you to sign these papers so we can get this whole thing over with. You won't even have to show up in court.'

Nora bit into a doughnut and brushed off the spray of sugar that powdered her shirt.

'Nora? When should I bring the papers by?'

She set the half-eaten doughnut down on the counter and reflected. 'Um, come this evening, if you want. Not too early, or I'll still be asleep. Say . . . seven-thirty?'

'Seven-thirty.'

'That won't cut into your dinner plans with what's-her-name?'

'Seven-thirty will be fine, Nora. I'll see you then. Just be there.' And he hung up before she could get in another dig.

Nora grimaced, then shrugged as she hung up. She finished the doughnut, feeling depressed. Despite herself, she'd started thinking about Larry again, and their marriage which had seemed to go bad before it had properly started. She thought about their brief honeymoon. She remembered Mexico.

It had been Larry's idea to drive down to Mexico – Nora had always thought of Mexico as a poor and dirty place filled with undesirables who were always sneaking into the United States. But Larry had wanted to go, and Nora had wanted to make Larry happy.

dependent

It was their *luna de miel,* moon of honey, Larry said, and the Spanish words sounded almost sweet to her, coming from his mouth. Even Mexico, in his company, had seemed freshly promising, especially after they escaped the dusty borderlands and reached the ocean.

One afternoon they had parked on an empty beach and made love. Larry had fallen asleep, and Nora had left him to walk up the beach and explore.

She walked along in a daze of happiness, her body tingling, climbing over rocks and searching for shells to bring back to her husband. She didn't realise how far she had travelled until she was shocked out of her pleasant haze by a sharp cry, whether human or animal she could not be certain. She heard some indistinct words, then, tossed to her by the wind.

Nora was frightened. She didn't want to know what the sounds meant or where they came from. She turned around immediately, and began to weave her way back among the white boulders. But she must have mistaken her way, for as she clambered back over a rock she was certain she had just climbed, she saw them below her, posed like some sacrificial tableau.

At the centre was a girl, spread out on a low, flat rock. The victim. Crouching over her, doing something, was a young man. Another young man stared at them greedily. Nora gazed at the girl's face, which was contorted in pain. She heard her whimper. It was only then that she realised, with a cold flash of dread, what she was seeing. The girl was being raped.

Nora was frozen with fear and indecision, and then the girl opened her eyes, and gazed straight up at Nora. Her brown eyes were eloquent with agony. Was there a glimmer of hope there at the sight of Nora? Nora couldn't be sure. She stared into those eyes for what seemed like a very long time, trying desperately to think of what to do. She wanted to help this girl, to chase away the men. But there were *two* men, and she, Nora, had no particular strengths. They would probably be pleased to have two victims. And at any time one of them might look up and see her watching.

Trying to make no noise, Nora slipped backwards off the rock. The scene vanished from her sight; the pleading brown eyes could no longer accuse her. Nora began to run as best she could over the uneven ground. She hoped she was running in the right direction, and that she would soon come upon Larry. Larry would help her – she would tell him what she had seen, and he would know what to do. He might be able to frighten away the men, or, speaking Spanish, he could at least tell the police what she had seen. She would be safe with Larry.

The minutes passed and Nora still, blindly, ran. She couldn't see their car, and knew the horrifying possibility that she was running in the wrong direction – but she didn't dare go back. A cramp in her side and ragged pains when she drew breath forced her to walk: she felt the moment when she might have been of some help, when she could have reached Larry in time, drain inexorably away. She never knew how long she had walked and run before she finally caught sight of their car, but, even allowing for her panic, Nora judged it had been at the very least a half an hour. She felt as if she had been running desperately all day. And she was too late. Much too late. By now, they would have finished with the girl. They might have killed her, they might have let her go. In either case, Nora and Larry would be too late to help her.

'There you are! Where'd you go! I was worried,' Larry said, slipping off the bonnet of the car and coming to embrace her. He sounded not worried but lazily contented.

It was too late. She did not tell him, after all, what she had witnessed. She never told him.

Nora became deathly ill that night in a clean, American-style hotel near Acapulco. Two days later, still shaking and unable to keep anything in her stomach, Nora flew back to her mother and the family doctor in Dallas, leaving Larry to drive back by himself.

It was the stench that woke her. Nora lurched out of her sleep, sitting up on the bed, gagging and clutching the sheet to her mouth, trying not to breathe in the smell. It was the smell of something dead.

Groggy with sleep, she needed another moment to realise something much more frightening than the smell: there was someone else in the room.

A tall figure stood, motionless, not far from the foot of her bed. The immediate fear Nora felt at the sight was quickly pushed out of the way by a coldly rational, self-preserving consciousness. In the dim light Nora could not tell much about the intruder except that he was oddly dressed in some sort of cloak, and that his features were masked by some sort of head mask. The most important thing she noticed was that he did not block her path to the door, and if she moved quickly . . .

Nora bolted, running through the apartment like a

rabbit, and bursting out through the front door into the courtyard.

It was late afternoon, the sun low in the sky but not yet gone. One of her neighbours, a Mexican, was grilling hamburgers on a little hibachi. He stared at her sudden appearance, then grinned. Nora realised she was wearing only an old T-shirt of Larry's and a pair of brightly coloured bikini pants, and she scowled at the man.

'Somebody broke into my apartment,' she said sharply, cutting into his grin.

'Want to use our phone? Call the police?'

Nora thought of Larry and felt a sudden fierce hatred of him: he had left her to this, abandoned her to the mercy of burglars, potential rapists, and the leers of this Mexican.

'No, thanks,' she said, her tone still harsh. 'But I think he's still inside. Do you think you could . . .'

'You want me to see if he's still there? Sure, sure, I'll check. You don't have to worry.' He sprang forward. Nora hated his eagerness to help, but she needed him right now.

There was no one in her apartment. The back door was still locked, and the screens on all the windows were undisturbed.

Nora didn't ask her neighbour to check behind every piece of furniture after he had looked into the cupboards: she was feeling the loathing she always felt for hysterical, overemotional reactions. Only this time the loathing was directed at herself.

Although one part of her persisted in believing she had seen an intruder, reason told her she had been mistaken. She had been tricked by a nightmare into running for help like a terrified child.

She was rude to the man who had helped her, dismissing him as sharply as if he were an erring servant. She didn't want to see the smug, masculine concern on his face; didn't want him around knowing he must be chuckling inwardly at a typical hysterical female.

Nora intended to forget about it, as she had forgotten other embarrassing incidents, other disturbing dreams, but she was not allowed.

She had a hard time falling asleep the next day. Children were playing in the parking lot, and her doze was broken time and again by their shouts, meaningless fragments of talk, and the clamour of a bicycle bell.

When, at last, she did sleep in the afternoon, it was to dream that she and Larry were having one of their interminable, pointless, low-voiced arguments. She woke from the frustrating dream with the impression that someone had come into the room and, certain it was Larry and ready to resume the argument in real life, she opened her eyes.

Before she could speak his name, the stench struck her like a blow – that too familiar, dead smell – and she saw the tall, weirdly draped figure again.

Nora sat up quickly, trying not to breathe in, and the effort made her dizzy. The figure did not move. There was more light in the room this time, and she could see him clearly.

The strange cloak ended in blackened tatters that hung over his hands and feet, and the hood had ragged holes torn for eyes and mouth – with a rush of horror, Nora realised what she was seeing. The figure was dressed in a human skin. The gutted shell of some other human being flapped grotesquely against his own.

Nora's mouth dropped open, and she breathed in the smell of the rotting skin, and, for one horrible moment, she feared she was about to vomit, that she would be immobilised, sick and at the monster's mercy.

Fear tightened her throat and gut, and she managed to stumble out of the room and down the passage.

She didn't go outside. She remembered, as she reached the front door, that she had seen that figure before. That it was only a nightmarish hallucination. Only a dream. She could scarcely accept it, but she knew it was true. Only a dream. Her fingers clutched the cool metal doorknob, but she did not turn it. She leaned against the door, feeling her stomach muscles contract spasmodically, aware of the weakness in her legs and the bitter taste in her mouth.

She tried to think of something calming, but could not chase the visions from her mind: knives, blood, putrefaction. What someone who had been skinned must look like. And what was he, beneath that rotten skin? What could that ghastly disguise hide?

When at last she bullied and cajoled herself into returning to the bedroom, the thing, of course, was gone. Not even the cadaverine smell remained.

Nightmare or hallucination, whatever it was, it came again on the third day. She was ready for it – had lain rigidly awake for hours in the sunlit room knowing he would come – but the stench and the sight was scarcely any easier to endure the third time. No matter how much she told herself she was dreaming, no matter how hard she tried to believe that what she saw (and smelled?) was mere hallucination, Nora had not the cold-bloodedness to remain on her bed until it vanished.

Once again she ran from the room in fear, hating herself for such irrational behaviour. And, again, the thing had gone when she calmed herself and returned to look.

On the fourth day Nora stayed at the motel.

If someone else had suggested escaping a nightmare by sleeping somewhere else, Nora would have been scornful. But she justified her action to herself: this dream was different. There was the smell, for one thing. Perhaps there was some real source to the smell, and it was triggering the nightmare. In that case, a change of air should cure her.

204

The room she moved into when she got off work that morning was like all the other rooms in the Posada del Norte. It was clean and uninspired, the decor hovering between the merely bland and the aggressively ugly. The carpet was a stubby, mottled gold; the bedspread and chair cushions were dark orange. The walls were covered in white, textured vinyl with a mural painted above the bed. The murals differed from room to room – in this room, it was a picture of a stepped Aztec pyramid, rendered in shades of orange and brown.

Nora turned on the air conditioning, and a blast of air came out in a frozen rush. She took a few toilet articles into the bathroom, but left everything else packed in the overnight bag which she had dropped on to a chair. She had no desire to 'settle in' or to intrude herself on the bland anonymity of the room.   *weird language*

She turned on the television and lay back on the bed to observe the meaningless interactions of the guests on a morning talk show. She had nothing better to do. After the network show was a talk show of the local variety, with a plain, overly made-up hostess who smiled, blinked, and nodded a lot. Her guests were a red-faced, middle-aged man who talked about the problems caused by illegal aliens, and a woman who discussed the ancient beauties of Mexico. Nora turned off the set halfway through her slide show featuring pyramids and other monuments in Mexico.

The television silent, she heard the sound of people moving in next door. There seemed to be a lot of them, and they were noisy. A radio clicked on, bringing in music and commercials from Mexico. There was a lot of laughter from the room, and Nora caught an occasional Spanish-sounding word.

Nora swore, not softly. Why couldn't they party on their own side of the border? And who ever carried on in such a way at ten o'clock in the morning? But she hesitated to pound on the wall: that would only draw attention to herself, and she didn't imagine it would deter them.

Instead, to shield herself, she turned on the television set again. It was game-show time, and the sounds of hysteria, clanging bells, and idiotic laughter filled the room. Nora sighed, turned the volume down a bit, and pulled off her clothes. Then she climbed under the blankets and gazed blankly at the flickering images.

She was tired, but too keyed up to sleep. Her mind kept circling until she deliberately thought about what was bothering her: the man in the skin. What did it mean? Why was it haunting her?

It seemed more a hallucination than an ordinary dream, and that made Nora doubly uneasy. It was too *real*. When she saw, and smelled, the nightmarish figure, she could never quite convince herself she was only dreaming.

And what did the hideous figure itself mean? It must have come crawling out of her subconscious for some reason, thought Nora. But she didn't really think she had just made it up herself – the idea of a man draped in another's skin stirred some deep memory. Somewhere, long before, she had read about, or seen a picture of a figure who wore the stripped-off skin of another. Was it something from Mexico? Some ancient, pre-Columbian god?

Yet whenever she strained to recall it, the memory moved perversely away.

And why did the dream figure haunt her now? Because she was alone? But that was absurd. Nora shifted uncomfortably in bed. She had no regrets about the separation or the impending divorce; she was glad Larry was gone. They should have had the sense to call it quits years before. She didn't want him back under any circumstances.

And yet – Larry was gone, and old two-skins was haunting her.

206

Finally, worn out by the useless excavations of her memory, Nora turned off the television and went to sleep.

She woke feeling sick. She didn't need to turn her head or open her eyes to know, but she did. And, of course, he was in the room. He would come to her wherever she fled. The stench came from the rotting skin he wore, not from a neighbour's garbage or something dead between the walls. He didn't look like something hallucinated – he seemed perfectly substantial standing there beside the television set and in front of the draperies.

Staring at him, Nora willed herself to wake up. She willed him to melt and vanish. Nothing happened. She saw the dark gleam of his eyes through ragged eye holes, and she was suddenly more frightened than she had ever been in her life.

She closed her eyes. The blood pounding in her ears was the sound of fear. She would not be able to hear him if he moved closer. Unable to bear the thought of what he might be doing, unseen by her, Nora opened her eyes. He was still there. He did not seem to have moved.

She had to get out. She had to give him the chance to vanish – he always had, before. But she was naked – she couldn't go out as she was, and all her clothes were on the chair beside the window, much too close to him. In a moment, Nora knew, she might start screaming. Already she was shaking – she had to do *something*.

On fear-weakened legs, Nora climbed out of bed and stumbled towards the bathroom. She slammed the door shut behind her, hearing the comforting snick of the lock as she pressed the button in.

Then she stood with palms pressed on the Formica surface surrounding the basin, head hanging down, breathing shallowly in and out, waiting for the fear to leave her. When she had calmed herself, she raised her head and looked in the mirror.

There she was, the same old Nora. Lost her husband, driven out of her apartment by nerves, surrounded by the grey and white sterility of a hotel bathroom. There was no reason for her to be here – not in this building, not in El Paso, not in Texas, not in this *life*. But here she was, going on as if it all had some purpose. And for no better reason than that she didn't know what else to do – she had no notion of how to start all over again.

Nora caught a glimpse of motion in the mirror, and then the clear reflection of the one who had come for her: the lumpish head with the mask of another's face stretched crudely over his own. She looked calmly into the mirror, right into the reflections of his eyes. They were brown, she realised, very much like a pair of eyes she remembered from Mexico.

Feeling a kind of relief because there was no longer anywhere else to run, Nora turned away from the mirror to face him, to see this man in his dead skin for the first time in a fully lighted room. 'She sent you to me,' Nora said, and realised she was no longer afraid.

The skin was horrible – a streaky grey with ragged, black edges. But what of the man underneath? She had seen his eyes. Suddenly, as she gazed steadily at the figure, his name came into her mind, as clearly as if he had written it on the mirror for her: Xipe, the Flayed One. She had been right in thinking him some ancient Mexican god, Nora thought. But she knew nothing else about him, nor did she need to know. He was not a dream to be interpreted – he was here, now.

She saw that he carried a curved knife; watched without fear as he tore seams in the skin he wore, and it fell away, a discarded husk.

Revealed without the disfiguring, concealing outer skin, Xipe was a dark young man with a pure, handsome face. Not a Mexican, Nora thought, but an Indian, of

208

noble and ancient blood. He smiled at her. Nora smiled back, realising now that there had never been any reason to fear him.

He offered her the knife. So easy, his dark eyes promised her. No fear, no question in their brown depths. Shed the old skin, the old life, as I have done, and be reborn.

When she hesitated, he reached out with his empty hand and traced a line along her skin. The touch of his hand seared like ice. Her skin was too tight. Xipe, smooth, clean and new, watched her, offering the ritual blade.

At last she took the knife and made the first incision.

her avoidance keeps her from making steps forward or acknowledging the changes in her life due to Larry's infidelity, but once she stops denying that she is unable to move forward, the loneliness + unhappiness + living w/o someone she was so dependent on lead to her relief + lack of fear when she resigns her self to taking her own life, the ultimate act of avoidance ↳ this extreme avoidance starts w/ the secret of the girl on the beach that she can't admit her failure to help to anyone

THE NEST

We found the house on the third day of hunting. It was in the country outside Cheltenham, half-a-mile from a small village: a tall, solid house standing on its own in an expanse of flat, weedy lawn surrounded by hedge.

I switched off the engine and we went on sitting in the car, staring up at the house, caught. The roof looked dilapidated, and the house had obviously stood empty for some time, but the yellow stone it was built of seemed to glow softly in the sunlight.

'Imagine living here,' Sylvia said softly.

'We could,' I said.

'Remember how we used to play we were the Brontë sisters? In a lonely old house on the moor.'

'You could go for long walks,' I said. 'I'd have tea waiting for you by the fire when you came in.'

She laughed, a brief, rich sound of uncomplicated pleasure.

'Let's go in,' I said, and we got out and followed the broken paving stones to the door.

'How old do you suppose it is?' Sylvia asked.

I shrugged. It was a simple, solid, stone box with a tile roof. For all I knew of architecture, it could have been twenty years old, or two hundred.

'I hope it's really old,' Sylvia said. 'There's something about an old house . . .'

The key turned stiffly in the lock, and we stepped into a narrow, rather dark entrance hall. Rooms opened to the left and right and a steep staircase rose directly ahead. My skin prickled. Sylvia touched my hand. 'It feels . . .' she said, very softly.

I nodded, knowing what she meant. It felt inhabited, or only very recently vacated – not like a house which had long stood empty. That made me cautious, and I left the door open behind us as we entered on our tour.

It was shockingly dirty. The two front rooms, large kitchen and tiny lavatory at the back; three bedrooms, and a bathroom upstairs were all filthy with litter. There were newspapers, empty cans, bottles, cigarette butts, contraceptives, food wrappers, indistinguishable scraps of clothing, dead leaves and twigs, and chunks of charred wood lying everywhere. But none of the windows were open or broken, there was no graffiti scrawled on the dirty walls, and no signs of a squatter's rough habitation. It was all just rubbish dumped or abandoned there for some unknown reason. And yet I couldn't lose the feeling that someone was living – or had been, until our arrival – amid all the mess.

We were together at first, touring the house, but somewhere along the way I lost Sylvia. I retraced my steps but could not find her. Outside, clouds had moved across the sun and the rooms were full of shadows. Once I froze at the sound of paper rustling in a corner. My skin crawled at the idea of the vermin that might be lurking there. I called Sylvia's name but there was no reply.

I went outside, but she wasn't waiting for me there; the garden was empty. A loud cawing drew my attention to the tall beech trees which stood close beside the house. Half a dozen rooks were perched low in one tree, but at my look they all flapped heavily away.

'We'd have to get the roof fixed,' Sylvia said from behind me.

I started and turned and saw her standing in the doorway. 'Where were you?'

'There's a big hole in it. Somebody covered it with plastic, but it's all shredded now – from the wind, I guess. Rain or anything could get in. The attic floor is all covered with –'

'I didn't know there was an attic.'

'Oh, yeah.'

'I didn't see any stairs.'

She walked down the path to join me. 'There aren't any stairs. The loft door is in the ceiling of my bedroom.' She giggled shyly. 'Well, what could be my bedroom. There was a box there, so I used that to climb up on, and then hauled myself up. Old monkey Sylvia.' She flexed her arms.

I could imagine Sylvia doing just that: seeing a trapdoor and pulling herself up through it without a thought for the consequences, without a fear. Headfirst into the unknown. It made me shiver, just to think of being in that dark, dank space beneath the roof.

'I suppose it would cost a lot to fix a roof,' Sylvia said, staring up at the rapidly scudding clouds.

'That's probably why the price of the house is so low,' I said.

'Is it?'

I nodded. 'It's the cheapest of all the ones we've looked at.'

'And the best.'

'You know what it is,' I said. 'It's the house we always dreamed of, as kids. The big, old house in the English countryside.'

'*Chez* Charlotte and Emily,' Sylvia said. 'I'll bet it's cozy in a gale.'

'It is a little isolated,' I said. That suited me, but Sylvia, I thought, liked parties and people, the bright lights of cities.

'That's what I want,' Sylvia said. 'It's perfect. I need a

212

change . . . I'm sick of cities, and city people. And I like England. I can see why you stayed here.'

I smiled slightly. She had been here barely a week. 'All right. Shall we hire someone to give us the bad news about the roof and the plumbing? Shall we make an offer?'

'Yes,' said Sylvia. 'Yes. Yes. Yes.'

I want to make it clear that the house was Sylvia's idea just as much as mine. At first she was even more enthusiastic than I was, impatient to get things moving to ensure that we had a house of our own by Christmas. She expressed no doubts, no serious reservations during all the negotiations. I did not bully her, or push her into something she did not want to do. Although I was the one who first suggested we take the money from the sale of our mother's house and, instead of dividing it in two, use it to buy one shared house, Sylvia seized upon my suggestion eagerly. It was not I, but she who said – I remember it distinctly – how nice it would be to live together again, and how cozy we would be in our little nest in the country. I do not understand how it all went wrong.

We weren't able to get the roof fixed right away, but the local carpenter and his brother rigged a tarpaulin over the hole to keep us snug and dry. Sylvia went up into the attic to supervise, despite my assurances that it was unnecessary and that the men should be left alone to their work. I stood outside in the rare, blessed sunshine and watched the activity on the roof. I couldn't hear anything Sylvia said, but every now and then her clear laugh floated out on the breeze. I could hear the men, for all the good it did me. The heavy, foolish way the younger one was flirting with Sylvia made me prickle with embarrassment. Fortunately, stretching a tarp over a hole is no great job, and even though Sylvia invited them in for a cup of tea afterwards, we didn't have to endure their clumsy society for long.

213

And yet, after they had gone, a stifling silence dropped, as if the tarpaulin had fallen in on us.

'All cozy and snug now, aren't we, Sylvia?' I said, forcing the cheer.

She looked from the clutter of cups and saucers down to her hands in her lap and began to twist her ring. It was the mate to mine, a platinum band set with rubies. They had been our mother's, the guard-rings she had worn on either side of her diamond wedding band.

'What's wrong?' I asked.

She shook her head swiftly, then said in a rush, 'Oh, Pam, what will I *do* here?'

I almost laughed. 'Do? Why, whatever you want. This is our home now. There's plenty for both of us to do, to fix it up, and in the spring we'll plant a garden. We can grow our own vegetables.'

'That's not what I mean. We're so much on our own out here. We don't know anyone. How will we meet people?'

'In the village,' I said. 'At church, in the pub, in shops. People are friendlier in the country than they are in London – it will be easy. Or we could have people come to visit. The house is big enough for guests.'

She still looked doubtful, brooding.

'Come on,' I said. 'You're not having second thoughts now. It's too late for all that. The house is ours now. You'll love it here – just give it a chance.'

'It's just . . . it's such a change from what I'm used to . . .'

'But that's what you said you wanted. And after Mother died whatever you did would have been a big change. How do you think you'd like living all by yourself in Edison? That boyfriend of yours wouldn't have been much help.'

'Stop it,' she said. 'I left him, didn't I? That's over.'

'I'm just trying to point out that you could be a lot worse off than you are. Think how miserable you would have been if you'd let that affair drag on. What could he

214

offer you? Nothing. He would never have left his wife, so you couldn't hope for marriage, or any kind of security –'

She glared at me. 'I never wanted security from him. I knew what I was doing. I wasn't trying to get him to marry me. It wasn't security I wanted – he gave me something else. Adventure, a feeling of excitement.'

'Oh, excitement,' I said. 'That'll do you a lot of good.'

'I don't expect you to understand. After mother died I felt I needed something else . . . he wasn't enough. That's why I came here. And it's over, so why do you keep bringing it up?'

She stood up, gathering the tea things together with a noisy clatter. As I watched her I wondered if she would ever, without me, have summoned the nerve to break up with her lover. I remembered how she had been at mother's funeral, how dazed and helpless, sending me those blue-eyed looks that begged for rescue. In moments of crisis she always turned to her big sister for help, and was grateful for my advice.

I remember, as clearly as if it had happened yesterday, an incident from our adolescence. We'd gone down to the drugstore as we often did, on an errand for our mother. Ready to leave, I had looked around for Sylvia. I found her at last in the shadow of a hulking, black-leather-jacketed boy. My immediate inclination was to go, and let Sylvia find her own way home. Boys, especially boys like that, made me uneasy. Usually they ignored me, but they were always hovering around my little sister, drawn to her blonde prettiness and easy charm.

Then Sylvia caught sight of me, and the look she sent was an unmistakable cry for help. My heart beat faster as I approached, wondering what on earth I could do. As I reached her side she said, 'Oh, gee, I've got to go – my sister's waiting for me.' She took my arm and – I didn't even have to speak to the monster – we were away.

Outside, safe, she began giggling. She told me how awful he was and how nervous she had been until she saw me. 'He's dropped out of school, imagine! And he wanted to take me for a ride on his motorbike – I couldn't think how to say no, how to get away without making him mad. Then, thank goodness, *you* were there to save me.'

I basked in her praise, believing that I *had* saved her from some awful fate. But only a week later I saw the horrible black leather jacket again: Sylvia's arms were tight around him as she sat on his motorcycle, and on her face was a look of blissful terror, beyond my saving.

On Christmas Eve I went looking for Sylvia. Upstairs all was dark, but still I called her name.

'I'm in here.'

Surprised, I went forward and found her sitting in her bedroom.

'All alone in the dark, Sylvia?' I switched on the bedside lamp.

'Don't.' She held up a shielding hand. I saw that she had been crying, and I sighed. There was a chair situated oddly in the centre of the room. I moved it closer to the bed and sat down.

'You're not doing yourself any good, Sylvia, sitting alone and crying. Anyway, he's not worth crying over.'

'How would you know? You never met him.'

'I know enough from what you told me. The facts speak for themselves: a married man, who couldn't even be bothered to come to mother's funeral, to be with you when he must have known how much you –'

'God, I wish I'd never told you! Can't you ever leave me alone, let me make my own mistakes?'

'If you really want to go back to him, I won't stop you.'

'You know it's too late.' She stared down at her lap,

216

looking like a sullen child. 'Anyway, I don't want to. I wasn't crying about *him*.'

I felt embarrassed and full of remorse. Of course. It was Christmas Eve – her first not spent with mother.

'Come on,' I said gently. 'You'll only make yourself feel worse, sitting up here alone. Come downstairs and help me decorate the tree. We always used to do that on Christmas Eve, remember? I've got a fire going and I thought I'd make some mulled wine. We'll put the *Christmas Oratorio* on – would you like that?'

'All right,' she said, her voice dreary. 'But in a minute. Just give me a minute alone.'

I hesitated, hating to leave her in such a mood. Her hand went out and switched off the light.

'Sitting alone in the dark,' I said. 'Well.' I stood up and moved uncertainly towards the door. 'You always used to be afraid of the dark.'

She gave a heavy sigh. 'Not for years, Pam. And it never scared me half as much as it did you.'

I left without answering. I was surprised, and a little shaken, to discover that she knew that about me. I had always been terrified of the dark. Even now a residual uneasiness lingered. But my own fear had always meant very little to me beside my obligation to protect my little sister. I had been her scout and protector, going ahead of her into darkened rooms to turn on the light and make certain no monsters lurked. I remembered the night my protectorate had ended, when Sylvia had turned on me, screaming, 'Leave me alone! Leave me alone! You never let me do anything! I'm not a baby, I'm not scared!' To prove it, to free herself from my loving care, she had rushed headlong, alone, into the terrifying dark.

On Christmas Day Sylvia vanished. It was to be the first of many such disappearances, although I didn't know that at the time. I had no particular reason for searching for her, but finding her room empty made me curious and I went on a circuit of the house. I hadn't heard her go out, and looking out of the window I saw that the car was still parked in the drive, and there was no one in sight. I went upstairs again, thinking that somehow I had missed her, but still the rooms were empty. In her room I found a straight-backed chair in an odd position, almost blocking the door. I had my hands on it to move it when I happened to glance up. The loft door was directly overhead.

I stared up, wondering. 'Sylvia,' I said loudly. 'Sylvia?'

Footsteps sounded, so close over my head that I winced. Then the door clattered open and Sylvia's head, the fine hair all tangled rat-tails, swung out and smiled. 'Hi.'

'What are you doing up there?'

'Cleaning.'

'On Christmas Day?'

'Sure, why not?'

'Well, it doesn't sound like much fun.'

'I got bored with reading. Anyway, I thought I'd better get it cleaned up before the roofers come.'

'There's no rush. We won't get anyone out to fix the roof until after the holidays.'

'I know. I just felt like doing it. Okay?'

'I thought we could take a walk.'

'Not right now.'

'It's lovely out.'

'Great, you go for a walk. Maybe I'll be finished when you get back. Have fun.' Her head swung up out of sight and the door – really nothing more than a flimsy piece of wood – came clattering down to close me out.

Having suggested a walk, I now felt obligated to go for one, but I was not in a good mood as I set out. Sylvia wasn't being fair, I thought. It was Christmas, after all: a special, family holiday. We should celebrate it by doing something together. Was that really asking too much of Sylvia? I argued it out with her in my imagination as I put on coat, hat, boots, and gloves, and by the time I had reached the road she had apologised and explained that cleaning out the attic was by way of being a present to me.

It was a cold, clear day and the air tasted faintly of apples. Since the ground was not too muddy, I soon left the road and struck off across the fields. I was travelling to the east of the house, up a hill, and the exertion of climbing soon had me feeling warm and vigorous. When I reached the top of the hill I paused to catch my breath and survey the countryside. Our house was easily picked out because it stood away from the village, amid fields and farmland, and my eyes went to it at once. The sight of it made me smile, made me feel proud, as if it were something I had made and not merely bought. There were the yellow stones of my house; there the bright green patch of the untended garden; there the spiky winter trees standing close to the east wall, like guardians.

I squinted and pressed my glasses farther up my nose, closer to my eyes, unable to believe what I saw. There was something large and black in one of the trees; something that reminded me horribly of a man crouching there, spying on the house. Absurd, it couldn't be – but there *was* something there, something much bigger than a rook or a cat. Something that did not belong; something dangerous.

I fidgeted uneasily, aware that if I ran down the hill now I would lose sight of it. It might be gone by the time I reached the house, and I might never know what it had been. If only I could see it better, get a better view.

Perhaps it was only a black plastic rubbish bag tossed into the branches by the wind and caught there.

As I thought that, the black thing rose out of the tree – rose flapping – and half-flew, half-floated toward the rooftop. And vanished.

Lost against the dark tiles? Suddenly I wondered about that tarpaulin. How tightly was it fixed? How easily could it be lifted? Could something still get in through the hole in the roof? Something like that horrible, black, flapping thing?

I thought of Sylvia alone in the attic, unsuspecting, unprotected. I moaned, and stumbled down the hill. I kept seeing things I didn't want to see. Something horrible looming over Sylvia. Sylvia screaming and cowering before something big and black and shapeless; something with big black wings. I would be too late, no matter how fast I ran. Too late. As I ran across the empty winter fields towards the house the tears rolled down my cheeks and I could hardly catch my breath for sobbing.

'Sylvia!' I could scarcely get her name out as I burst in the house. I felt as if I had been screaming it forever. 'Sylvia!' I staggered up the stairs, catching hold of the flimsy rail and foolishly using it to haul myself upward. 'Sylvia!'

I could hear nothing but my own ragged breathing, my own voice, my own thundering feet. I stood in her room, too frightened to mount the chair and push open the door. 'Sylvia!'

Above me, the board clattered and was pulled away, and Sylvia looked out, flushed, angry, concerned. 'What is it?'

I caught the back of the chair and held it. Finally I managed to whisper, 'Come down. Now. Please.'

She frowned. 'All right. But I wish you'd tell me ...' Her head drew back and her feet came down, flailed a moment, then found purchase on the chair seat. She let herself down and pulled the door shut after her.

I caught her arm. 'You're all right?'

'Yes, of course I'm all right. You look awful. What's wrong?'

'I saw something ... from the hill ... I was looking

down at the house and I saw it. Something big and black, crouching in the tree where it shouldn't have been. And then it flew towards the roof. And then I couldn't see it anymore, and I thought it might have got in, through the hole, you know.'

She regarded me uneasily. 'What must have got in? What did you see? A bird?'

I shook my head. 'Something bigger. Much, much bigger. Like a man. It flew, but it wasn't a bird. It couldn't have been. Not an ordinary bird. It was huge and black and flapping. I was afraid. I knew you were up in the attic, and with that hole in the roof – you said yourself, anything could get in. Anything. I saw it. I was so afraid for you.'

'I think you'd better sit down and rest,' Sylvia said. 'I'll make you some tea.'

'You didn't see anything? Nothing came into the attic?'

'You can see I'm all right.'

'You were alone? Nothing came in?' *no answer*

She led me out of the room and I followed her downstairs, desperate for reassurance, wanting to hear her say that there had been nothing in the attic with her. Instead she said, 'I don't understand what you think happened. Tell me again what you saw.'

I was silent, trying to remember. It was suddenly difficult to sort out fact from fantasy, the reality of what I had seen from the terrifying vision which had obsessed me while I struggled back to the house. Sylvia threatened; Sylvia engulfed or embraced by something, by someone ... 'I don't know,' I said at last. 'I saw something. I don't know what it was.'

The Monday after Christmas I went to Cheltenham to pick up some material for curtains – and went alone. Sylvia wasn't interested in going, although I had planned the trip as a treat for her.

'We could make a day of it,' I said. 'Do some shopping, have a meal, see a film – whatever you like.'

Sylvia only smiled and shook her head.

'Why do you want to stay here alone? What will you do while I'm gone?'

'What makes you think it will be anything different from what I do while you're here?'

I hadn't meant that at all, but her words awakened suspicion. 'Please come,' I said. 'It'll do you good to get out of the house.'

She smiled. 'I'll take a walk. That'll get me out of the house. It's a nice day for it. I haven't really explored the neighbourhood yet.'

And so I drove away on my own, feeling uneasy. Once in Cheltenham I had no urge to linger. I bought the material, filled the petrol tank, and drove back home without stopping for so much as a cup of coffee.

The house did not feel empty when I came in. Sylvia might have gone out for a walk, I knew, but I went through the house quietly, looking for her. I was on the upstairs landing when I heard the sound; I'm sure it would not have been audible downstairs. The sound came from the attic, directly overhead. It was a rustling, scrabbling sort of sound, with the occasional small thump, as of something moving around. I stopped breathing and stood still, staring at the featureless white ceiling, so low I could almost have reached up and touched it, to feel the movements on the back of my hand. The scrabbling sound gradually retreated as I listened, and finally stopped.

I bolted down the stairs and out of the front door. It would have to come out through the hole in the roof – I was sure of it. I might see it on the roof or in the high branches of the tree nearest the house. I would be able see what I had seen from the hill, and this time, perhaps, I would recognise it. It would have been a reward to see anything, even a rook, but although I circled the house, craning skyward, I saw nothing that moved against the dark roof or the pale sky. Finally I gave up and went into the house.

Sylvia was in the hall. I wondered how she had managed to slip past me. She looked flushed and slightly out of breath.

'Your shirt-tail's out,' I said.

She smiled vaguely and stuffed it back into her jeans.

'Did you have a nice walk?'

'Mmm, lovely.' She drifted away towards the kitchen.

'I heard something just now. In the attic.'

She stopped and looked back at me. 'When? I thought you just got back?'

'I did just get back. I went upstairs to look for you and heard something moving in the attic. So I went outside to see if there was anything on the roof.'

She went on looking at me.

I shrugged, admitting defeat. 'I didn't see anything.'

She turned away. 'You want coffee or tea? I'm going to put the kettle on.'

'Coffee. Thanks.' I watched her walk away from me.

It proved remarkably difficult to get someone to agree to come out and fix the roof before March. In this part of the world, it seemed, one booked roof repairs farther ahead than wedding receptions or holidays. I complained about it to Sylvia, who was indifferent.

'So what? There's no rush. There's that tarp over the hole to keep the rain out.'

'That was supposed to be a temporary thing,' I said. 'And what if it's got loose? We've had some windy nights. It might be flapping free, letting things in.'

She looked at me with a little half-smile. 'Do you want me to go up and check that it's still in place?'

'Up on the roof, you mean?'

'I can see it from the attic. I can touch it, for that matter.'

I shrugged. 'Well, I could go up into the attic and see for myself.'

'Of course you could.' She looked back down at her magazine, smiling to herself. She was curled up in one of the two matching armchairs I had arranged on either side of the wood-burning stove. The ruby chips on her finger glittered as she turned a page.

'Do you know, I've never actually been into the attic?' I was certain, as I asked, that she knew.

'Well, you're not missing much,' she said calmly. She continued to read, and I paced the room, which I'd made comfortable and appealing with carefully selected furniture, dark brown curtains, and a beige carpet. I wondered if she knew that I was afraid of the attic – that dirty, dark place where *something* might lurk. She seemed so cool . . . But then maybe I was imagining things. Maybe she had nothing to hide. I should go up to the attic and see for myself, settle my mind and end these fantasies. But at the thought of climbing up there, poking my head up into the unknown darkness, my knees went weak and there was a tightness in my chest. No. There was no need to go up. If anything ever came into the attic, Sylvia would surely tell me, and ask for my help, just as she had at our mother's grave, and a hundred times before.

The grey winter days dragged slowly by. It seemed always to be raining, or to be about to rain. I drew up lists of the improvements we would make in our house, the things we needed to buy, the vegetables and flowers we would grow in our garden.

Sylvia's disappearances became more frequent. Sometimes she claimed to have been out for a walk – yes, even in the rain – and sometimes that she had been in the house all along. I had to be careful. She was suspicious of my ques-

224

tions, and I didn't want to provoke her. Let her tell me all, in her own good time. I never mentioned the attic, or the sounds I heard at night. I pretended that I noticed nothing, and I waited.

And then one night I woke and knew that something was wrong. It was late: the moon was down and there was no light. The darkness lay on me like a weight. I got up, shivering, and wrapped myself in my dressing gown. As I stepped out of my room I could see that Sylvia's door was shut and no light came from beneath it.

She's asleep, I thought. *Don't disturb her.*

But even as I cautioned myself I was shuffling forward, and my outstretched hand had grasped the doorknob. When the door was open I could see nothing in the blackness, and there was no sound. I reached for the light switch. Squinting in the harsh light, I saw that Sylvia's bed was empty.

I leaned against the door frame, blinking miserably at the undisturbed bed. She hadn't even slept in it.

Then I heard the noise.

There was someone in the attic. The sounds were soft but unmistakable, the sounds of movement. Floorboards creaked gently, rhythmically beneath a moving weight, and there was a jumble of softer sounds as well. I held my breath and listened, struggling to make sense of what I heard, trying to separate the sounds and identify them. I closed my eyes and held tightly to the door frame. Above me, the soft sounds paused, continued, paused, continued. Was it: cloth against flesh, flesh against flesh, a struggle, an embrace, a sob, a breath, a voice?

I snapped off the light and the loud click made me shudder. They might hear. I scuttled out of the room, back through darkness to my bed, terrified the whole way that I would hear the wooden slide of the trapdoor and the sound of something coming after me.

225

The door to my room, like the doors to all the other rooms, had a keyhole but no key. I pushed my bedside table against the door, knowing it was no protection, and huddled on my bed, shaking. I wiped the tears off my face and listened. I could hear nothing now, but I did not know if that was because of the location of my room, or because there was nothing more to hear. I took the edge of the sheet into my mouth to keep from making a sound and tried not to think. I waited for morning.

But it was some time before morning when I heard the motorbike on the road below the house. Listening to the approach, the pause, and then the sound of it roaring away again, it struck me that I had heard that same sequence of sounds outside the house more than once before. As I puzzled miserably over that, I heard the front door open.

Fear and sorrow drained away, leaving me empty, as cold as ice. I heard Sylvia climbing the stairs. I knew that laboured, guilty tread well, having heard it many nights when she was in high school, sneaking home late from her dates.

I met her on the landing.

'Pam!' Her face whitened, and she moved a little backwards, hand clutching the stair rail as if she would retreat downstairs.

'We'll have to get that roof fixed,' I said calmly. 'No more excuses. It can't wait. I don't care what it costs, if we have to get someone to come all the way from London, whatever it takes, we can't go another day with that hole in the roof.'

'What?'

'Anything could get in,' I said. 'You said so yourself. Anything could get in. Or get out. Come and go, day or night. It's an easy climb from the roof down that big beech tree.'

Sylvia gave me a cautious, measuring look, and took

226

my arm. 'Pam, you've been dreaming. I'm sorry I woke you. I was trying to be quiet. Now go on back to bed.'

I pulled away. 'I didn't dream those sounds. You can't fool me. I didn't dream your empty bed. What were you doing up there?'

She exhaled noisily. 'I was out.'

'Yes, I heard you come in. That's always your excuse when you disappear – you were out. Out for a walk, even in the middle of the night. I know where you really went, and I'm sick of your stories. I want the truth. I want to know what's going on up there.'

Sylvia's face was hard. 'I don't care what you want. I don't care what you think. I don't have to tell you anything. I don't have to explain myself to you.' She pushed past me, into her room, and closed the door.

I said, 'You think I'm afraid to go up there, don't you? You thought I'd never find out. Well, you were wrong.'

She did not answer, although I waited, and finally I went back to my room. Through the wall I heard the faint sounds of Sylvia moving about, then the snapping of a light switch, and then only silence. I listened for the rest of the night, but she didn't move again. Only her bed creaked occasionally, as she turned in her sleep.

When the sky turned pale and grey morning lit the room I dressed myself in jeans, pullover, and boots. As an afterthought I pulled on a pair of heavy gloves and hefted a flashlight in my hand like a weapon. I knew that if I thought about what I was going to do I would be too frightened to go on. I had to do it, not for myself, but for Sylvia. _denial_

She didn't stir when I entered her room. I stood for a moment, looking at her sleeping shape humped beneath blankets, remembering her anger. All our lives I had helped her, and she had rarely been grateful. But I didn't need her gratitude. I wanted her safety.

There was no way to enter the attic other than head-

227

first, and with difficulty. I set the chair below the door and hesitated, sweat trickling down my back at the prospect of pulling myself up, defenceless, into the unknown. Finally I went ahead and did it, climbing onto the chair, lifting aside the lightweight board that served as a door, and then, wriggling and straining, hauling myself up through the opening as quickly as I could.

I found myself in a low, dim, dusty space piled with litter. Covering the floorboards thickly were leaves, twigs, fragments of board and brick, scraps of paper, dust, soil, and dead insects. Just the sort of place I hated most. If Sylvia had cleaned up, I could see no sign of her work. I switched on the flashlight and pointed it around, wishing the light had a purifying as well as illuminating power. I played it on a huge heap of rubbish which must have piled up and remained untouched for ages. Bits and pieces of it were recognisable within the mess as fragments of newspaper, food wrappings, and cloth. There was so much of it that I wondered dazedly if the previous owners of the house could have been so far gone as to use their own attic as a rubbish dump.

A rubbish dump. That's what I thought, shining the light at it. Bits and pieces blown in through the hole in the roof or deliberately left by tenants. Bits of newspaper, cloth, wood, and cardboard plastered together with mud and hay, twigs and leaves, and bits of string to form a coherent whole.

Rather like a nest.

But it was *huge*. It couldn't be. Why, it was nearly as tall as I was, and wider than my bed. What kind of animal –

Ridiculous. And yet, now that I had thought of it, I could not stop seeing the big pile as a nest, a shelter of some kind. There was a pattern to it: it was a deliberate construction, not a random pile at all. Something or someone had built it.

Feeling sick at the thought, I stepped closer, holding my light before me. I was hoping that, if I saw it more clearly, or from some other angle, the illusion of structure would collapse. I began to circle it.

Then I found the entrance. My attention was drawn by a white cloth, the brightness of it startling against the mottled grey-brown of everything else. As I bent down to take a closer look, I saw that it was lying half-in, half-out of a narrow, moulded entranceway. My light showed me a short, narrow crawl-space which took a sudden, sharp turn, cutting off visual access to the interior. It was big enough for me to enter on hands and knees, but the idea was too horrible to consider.

Feeling like a coward, but unable to force myself on, I grabbed hold of the white cloth and pulled it free.

I looked down at what I held in my hands. It was one of Sylvia's nightgowns.

Somehow, I got down out of the attic. I stood in Sylvia's room, my heart pounding hard enough to make me sick, and I watched her sleep, and I did not scream.

The pest control man agreed to come out that very day. I suspect he pegged me as an hysterical woman, but at least he was willing to drive out to the house with his full arsenal of traps and poisons and see what might live in the attic.

He was a big, beefy, red-faced, no-nonsense sort of man, and I wondered how his composure would stand up to the sight of that nest in the attic. He stared, stolid and faintly contemptuous, and I struggled to describe what I had seen.

'What sort of thing would build such a nest? And in an attic? What could be living up there?' I asked him.

He only shrugged. 'I'm sure I couldn't say. I'll have a look.'

I had roused Sylvia before his arrival. Now she stood by and said nothing as this solid, sensible man climbed into the attic. My nerves were singing; I couldn't bear to be so close to her. Abruptly I turned and went away downstairs where I could sit and shake without having to explain myself. I had wadded up Sylvia's nightgown and thrown it on the floor while she still slept. I had not been able to confront her with it, and she had not mentioned it to me.

When the man came down out of the attic his manner was unchanged and he gave his ponderous, practical report.

'You do have mice, and spiders. An old house like this, with the fields so close, it stands to reason. You might want to get a cat. Good company they are, too, cats. I saw no sign of rats, so you can be easy on that. You want to get that roof fixed, of course, and clear up all that mess. I can put down poison and traps . . .'

'I don't care about mice,' I said sharply. 'What made that nest, that's what I want to know. You're not telling me it was built by mice?'

'Stands to reason they'd nest there,' he said.

'I'm sure it does. But what built that huge nest in the first place?'

He looked a shade uncertain. 'Maybe you'd like to come up and point it out to me. Maybe I don't know which nest you mean. Maybe I missed it.'

'You can't possibly have missed it! It's huge – I've never seen anything like it. Five feet tall, at least, and made of twigs and straw and mud and bits of old newspaper and –'

'You mean that heap of rubbish? Shocking the way it's piled up, isn't it? It's because of that you've got the spiders and the wood-lice and everything.'

'It's not just a rubbish heap,' I said patiently. 'It's a nest. *The* nest. If you'd looked at it properly you would have seen that it didn't just grow, it was put together as a shelter,

230

with an entranceway and everything. If you were doing your job, you should have seen that. You just left it?'

He gave me a blank, steady look. 'It's not my job to clean up other people's rubbish. Not very pleasant sorting through it to see what might live there, but I poked my stick in and turned it over and stirred it around. That's how I know about the mice and all. It's no wonder you've got them, a mess like that. You need to get it cleaned up. Hire someone, if you don't fancy tackling it yourself. Once you've got that lot cleared away and the roof fixed you won't have any trouble.'

I recognised the sort of man he was. If he couldn't understand something, then for him it did not exist. There was probably no way I could get him to see what I had seen. Well, it didn't matter, and I agreed with his advice. 'Could you recommend someone to clear it away for me?'

'I do have a nephew who does the odd job,' he said. 'Since you ask.'

The nephew came out that same afternoon to do his work, as did a team of roof menders for a preliminary survey. Getting the roof mended took a full week and more. It could be done no faster, no matter how I stressed the need, no matter what bonuses I promised. Winter days were short. They told me they would do the best they could.

During this period, when the house was always full of workmen, Sylvia and I barely communicated. She went out, most days, and did not tell me where she went. But these were not like her previous disappearances, and so they did not worry me. I saw her go out through the front door every time, and saw her walk down the road and turn towards the village. She did not return until after dark, when the house was empty and still again. I saw those days as a precarious interval: once I had made the house safe there would be time to talk, opportunity to mend the rift that had come between us.

Finally it was done. The roof was fixed and the house was whole again. Sylvia and I sat in the warm front room that evening, each in an armchair with a book. I couldn't concentrate on mine; I looked around, admiring the harmony of the room, the warm conjunction of colours and furnishings, all so carefully chosen.

Sylvia said, 'You're happy here.'

I smiled. 'Of course. Aren't you?'

She didn't answer and I wished I hadn't asked. 'You will be,' I said. 'Give it time.' I hesitated, and then added, very low, 'I did it for you.'

'I know how much this house means to you,' Sylvia said. 'And you're happy here. This is your place. I wouldn't expect you to give it up just because I . . . you wouldn't have to pay me back, even though it was half my money.'

'What are you talking about?'

'I mean if I was to go away.'

'But why should you?'

She shrugged and shifted in her chair. 'If I . . . stopped wanting to live here.'

'Have you?'

'If I was to get married. You wouldn't want my husband to move in here with us?'

'No, of course not.' The idea made me tense. 'But why talk about that now? It's not likely to happen for years. Is it? There's not someone now . . . someone you want to marry?'

She sighed and fidgeted and then suddenly glared at me. 'No. There isn't anyone I want to marry. But someday, maybe, I'll meet a man I do want to marry. And then I'll want to go away and live with him. That fantasy we had as children would never work, you know. We're not going to marry two brothers and all live together in one house! Someday I'll want a house of my own –'

'Then what's this?' I demanded. '*This* is your house.

You can't go on waiting for your life to start with your husband. You're not a child, you're grown up and you made the decision to come live here with me. This is *our* home; we have an equal responsibility for it. If you're not happy here, then we can sell it and move somewhere else. We're not trapped. Only a child would talk about leaving like that, as if the only choice you can see is between running away and staying. Just tell me what you want, and we'll work together for it.'

'Maybe I want something you can't give me.'

'Oh? And what's that? Excitement? True love? What is it you want?'

'I don't know,' she muttered, suddenly unable to meet my eyes.

'Well, if you don't know, *I* certainly don't. You can't go through your life expecting other people to solve your problems for you, and give you what you want, you know. You've got to accept responsibility for your own life at some point.'

'I'm trying to,' she said softly, staring into her lap.

'Sylvia, please tell me about it. I'll try to understand, but you must give me the chance. Don't blame me too much – I was trying to help. I wanted to save you.'

She stared at me. 'What are you talking about?'

I wanted to scrape that fake innocence off her face with a knife. I wanted to slap her, to hurt her into honesty. These lies, the unspoken words kept us apart. If she would only confess we could begin again, start clean.

'The attic,' I said, watching her like a hawk. I cleared my throat and began again. 'Now that the roof has been fixed, and all that garbage cleared out, we could use the attic as another room. You could buy some paints and make it your studio.'

'Why do you keep going on about that?' she cried.

'Going on about what?'

233

'About my painting! As if I did!'

'You used to. You were very good.'

'I never did.'

'Now, Sylvia, you know – '

'All I ever did was take an art class when I was fourteen. Because I had to do *something,* everyone did, and if I didn't find something of my own I'd have had to take dancing classes with *you.* That's all it ever was.'

I'd let her evade the real issue long enough. 'But what about the attic?'

She threw herself out of her chair. 'Oh, do what you like with it! I don't care. Just don't fool yourself that you're doing it for me.' She was on her way out of the room as she spoke.

'Sylvia, wait, can't we talk?'

'No, I don't think we can.' She didn't look back.

Later that night, after I had gone to bed, I heard Sylvia moving around restlessly in her room. Then I heard the soft, unmistakable clatter of the attic door.

I held my breath. She was safe; I knew she was safe. The attic was clean and bare and utterly empty, and the roof was intact. But I had to know what she was doing up there. Since she wouldn't tell me, I would have to find out for myself. I rose from my bed and went onto the landing, where I could hear.

I heard her footsteps, light and unshod, making the softest of sounds against the wood floor. She was walking back and forth. Pacing. First slowly, then more quickly, almost in a frenzy. She began to cry: I heard her ragged, sobbing exhalations. She said something – perhaps called out a name – but I could hear only the sounds, not the sense of them. The cold air on the landing made me shiver, but I worried more about Sylvia, barefoot and in her thin nightdress in the unheated attic. I longed to go and comfort her, but I knew she would reject me. She

234

needed time to adjust, time to accept what I had done for her. Finally I went back to bed, leaving her to her lonely sorrow.

It was mid-morning when I awoke, and the room was filled with sunlight. My heart lifted with pleasure. It would be a beautiful day for a long drive in the car. There was a ruined castle not far away that Sylvia would love. We could take a picnic lunch with us.

When I had dressed I went to her room and flung open the door. 'Wake up, sleepyhead!'

The words rang embarrassingly in the empty room. I saw that the bed had not been slept in.

My heart thudded sickeningly and I tasted something bitter. If, after all my care –

Then I had a sudden, sane vision of Sylvia, exhausted ~~>~~ NOT and sleeping alone on the floor of the attic, worn out with crying. I went up to fetch her.

But the attic was empty. Or nearly. Something glittered on the bare boards and I saw that it was Sylvia's ring, her half of the pair our mother had left us. I knew how much Sylvia had cherished it. She would never have lost it, never left it behind carelessly. But there it was, and Sylvia was gone.

I searched the house and found that she had taken away a bag of clothes. She had left no note.

The day passed and faded into night, but Sylvia did not return or call. Had she been seduced away, kidnapped? She hadn't said anything about leaving. She must mean to come back, she must.

As the days blended one into the other in the still, silent house, I asked myself again and again why she had gone. I asked myself how I could have prevented it, and I found a hard answer. By trying to keep her, I had forced her to go. I had been too severe, too self-centered. I had held her too tightly, refusing to let her have any life of her own. She was a woman, not a child, and her rebellion was natural. I had driven her away.

'Maybe I want something you can't give me,' she had said. But what she wanted was so horrible! The memory of that dark, filthy den in the attic, her discarded nightgown shimmering whitely against it, still sent a shudder through me. I would not, could not, follow her there. Our childhood fantasy of marrying brothers had never seemed more impossible.

But why couldn't we both have what we wanted? Why did I have to live without her? Understanding more now, I was willing to give more, even to share her, if she would only come back. I would no longer try to change or bind her; I would leave the attic, and her life up there, strictly alone. She could bring her husband, or whatever he was, to the house and I would not interfere. If only I could tell her so. If only she would give me another chance.

One day I went up to the attic with the toolkit and set to work on the roof. The hammer did no good at all, and I broke my knife and screwdriver against it. Finally I went down to the village and bought an axe. I was soaking with sweat and rain and my hands were bleeding before I was through, but I got it done at last. The new hole was even bigger than the old; quite big enough for anything to get through. I stuck my head out, scaring off a couple of rooks who had come to examine my work, and I looked around at the heavy grey sky and the bare trees, searching for something large and black flapping on the horizon. I saw nothing like that. The rain ran into my eyes and I retreated.

We hadn't been in the house long enough to acquire much in the way of rubbish, but I took the old newspapers and magazines we'd been saving to recycle, and the bag of garbage from the kitchen, and carried it all up to the attic. Working fast in the gathering dark and cold rain, I raked up a sackful of dead leaves and twigs from the garden, and picked up broken branches from beneath the trees. Still it wasn't enough, so I took the axe to a couple of chairs, tore the stuffing out of my pillows, and scissored up a few old clothes.

It's a start, anyway. A sign of my goodwill. All I can do now is wait. And so I do, lying in Sylvia's bed every night, listening for noises from above.

After their mother died, Emily made it her purpose to fill the role + take care of Sylvia, but this is detrimental to their relationship — Sylvia wants a temporary escape but Emily wants to keep her in sight always!

The roof entry to the attic house represents a way for something to get to Sylvia but really she uses it as a place of her own since Emily won't go there.

The black thing wasn't real, nor was the nest — just what Emily imagined was taking her sister from her — Sylvia just wanted to live her life w/o doing every little thing together w/ her sister, so she was driven away be Emily's constant concern presence + control